Five interesting things about Rachel Gibson:

1. Growing up, I didn't like to read. I liked to play tetherball and wanted to be a tetherball champion.

2. I have a deadly fear of grasshoppers.

3. I am a shoe-aholic. I think ugly shoes are an abomination of biblical proportion.

4. I love to read the tabloids. Especially the ones featuring stories such as Bat Boy and women having Big Foot's baby.

5. I write romantic novels, but I hate overly sentimental movies and sappy love songs.

By Rachel Gibson

True Love and Other Disasters

Rachel Gibson

little
black
dress

First published in 2009 by
AVON BOOKS
An imprint of HARPERCOLLINS PUBLISHERS, USA

First published in Great Britain in 2009 by
LITTLE BLACK DRESS
An imprint of HEADLINE BOOK PUBLISHING

A LITTLE BLACK DRESS paperback

1

Cataloguing in Publication Data is available from the British Library

ISBN 978 0 7553 4598 4

Typeset in Transit511BT by Avon DataSet Ltd,
Bidford-on-Avon, Warwickshire

Printed and bound in Great Britain by
Clays Ltd, St Ives plc

Headline's policy is to use papers that are natural, renewable and
recyclable products and made from wood grown in sustainable forests.
The logging and manufacturing processes are expected to conform to the
environmental regulations of the country of origin.

HEADLINE PUBLISHING GROUP
An Hachette UK Company
338 Euston Road
London NW1 3BH

www.littleblackdressbooks.com
www.headline.co.uk
www.hachette.co.uk

The night before Virgil Duffy's funeral, a storm pounded the Puget Sound. But by the next morning, the gray clouds were gone, leaving in their place a view of Elliott Bay and the spectacular skyline of downtown Seattle.

Sunlight cut across the grounds of his Bainbridge estate and in through the towering windows. Among the guests honoring him at his wake, there were those who wondered if he was up in heaven controlling the notoriously gray April weather. They wondered if he'd been able to control his young wife, but mostly they wondered what she was going to do with the pile of money and NHL hockey team she'd just inherited.

Tyson Savage wondered that himself. The voices pouring from the formal living room drowned out the sound of his Hugo Boss dress shoes as he moved across the parquet flooring of the entry way. He had a really bad feeling that the Widow Duffy was going to screw up his chance at the cup. The bad feeling bit the back of his neck and had him adjusting the tight knot of his tie.

Ty walked through the double doors and into a large room that reeked of polished wood and old money. He spotted several of his teammates, spit and polished and looking slightly uncomfortable amongst the Seattle elite. Defenseman Sam Leclaire sported a black eye from last week's game against the Avalanche that had resulted in a five-minute penalty. Not that Ty held a muck-up in the corner against a guy. He also had a reputation for throwing the gloves, but unlike Sam, he wasn't a hothead. With only three days to go before the first playoffs game, the bruises were bound to get a hell of a lot worse.

Ty stopped just inside the door, and his gaze moved across the room and landed on Virgil's widow standing within the sunlight spilling through the windows. Even if the sun hadn't been shining in her long blond hair, Mrs. Duffy still would have stood out amongst the mourners surrounding her. She wore a black dress with sleeves that reached just below her elbows and a hem that touched just above her knees. It was just a plain dress that looked anything but plain as it poured over her incredible body.

Ty had never met Mrs. Duffy. A few hours earlier, at St. James Church, was the first time he'd seen her in person. He'd heard about her though. Everyone had *heard* about the billionaire and the Playmate. He'd heard that several years before the Widow had snagged herself a rich, old man, she'd been working a stripper pole in Vegas. According to the gossip, one night while she'd been rocking her acrylic heels, Hugh Hefner himself had walked into the club and spotted her onstage. He'd put her in his magazine, and twelve months later, he'd made her his Playmate of the Year. Ty hadn't heard how she'd met Virgil, but how the two had met didn't matter. The old man dying and leaving his team to a gold digger did. One whole hell of a lot.

The talk in the locker room at the Key Arena was that Virgil had had a massive heart attack while trying to please his young wife in the sack. The rumor was that the old man had blown out a heart valve and died with a big ol' grin on his face. The mortician hadn't been able to remove it, and the old man had gone into the cremation oven wearing a hard-on and a smile.

Ty didn't care about rumors, and he didn't care what people did or whom they did it with. If it was good, bad, or somewhere in between. Until now. He'd just signed his contract with the Seattle Chinooks organization three months ago, partly because of the money the old man had offered him, but mostly for the captaincy and a shot at Lord Stanley's cup. Both he and Virgil wanted that cup, but for different reasons. Virgil had wanted to prove something to his rich friends. Ty wanted to prove something to the world: that he was better than his dad, the great Pavel Savage. The cup was the one thing that had eluded them both, but Ty was the only one who still had a shot at it. Or at least he'd had a good shot until Duffy croaked right before the playoffs and left the team to a tall, blonde Playmate. Suddenly Ty's chance at the biggest trophy in the NHL was in the hands of a trophy wife.

'Hey, Saint,' Daniel Holstrom called out as he approached.

Ty had been given the nickname 'Saint' his rookie year, when after a night of especially wild partying, he'd played like shit the next day. When the coach benched him, Ty had claimed he had a flu bug. 'You're like your father,' the coach had said, with a disgusted shake of his head. 'A damned saint.' Ty had been trying and sometimes failing to live down the reputation ever since.

He looked across the shoulder of his navy blazer and into the eyes of his teammate. 'How's it goin'?'

'Good. Have you given your condolences yet to Mrs. Duffy?'

'Not yet.'

'Do you think Virgil really died while doing his wife? He was what? Ninety?'

'Eighty-one.'

'Can a guy still get it up at eighty-one?' Daniel shook his head. 'Sam thinks she's so hot she could raise the dead, but frankly I doubt that *even she* can work miracles on old equipment.' He paused a moment to study the young widow as if he couldn't quite make up his mind. 'She is smokin' hot.'

'Virgil probably had pharmaceutical help, eh?' Ty's own father was in his sixties and was still getting it on like a teenager, or so he said. Viagra had given a lot of men back their sex lives.

'That's true. Isn't Hefner in his eighties and still having sex?'

Or so he claimed. Ty unbuttoned his jacket. 'See ya later,' he said and moved through the crowd, which ranged in age from old as dirt to a few teenagers whispering in the corner. As he walked straight for the 'smoking hot' Mrs. Duffy, he nodded to several of the guys, who looked slick and a little uncivilized decked out in designer suits.

He stopped in front of her and held out his hand. 'I'm sorry for your loss.'

'Thank you.' A slight frown creased her smooth forehead and her big green eyes looked up into his face. She was even more beautiful and looked much younger up close. She placed her hand in his; her skin was soft and her fingers a little cool. 'You're the captain of Virgil's hockey team. He always spoke highly of you.'

It was her hockey team now, and what she did with it was up for speculation. He'd heard she was going to sell it. He hoped that was true and that it happened soon.

Ty dropped her hand. 'Virgil was a great guy.' Which everyone knew was a stretch. Like a lot of extremely wealthy men used to getting their way, Virgil could be a real son of a bitch. But Ty had gotten along with the old man because they'd shared the same goal. 'I enjoyed our long talks about hockey.' Virgil might have been eighty-one, but his mind had been sharp and he'd known more about hockey than a lot of players.

A smile curved her full kiss-me-baby lips. 'Yes. He loved it.'

She wore very little makeup, which surprised him given her former profession. He'd never met a Playmate who didn't love to paint her face. 'If there is anything the guys and I can do to help you out, let me know,' he said without much sincerity, but since he was the captain of the team, he figured he should offer.

'Thank you.'

Virgil's only child stepped forward and whispered something in the Widow's ear. Ty had met Landon Duffy on several occasions and couldn't say that he liked him much. He was as ruthless and driven as Virgil, but without the charm that had made his father such a success.

The Widow's smile faltered and her shoulders straightened. Anger flashed in her green eyes. 'Thank you for coming, Mr. Savage.' Like a lot of Americans, she'd mispronounced his name. It wasn't savage, like in *beast*. It was pronounced Sah-vahge.

Ty watched her turn and walk away, and he wondered what Landon had said. Obviously, she hadn't liked it. His gaze slid down her blond hair to her nicely rounded behind in the plain black dress that looked anything but plain. He wondered if Virgil's son had propositioned her. Not that it mattered. Ty had more important things to worry about. Namely, this

Thursday's game in Vancouver when they'd take on the dual threat of the Sedin twins in the playoffs opener. Until three months ago, Ty had been captain of the Canucks, and he knew better than anyone to never underestimate the boys from Sweden. If they were on their game, they were a defenseman's worst nightmare.

'Have you seen the pictures?'

Ty removed his gaze from the Widow's departing ass and looked over his shoulder at his teammate, all-round shit-disturber, Sam Leclaire. 'No.' He didn't have to ask what pictures. He knew and had never been interested enough to search them out.

'Her boobs are real.' Out of one corner of his mouth Sam added, 'Not that I looked.' He tried to appear innocent, but the black eye ruined it.

'Of course not.'

'Do you think she can get us invited to the Playboy Mansion?'

'See ya tomorrow,' Ty said through a laugh and moved toward the entry. He walked out the huge double doors of the brick mansion and the chilly breeze brushed his face. He paused to button his jacket and the sound of the Widow Duffy's voice carried on the breeze.

'Of course I want to see you,' she said. 'It's just such a bad time.'

Ty glanced at her, standing a few feet away with her back to him. 'You know I love you. I don't want to argue.' She shook her head and her hair brushed the middle of her back. 'Right now is impossible, but I'll see you soon.'

She moved toward the side of the house and Ty continued down the steps. He wasn't shocked that Mrs. Duffy had what sounded like a lover on the side. Of course she did. She'd been married to an old man. An old man who'd just given her his hockey team.

Ty didn't like to think of all the ways that could screw up his chances at the cup, but of course it was always first and foremost in his mind. Virgil's death could not have come at a worse time. Any sort of uncertainty could and would affect the players, and not knowing who was going to buy the team or what changes the new owner would implement, was a big question mark hanging over them like an axe. But worse than the uncertainty was the thought of being owned by a stripper turned Playmate turned trophy wife. It was enough to make the bite at the back of his neck clamp down a little harder.

As he moved toward his black BMW, Ty pushed everything out of his brain but his latest obsession. He put Virgil's widow, the impending buyout, and the upcoming game out of his mind. For a few hours, he wasn't going to worry about the widow's plans for the team or the game against the Canucks.

For most of his life, Ty had always tried to curb the wild Savage impulses that could get him in trouble, but he had one true weakness that he regularly indulged. Ty loved nice cars.

He slid inside the soft leather interior and fired up the M6. The low, throaty growl of the 5.0-liter V-10 engine hummed across his skin as he slid a pair of Ray-Ban aviators onto the bridge of his nose. The mirrored lenses shaded his eyes from the bright afternoon sun as he pulled out of the gated estate and headed toward Paulsbo. He opened up the 500 horses under the Beemer's hood and took the long way home.

Faith Duffy closed her cell phone and looked out across the emerald expanse of lawn, carefully tended beds, and sputtering fountains. The very last thing she needed right now was a visit from her mother. Her own life was uncertain and scary, and Valerie Augustine was an emotional black hole.

Her gaze skimmed the busy waters of Elliott Bay, and she folded her arms across her chest and rounded her shoulders against the cool breeze blowing the hair about her face. Last night she'd dreamed she was working at Aphrodite again. Dreamed that her long blond hair blew about her head as Motley Crue's 'Slice of Your Pie' pounded from the speakers above the main stage inside the strip club. In the dream, pink laser light slashed across her long legs and six-inch acrylic platforms as she slowly ran her hands down her flat stomach. Her palms slid over her crotch, covered in a tiny plaid skirt, and her fingers gripped the chair between her bare thighs.

Faith hated that dream. She hated the panic and the

knot of fear the dream always left in her stomach. She hadn't had that dream in years, but it was always the same. She always turned sideways on the chair, arched her back, and slowly lowered her head toward the stage as her hands unbuttoned her little white blouse. The pink light cut across her as she balanced on the seat of the chair and brought her legs up. She slid one foot down her calf as her big breasts spilled free of the blouse and threatened to fall out of her red sequined demi-bra. As always, men lined the edges of the stage, watching her with hot eyes and slack mouths.

'Layla.' They chanted her stage name while clinching money in their tight fists.

In the dream, an I-know-you-want-me smile curved her mouth as Vince Neil and the boys sang about a sweet smile and another slice of pie. Inside the gentlemen's club, three blocks off the Las Vegas strip, Faith placed her hands on the floor by her head and executed a perfect walk over until she stood with her feet a shoulders' width apart. She tossed her shirt to the side and rocked her hips as she bent forward at the waist. She slid the tiny plaid skirt down her thighs and legs, and she stepped out of the skirt wearing a red G-string that matched her bra. The heavy bass and drumbeat thumped the stage and the bottoms of her acrylic platforms as she became the object of male fantasy, manipulating them into digging deep into their wallets and handing over their cash.

The dream always ended the same. Her stash of

money always evaporated like a mirage, and she always woke gasping. Anxiety beating her chest and stealing her breath. And as always, she felt like a helpless little girl again. Alone and terrified.

Women who claimed they'd rather starve than strip had probably never had to make that choice. They'd probably never had to eat hot dogs five days in a row because they were cheap. They'd probably never fantasized about tables of Big Macs and fries and ramekins filled with crème brûlée.

Faith turned her face toward the breeze and took a deep breath. She should go back inside. It was rude to neglect Virgil's friends at his wake, but most of them had never really liked her anyway. As for his family – well, they could all go to hell. Every last one of them. Not even on this day, of all days, had they put aside their bitterness.

Virgil was gone. She still couldn't believe it. Just a week ago he'd been telling her stories about all the amazing things he'd done in his long life, and now . . .

Now he was gone and she felt horribly alone. She was raw and drained from burying her husband and the best friend she'd ever known. She knew that some people hadn't liked Virgil. In his eighty-one years, he'd made a lot of enemies. But he'd been good to her, especially at a time when she hadn't always been good to herself.

Even after his death, he was still being good to her. Virgil had endowed his various charities, and the bulk of his billion-dollar estate had gone to his only child, Landon, and Landon's three children and eight grand-children. But he'd left Faith the penthouse in Seattle, fifty million dollars in the bank, and his hockey team. A smile lifted her lips as she thought about how much that had pissed off his family. She was sure they all thought she'd schemed and connived to get her hands on all that money. That she'd traded twisted sexual favors for the hockey team, but the truth was that Virgil had known she hadn't cared about the team. She wasn't into sports and had been as shocked as everyone else that Virgil had left the Chinooks to her. She suspected Virgil had done it because Landon had never made any secret of the fact that he expected to inherit the team. Once he owned the Chinooks, Faith knew she'd be banned from the skybox. Which, really, would have been no hardship for her. She had no interest in hockey. Sure, she'd gone to some of the games with her husband, but she hadn't really paid much attention to the action down on the ice. She'd spent her time up there tuning out the contentious Duffys and looking through binoculars for hideous outfits and idiot drunks in the seats below. On a good night at the Key Arena, she might spot an idiot drunk *wearing* a hideous outfit.

Unlike Faith, Landon had more interest in the games and had been counting down the days until he could get his hands on the team. Owning a professional sports team was a sign of extreme wealth. A membership in an exclusive club that Landon had wanted badly. A membership his father had now denied him.

Landon might have been Virgil's only son, but they'd despised each other. Landon had never attempted to conceal his disapproval of Virgil's life or his hatred for Virgil's fifth wife, Faith.

She moved down the long carpeting in the upstairs hall and into the bedroom suite she'd shared with Virgil. Several men from a moving company were packing her clothes into boxes while one of Landon's lawyers hovered in the background, making sure Faith didn't take anything that they didn't feel belonged to her. She ignored the movers and brushed her hand across the back of Virgil's worn leather chair. The seat was indented from years of use and Virgil's reading glasses sat on the table on top of the book he'd been reading the night he'd died. Dickens, because Virgil had an affinity to David Copperfield.

That night, five days ago, she'd been lounging in the chair next to her husband and watching a rerun of *Top Chef*. On the television, as Padma judged the best *amuse-bouche*, Virgil had sucked in a sharp breath. She'd looked over at him. 'Are you okay?' she'd asked.

'I'm not feeling well.' He'd set his glasses and book aside and raised a hand to his sternum. 'I think I'll go to bed.'

Faith put down the remote, but before she could rise to help him, he slumped forward and gasped, his age-spotted hand falling to his lap.

The rest of the night was a blur. She remembered yelling his name and cradling his head in her lap while she talked to the 911 operator. She couldn't recall how he came to lie on the floor, only looking down into his face as his soul slipped from his body. She remembered crying and telling him not to die. She'd pleaded with him to hang on, but he hadn't been able to.

It had all happened so fast. By the time the paramedics had arrived, Virgil was gone. And instead of his family being grateful that he hadn't died alone, they hated her even more for being there at the end.

Faith walked into the bedroom and grabbed the Louis Vuitton suitcase she'd packed with a few changes of clothes and the jewelry Virgil had bought her throughout their five years of marriage.

'I'll need to search that,' Landon's lawyer said as he stepped into the room.

Faith had a few lawyers of her own. 'You'll need a warrant,' she said as she brushed past him, and he didn't try to stop her. Faith had been around too many truly scary men to be intimidated by one of Landon's bullies. On her way out of the sitting room, she grabbed her black Valentino coat. She slipped Virgil's copy of *David Copperfield* into her Hermès bag and headed toward the front of the house. She could have left by the back entrance, the servants' stairs, and save herself from running into Virgil's family, but she wasn't about to do that. She wasn't about to sneak away like she'd done something wrong. At the top of the stairs, she shoved her arms through the sleeves of her coat and smiled as she remembered her continual argument with Virgil. He'd always wanted her to wear mink or silver fox, but she'd never felt comfortable wearing fur. Not even after he'd pointed out that she was a hypocrite because she wore leather. Which was true. She loved leather. Although these days, she exercised taste and moderation. Something her mother had yet to discover.

As she moved down the long, winding staircase, she forced a smile in place. She said good-bye to a few of Virgil's friends who'd been kind to her, and then slipped out the front door.

Her future was wide open. She was thirty years old and could do anything she wanted. She could go to school or take a year off to lie around on a warm beach somewhere.

She looked back at the three-story brick mansion where she'd lived with Virgil for the five years of their marriage. She'd had a good life with Virgil. He'd taken care of her, and for the first time in her life, she hadn't had to take care of herself. She'd been able to relax. To breathe and have fun and not worry about survival.

'Good-bye,' she whispered, and pointed the toes of her red leather pumps toward her future. The heels of her shoes clicked down the steps and toward the garage around the back as she made her way to her Bentley Continental GT. Virgil had given her the car for her thirtieth birthday last September. She tossed the suitcase in the trunk then hopped inside and drove from the estate. If she hurried, she could just make the six-thirty ferry to Seattle.

As she drove through the gates, she again wondered what she was going to do with her life. Other than the few charities she helped chair, there was no one who needed her. While it was true that Virgil had taken care of her, she'd taken care of him, too.

She took her sunglasses from her purse and slid them onto the bridge of her nose.

And what the heck was she going to do with his hockey team and all those tough, brutal players? She'd met some of them at the yearly Christmas party she always attended with Virgil. She especially remembered meeting the big Russian, Vlad, the young Swede, Daniel, and the guy with the perpetually bruised face, Sam, but she didn't know them. To her, they were just members of the twenty-some-odd men who, as far as she could tell, liked to fight and spit a lot.

It was best that she sell the team. Really, it was. She knew what they thought of her. She wasn't a fool. They thought she was a bimbo. A trophy wife. Virgil's arm candy. They'd probably passed around her *Playboy* layout. Not that she cared about that. She wasn't ashamed of the pictures. She'd been twenty-four years old and had needed the money. It had beaten the hell out of stripping, introduced her to new people, and provided new options. One of those options had been Virgil.

She slowed the Bentley at a stop sign, looked both ways, then blew through the intersection.

Faith was used to men staring at her. She was used to men judging her by the size of her breasts and assuming she was dumb or easy or both. She was used to people judging her by her profession or because she'd married a man fifty-one years older than herself. And really, she didn't care what the world thought. She'd stopped caring a long time ago, when the world had walked past her as she'd sat outside the Lucky Lady or the Kit Kat Topless Lounge waiting for her mama to get off work.

The only thing she'd been born into this world with was her face and body, and she'd used them. Caring what people thought about that gave them the power to hurt her. And Faith never gave anyone that kind of power. No one except Virgil. For all his faults, he'd never treated her like a bimbo. Never treated her as if she were nothing. Sure, she'd been his trophy wife. There was no denying that. He'd used her to prop up his enormous ego. Like Virgil's hockey team, she was something he owned to make the world envious. She hadn't minded. Not at all. He'd treated her with kindness and respect, and he'd provided her with what she wanted most. Security. The kind she'd never known, and for five years she'd lived in a nice, safe bubble. And even though her bubble had burst and it felt like she was free-falling, Virgil had made sure she would have as soft a landing as possible.

She thought of Ty Savage, with his deep, rich voice

and his slight accent. 'I enjoyed our long talks *aboat* hockey,' he'd said, referring to Virgil.

Faith had been around a lot of good-looking men in her life. She'd dated a lot of them too. Men like Ty whose looks could steal your breath, hit you like a club, and turn your head completely around. His dark blue eyes were lighter blue in the center, like tiny bursts of color. A lock of his dark hair touched his forehead, while fine strands curled about the tops of his ears and the back of his neck. He was tall and built like a Hummer, but he was a little too volatile for Faith's tastes. Perhaps it was the hetero-juices pounding through the man's system and rolling off him like toxic vapors. Perhaps it was the scar on his chin that made him look a little dangerous. Little more than a thin, silvery line, the scar looked scarier than Sam's black eye.

She thought of her hand in his warm, firm palm as he offered his help. Like a lot of men, Ty Savage said all the right things but he hadn't meant them. Men seldom did. Virgil had been the only man she'd ever known who had kept his promises. He'd never lied to her, even when it would have been easier. He'd shown her a different way to live her life, other than the way she'd been living. With Virgil she'd been safe and happy. And for that, she would love and miss him forever.

Thousands of booing fans marked Ty's return to the General Motors Place arena in Vancouver. Dozens of banners hung from the stands, the sentiments ranging from 'Fallen Saint' and 'Saint's a Traitor' to Ty's personal favorite, 'SUCK IT, SAVAGE.'

For seven seasons he'd worn a Canucks jersey. For the past five there'd been a *C* just below his left shoulder, and he'd been treated like a conquering hero. Like a rock star. This season he still wore a *C*, only he'd traded a killer whale for a salmon swatting a puck with its tail. Players were traded all the time. At least he hadn't waited until right before the deadline to accept the offer of more money and – something infinitely more valuable than gold – a better shot at the cup.

For more than a season it had been known that he wasn't happy with Vancouver management and the direction of their coaching staff. Then, shortly after Christmas, Seattle's captain, Mark Bressler, had been involved in a horrible car wreck and the team was left without its leader. The Seattle organization had made

Ty an offer he didn't feel he could refuse and he'd made the trade. There were a lot of people in the press and the entire country of Canada, including his father, who thought he should feel bad – like a traitor. But he didn't.

At least the fans weren't throwing things at him tonight, which was a shock considering how betrayed they'd felt by his defection 120 miles south.

A smile twisted one corner of his mouth as he jammed his helmet on his head and skated toward center ice to face off with his former teammate, Markus Naslund. He skated past the face-off circle twice for good luck and then stopped in the middle.

'How's it, Nazzy, eh?' he asked.

'Suck it, Saint,' Markus said through a grin.

Ty laughed. He liked Nazzy. Respected his skills on the ice, but it was his job tonight to make him wish he'd stayed home. Ty knew the opposition better than he knew the players on his own team, had played with them longer, but the Chinooks had the best 5-on-5 team in the league while their power play unit accounted for one quarter of the team's extra-man goals. When the Chinooks were on fire, they dominated the ice with speed, brute strength, and hockey sense.

But that night in Vancouver, there was something weird in the air. Ty didn't believe all that much in being jinxed. Sure, he always skated past the face-off circle twice before entering it, but he really wasn't a super-stitious guy. He believed in skill more than some intangible bad luck. He was one of only a handful of players who shaved during the playoffs.

There was definitely something hinky about this game though. From the drop of the first bouncing puck, things did not turn in the Chinooks' favor. The defense had a hard time moving the puck up to the offense, and like the rest of the team, Ty couldn't find a cohesive rhythm. He crashed the net but had difficulty getting the puck into scoring position.

Shots ricocheted off the pipes and the game deteriorated into old-time hockey by the middle of the second period. Sam Leclaire and enforcer Andre Courture spent most of their time in the penalty box for 'innocently' tripping, elbowing, slashing, and roughing in the corners.

In the last seconds of the game, Ty finally felt in his zone and tore across ice with the puck in the curve of his stick. He knew the Vancouver goalie caught left and he deked right. The *shh-shh* of his skate was drowned out by the pounding in his head and the screaming crowd. He brought his stick back and fired at Luongo's five-hole. The blade slapped the ice and shattered. Ty watched in disbelief as the puck slid wide and the final buzzer sounded. The score: Seattle – 1; Vancouver – 2.

A half-hour later, Ty sat in the guest locker room staring at the carpet between his bare feet. He had one towel wrapped around his waist and one around his neck. His teammates stood in front of their lockers, toweling off and getting dressed for the flight home.

The only good thing to come out of that night was that Coach Nystrom had banned the press from the locker room.

'We're going to put that game behind us,' Coach Nystrom said as he walked into the room. He shoved his hands in the pockets of his dress pants. 'The other coaches and I will take a look at the game tapes and try to figure out what the hell happened tonight. When we meet Vancouver again Saturday, we'll be better prepared.'

'Game waz jinx,' Vlad 'The Impaler' Fetisov said as he stepped into his pants.

Forward rookie Logan Dumont crossed himself. 'Felt like it to me, too.'

Ty stood up and pulled the towel from around his neck. It was too early in the playoffs to get spooked. 'One bad game doesn't make a bad playoffs season, and it doesn't mean we're jinxed.' In practice they worked like a well-oiled, unbeatable machine. On game nights, they didn't jell quite so well, and Ty could think of only one way to turn that around. 'Poker night,' he said. 'I'll get back to you all on the time and place. Bring cash and be prepared to lose.' The Chinooks loved poker and there was nothing like their love of poker to inspire a little male bonding. When Ty was a rookie, the guys had taken him to a strip club to initiate him. When he was traded to Vancouver, they'd bonded at Mugs and Jugs. Ty had never particularly liked strip clubs. Ironic, given the current owner of the Chinooks.

He dropped the towel and ran his fingers through his damp hair. He had heard that morning that the Widow was planning to sell the team to Virgil's son, Landon. The little Ty knew of Virgil's son, he pretty much figured that Landon was a massive tool. But he also figured it was better to be owned by a tool than a clueless trophy wife.

'Who's gonna bring the cigars?' defenseman Alexander Devereaux asked as he buttoned his dress shirt.

'Logan,' Ty answered and lowered his hands to the towel knotted at his waist. 'And make 'em Cuban, eh?' The thick cotton fell to his feet and he opened his sports bag sitting on the bench. He pushed aside an old issue of *Playboy* that Sam had given him and grabbed a pair of clean underwear. Even though he really didn't have a burning urge to see Mrs. Duffy in the buff, he'd probably take a look at it when he got home.

'Me?' Logan shook his head. 'Why me?'

' 'Cause you're a rookie,' Sam answered the obvious.

Ty pulled on his black boxer briefs and adjusted his junk. The Vancouver press would be waiting for him and he wasn't looking forward to the walk from the locker room to the bus. The sportswriters had been brutal when he was traded. He didn't expect that they'd go easier on him tonight.

And he was right. He got three steps out of the locker room before the first question was fired at him.

'The Chinooks only had sixteen shots on goal

tonight. What happened to "The Firing Squad"?' a reporter from the *Vancouver Sun* asked, referring to the forward line of Ty, Daniel Holstrom, and Walker Brookes.

Ty shook his head and kept on walking. 'It wasn't our night.'

'With the organization in so much turmoil and up for sale,' another reporter commented, 'that has to affect your play and your chances at the cup.'

'It's early in the playoffs season.' He shoved up one corner of his mouth and didn't miss a beat. 'I'm not worried about it,' he lied.

'Savage! You traitor. How does it feel to be owned by a woman?'

He kept walking.

'I hear she's going to paint your locker room pink.'

'No. Salmon,' another reporter added. 'And put bunny ears on your fishy.'

'Does she sign your check wearing her tail?' That got them all laughing.

Even though they weren't the least bit funny, Ty smiled and laughed along with the reporters. 'I don't care what Miss January wears when she signs my check. Just as long as she signs.'

'What about the announcement that she's in talks to sell the team?'

'Don't know anything about it.' Except that he hoped it was all wrapped up soon. Protracted negotiations would affect the team. He held up one hand and walked out the back door of the arena. 'Good night, gentlemen.'

It was Miss July. She'd been Miss July.

'It wasn't enough that you are a shameless gold digger. You've turned my father's team into a laughing-stock. You're an embarrassment.'

Faith looked up from the sports section on the table in front of her. If Ty Savage was going to make a derogatory comment about her, he could have at least gotten the month right. 'Your father gave me the team,' she pointed out. 'He wasn't embarrassed by me.'

Landon Duffy frowned across the table from her. He looked so much like his father it was disconcerting, but while Virgil's icy blue-gray eyes could be shrewd, Landon's were cold. And today they were downright frozen over, letting her know just exactly how much he resented having to pay 170 million for a team he considered his. 'He was a senile old man and easily manipulated.'

'Not so easily, or we wouldn't be here. You'd already have the team instead of me.' Landon was one of the few people who intimidated her. A lot, but that didn't mean she had to show it. She looked to the left at her attorney. She didn't have to be here today. Her lawyers could have handled everything, but she didn't want Landon to know he scared her. 'Let's get this over with.'

Her attorney slid a letter of intent across the table to

Landon and his team of lawyers. As they looked it over, Faith thought about her own lawyer's advice that they should entertain other offers. He'd said something about long-term tax advantages, operating-cost certainties, salary caps, and cross merchandising that would attract other potential owners and drive up the price. Faith wasn't interested in the money. Just that she end any future dealings with the Duffys.

If Landon had been a different man, a nicer man, she probably would have just given the team to him. The fifty million Virgil had left her was more than enough money. But, she supposed, if Landon had been a different man, a nice man, his father would have left him the Chinooks in the first place. And if Virgil had been a different man, a more forgiving man, he would not have seen to it that his son pay dearly for their contentious relationship.

Faith stood and smoothed the creases out of her camel hair skirt. 'I'll leave you gentlemen to discuss the details.' She grabbed her red wool coat from the chair beside her. She turned to her lawyer and said, 'I'll be at the Chinooks offices in a meeting with management to let them know of my decision.' She didn't know the coaches or any of the management, but she figured they deserved to know what was going on. And she figured it was her place to tell them rather than let them hear it from her lawyers or from the media. She'd tell them how much the organization had meant to Virgil, and reassure them that they'd be in capable hands with

Landon. As much as she hated Landon, that much was true. 'Call me when you're finished here.'

Landon signed his name with a flourish and then looked up. 'Make sure you don't take anything out of that building. Nothing there belongs to you.'

Lord, his continual insinuations that she was a thief were tiresome, but something she wouldn't have to put up with for long.

'Everything there belongs to me until we sign the final papers and your check clears.'

'Just remember what I said, *Layla*,' he added, using her stage name.

She grabbed her clutch from the table and held it against the turmoil twisting a knot in her stomach. She'd dealt with men like Landon for most of her life. Demeaning men who were offended by her mere presence even as they undressed her with their hot eyes. No matter that she wore a sweater that covered her from her chin to her wrists, and her skirt hit just below her knees, to them she would always be a stripper who took her clothes off for money. No matter that they were the heads of philanthropic organizations that raised money for the less fortunate. They resented her for daring to breathe their exclusive air.

It was on the tip of her tongue to tell Landon what he could do with himself. She could feel Layla coming to the surface to kick ass and take names. But that's what Landon wanted, and she could almost hear Virgil whispering in her ear. *Landon's a pissant. Don't let him win. Don't let him see that he gets to you.* Faith clamped her teeth shut and her mouth curved into a pleasant smile, a trick she'd learned since becoming Virgil's wife. She shook her head as if to say he couldn't bother her, and the end of her ponytail brushed the backs of her shoulders. She did not want to let Layla out. Layla was trouble, and Faith did not want Landon to win. 'Good day, gentlemen.'

The heels of her Christian Louboutin leopard-print pumps tapped across the hardwood floors of the law office. She shut the door behind her and pulled a breath of clean air deep into her lungs. That had been close. She hadn't let Layla out in a long time. Not since she'd had to pretend that she liked having men stuff money in her G-string. Layla was a fighter and a survivor, and she'd tell Landon to kiss her ass.

She pushed away from the door and threaded her arms through the sleeves of her coat. One of the benefits of selling the team was that she'd be free of Landon and his family. No more picking her way through that fractious web.

The drive to the Key Arena took twenty minutes and gave Faith a few extra minutes to tell herself she was doing the right thing. Virgil had left the Chinooks to her, not Landon, but it had probably been his intent that she sell the team to her stepson. Right? Or would he have been angered by her decision? She just didn't know, and she wished Virgil had talked to her about it before he'd died.

A cool drizzle wet the windshield of the Bentley as she pulled into the parking garage and into a reserved space. The business offices for the Chinooks were on the second level, and everyone was already seated when she walked into the room. She recognized most of the men sitting at the long table from Virgil's funeral. 'Hello,' she said as she made her way to a vacant chair in the middle. 'I hope I haven't kept you all waiting,' she added, even though she knew she was right on time.

'Not at all.' General manager Darby Hogue stood and offered his hand across the table. His brown eyes were as warm as his palm. 'How are you doing?'

'Better.' Which wasn't necessarily true. She missed Virgil every day, and there was a large hole in her heart. 'Thank you for asking.'

Darby reintroduced everyone in the room, starting with executive management, continuing around the table to include the hockey operations staff and concluding with the big captain of the Chinooks sitting at the far end of the table. Roughly eight men and her. Some of them more rough than others. Or rather, *one* more rough than the others.

The last time she'd seen Ty Savage, he'd appeared more civilized, in his designer suit. Today his volatile blue-on-blue eyes looked across at her from beneath his black brows, and he didn't look civilized at all. His arms were folded across his muscular chest covered in a white T-shirt. The words 'Chinooks Hockey' were

printed in black up one of the long sleeves. It was just
after noon and he already sported a five-o'clock
shadow. 'Hello, Mr. Savage.' Why the captain of the
team needed to be in on the meeting, she didn't know.
Although she supposed it didn't matter.

One corner of his mouth lifted, like she'd amused
him. 'Mrs. Duffy.'

She set her clutch on the table and took off her coat.
One of the coaches rose and helped her. 'Thank you,'
she said as he hung it on the back of her chair. She
pulled down the long sleeves of her cream angora
sweater to cover her wrists and directed her attention
to the faces around her. 'My late husband loved this
organization. He loved hockey and used to talk about
trades and averages against and front-end deals. I'd
listen to him for hours, but I never had any idea what
he was talking about.'

She smoothed the back of her skirt and sat. 'That's
why I've decided to sell the team to someone who has
the same passion for the game as Virgil.' A lump formed
in her throat and she wondered yet again if she was
doing the right thing. She wished she were certain. 'A
half-hour ago, Landon Duffy signed a letter of intent to
buy the franchise.' She expected applause. Something.
She looked across at the table for some sign of relief,
but oddly, she didn't see any. 'When the sale is final,
we'll hold a press conference.'

'When will that be?' Coach Nystrom asked.

'A few weeks.' She folded her hands on the table in

front of her. 'Landon assures us that nothing will change.'

Someone farther down the table said, 'We heard he's thinking of moving the team.'

Faith had not heard that. If it happened, Virgil would roll over in his grave. 'When did you hear this?'

'I got a call this morning from Sports Center asking to confirm it.'

'He didn't mention it, so I assume he plans to leave the team here in Seattle.' She shook her head. 'Why would he move the team?'

'Money,' Darby explained. 'We're still recovering from the lockout, and another city might offer him a new stadium with better concession deals and lower labor costs. A new city might give him more lucrative television contracts and better tax incentives.'

A frown creased Faith's forehead and she sat back in her chair. She knew about the 2004–2005 NHL lockout. She and Virgil had been married a short time, and she remembered him flying off to meet with the players union, and the impasse that had resulted in the cancellation of the entire hockey season. She remembered a lot of swearing. Much worse than she'd ever heard in any strip club.

The door to the conference room opened and Landon entered, followed by two lawyers. She wasn't all that surprised to see him. 'Have you finished telling them the good news?' he asked, all smiles, as if he were an avenging angel sent to save the Chinooks from her clutches.

She stood. 'We're still discussing the details.'

'I'll take over from here,' he said, sounding like the CEO that he was in his four-thousand-dollar suit.

'You don't own the team yet, Landon. I don't believe you can legally discuss anything.'

He waved his hand, dismissing her. 'Run along.'

She felt her cheeks flush. From anger or embarrassment, she didn't know. Maybe both. She stood a little straighter and squared her shoulders. 'If you want to talk to the coaches and staff, you'll have to wait outside until we're finished.'

His smile fell. 'Like hell, Layla.'

No maybes about it now. She was both mad *and* embarrassed. To call her Layla in the lawyers' offices had been bad enough, but here in a room filled with these men was far worse. He meant it to be degrading. To remind all the men in the room of her former profession. If Virgil were alive, Landon wouldn't have been so openly disrespectful. Not in public, anyway. Now he felt free to publicly insult her. 'I said wait outside.' Then she smiled and used the nickname he hated, 'Sprout.' She didn't know why he hated his nickname so much. 'Sprout' was kind of cute, and lots of kids had gone through adolescence called far worse.

Apparently Landon didn't think so, and his icy gaze got all frosty again and he took a step toward her. 'For five years I've been forced to tolerate you,' he said as a vein on his forehead popped out. 'Not anymore. If you don't leave, I'll have security take you out with the rest of the trash.'

Anger clutched her stomach and burned her cheek, and before she gave it a thought, she opened her mouth and said, 'I've changed my mind. I'm not selling the team. I'm keeping it.'

Landon stopped dead in his tracks. 'You can't do that.'

Momentarily satisfied at her power to slap him down, she smiled. 'I can do whatever I want. And what I want is to keep the team your father gave *me*.' God, she wanted to hurt him. To call him names and spit in his face. To give him a good hard knee between the legs. In another life she would not have hesitated, but Mrs. Duffy did not knee men in the nuts. Virgil had taught her that. 'Stay away from my hockey team.'

He took a few more steps and reached for her. Before she could react, a big body stepped in front of her and she was suddenly staring at a wide back and white cotton T-shirt.

'It might be best if you leave now, Mr. Duffy,' Ty Savage said. 'I don't want to see anyone get hurt.' Faith wasn't sure if he meant her or Landon. 'And I would sure hate to read in the papers that Mrs. Duffy had you hauled out by security.'

From behind Ty's back she heard Landon's lawyers say something, and then Landon said, 'This isn't over, Layla.' After a few tense seconds, the door slammed shut behind him and Faith let out a pent-up breath. Her cheeks burned. She'd endured her share of humiliation. Some of it, admittedly, self-inflicted, but this felt like the time in elementary school when Eddie Peterson pulled up the back of her dress at the drinking fountain and exposed her holey pink underwear for the entire first grade.

Ty turned and spoke to her, 'What did you do to make the man hate you so much?'

She looked up past the white scar on his chin surrounded by stubble, over his mouth and into his blue-on-blue eyes. 'I married his father.' She gave in to her weak knees and sat. 'Thank you for stepping in.'

'Don't mention it.'

Her hands shook and she pulled them into her lap. 'I guess I'm not selling the team,' she said, dazed, and to no one in particular. She turned and looked at the stunned faces around her. She knew the feeling. She was just as stunned by her announcement.

'I've never seen a man treat a lady like that,' Darby said with a shake of his head.

Landon didn't think she was a lady, and the last thing she wanted to do was talk about Landon and what he thought of her. 'I suppose I'll need a crash course in hockey.' Her face felt a little numb from the shock.

'You can hire an assistant,' one of the coaches suggested. 'Virgil had one until the lockout. After that, I don't know what happened to Jules.'

She'd never heard of a Jules. 'Jules?' Her voice sounded strange and she had to fight the urge to put her forehead on the table and groan. *What had she just done?*

'Julian Garcia,' Darcy answered. 'I'll see if I can dig up his number for you.'

'Thank you.' She guessed she was keeping Virgil's team. At least for now, and she really didn't know what else to say but, 'I'll do what I can to make sure you all get the Stanley Cup. That was Virgil's dream and I know he was looking at acquiring players to make the team even stronger.' Or at least she thought she'd heard him mention it.

'The trade deadline has passed. Our roster is set, but next season we sure could use a guy in the blue zone with a mean right hook,' someone at the end of the table said.

Faith wasn't sure what that meant, but no one seemed to notice, as they talked over and around her in rapid-fire succession as if she wasn't even there.

'Someone who can defend as well as fight.'

'We've got Sam.'

'Liking to fight and intimating your opponents are two different things,' Ty added to the conversation as he took his seat at the end of the table. 'Sam's better feeding the puck up ice than he is at fighting. No one's afraid of Sam.'

'That's true.'

'Andre and Frankie are both coming along.'

'Not fast enough. We need someone like George Parros, but who can shoot the puck like Patrick Sharp.'

'Someone like Ted Lindsay.'

Coach Nystrom said, 'Yeah, like "Terrible Ted."'

They all nodded as if 'Terrible Ted' was their guy. Faith's head was spinning and the conversation swirling around her made her feel as if she might hyperventilate. She had every right to hyperventilate; her life was spinning out of control, but she figured she probably shouldn't pass out on her first day as owner. It might look bad. 'How much to get this guy? This Terrible Ted?' she asked in an effort to join the conversation and not appear so absolutely clueless.

The conversation came to a halt and their heads pivoted to stare at her. Somehow she'd rendered them all speechless. All except Ty Savage. His eyes squinted as if he was in pain. 'We're fucked.'

'Saint, there's a lady in the room,' a man in a Chinooks cap admonished.

'Sorry.' Then Ty tilted his head back and said, 'We're screwed like a crack whore on payday, eh?'

She looked across at Darby. 'What?'

'Ted retired in nineteen sixty-five.' He tried to give her a comforting smile but it looked as pain-filled as Ty's squinty eyes. 'Before you were born.'

'Oh.' She guessed that meant Terrible Ted wasn't available. So much for not *appearing* clueless.

'Then she looked at us with those big green eyes and asked how much to get Terrible Ted to play for the Chinooks?'

Pavel Savage choked on the beer he held to his lips and lowered the mug to the table. 'You're screwed.' He wiped the back of his hand across his mouth.

Ty nodded and took a long drink of his Labatt's. His father had shown up at his house an hour ago, unexpected. Like always. 'Yep. That's what I said.' He set down the bottle and picked up his driver. Since his father's arrival, the two of them had talked about last night's game against Vancouver and Round Two, tomorrow night. They'd talked about Virgil's death and what it meant for Ty's chances at the cup. 'The GM suggested she dig up Virgil's old assistant.' He stood with his feet a shoulders' width apart and placed the club behind the golf ball. 'I don't care how many assistants she hires to tell her the difference between a cross check and slashing, she'll never have what it takes.' He brought the club back behind his shoulder and swung. The ball shot across the room and into the center of the big net at the other end. When he'd bought the house on Mercer a month ago, he'd bought it because of the huge media room that would allow him to practice long drives inside. A wall of windows looked out at the lake and the city of Seattle beyond. At night the skyline was spectacular. 'The old man could not have died at a worse time, but at least he created a strong front line before he croaked.'

'That is some comfort. God rest his soul,' Pavel murmured as he looked down at the little radar unit monitoring Ty's speed and tempo. The speed read 101, and Pavel's dark brows lowered. 'Is she as beautiful as her pictures?'

'I haven't seen her pictures.' Ty hooked another ball with his driver and lined it up on the golf mat next to the radar. He didn't have to ask whom his father was talking about. 'I don't give a shit about her pictures.' After she'd announced earlier that afternoon that she was not selling the team, the Chinooks PR department had issued a statement to the press that landed Faith Duffy on every channel of the local news. They'd dug up film footage of her walking into an event with Virgil and had spliced it with footage of her wearing a low-cut dress from her *Playboy* days and smiling with Hugh Hefner.

Ty's phone had rung nonstop, with reporters wanting to know how he felt about the new owner, and instead of answering, he'd unplugged his phone. After Landon's behavior, Ty was certain Virgil's son wouldn't have been a better choice. The man's judgment was obviously flawed and influenced by emotion and personal motivations, which was never good in an owner. Now suddenly, a Playmate was the better of the two choices. How had that happened? 'You've seen the photos, I imagine.'

'No. I have not.' Pavel's eyes pinched at the creased corners as he watched Ty swing.

The ball shot across the room and hit the red center of the net.

'That's surprising.' Ty glanced at the radar, then at his father: 113. He recognized that squinty glint. Pavel was sixty-five and as competitive as ever.

'Not so much.' He shrugged and motioned for Ty to hand him the club.

'You couldn't find an old *Playboy*.'

'No.' Pavel lined up a ball beside the radar.

Ty didn't tell his father that he had the magazine in his gym bag right across the room. There was just something wrong about showing it to the old man, especially when he hadn't even seen it himself.

'But then I really didn't try. There are a lot of beautiful women in this world, why spend unnecessary time and energy on one?' Which summed up Pavel's relationships with women. Even those women he'd married. He swung and the ball flew across the room and into the net. The radar flashed 83. Not bad for a man Pavel's age, but of course it wasn't good enough to beat his son.

'The grip on your club is hinky,' he said and handed Ty the driver. 'I'm tired. I'm going to bed.'

There was nothing wrong with his grip and Ty shot a few more balls into the net just to prove it. A little after ten, he flipped on his big-screen TV and settled onto the overstuffed moss-colored couch to watch the news. He thought about tomorrow night's game and the Sedin twins.

He thought of Faith Duffy and hoped like hell that her announcement not to sell the team didn't throw the Chinooks off their game. Knowing who was going to end up owning the Chinooks was better than not knowing, but not by much.

He thought about the way she'd looked that afternoon. First composed and together, then obviously shaken. Landon had called her 'Layla,' which Ty figured had probably been her stripper name. Virgil's son was an asshole. No two ways about it. To purposely degrade any woman in public was a nasty thing to do, but to do it to his former stepmother in front of a roomful of people showed a nasty arrogant streak that had made Mrs. Duffy look like the classier of the two. She'd stood there, toe to toe, with her head high and her back straight, and Ty had to give her points for not dissolving into tears or cussing like the irate stripper she'd once been.

He raised his beer to his lips and took a long drink. She didn't dress like a stripper. Not even like a more subdued Playmate. No bright colors or tight T-shirts ripped in strategic places. No tight jeans or short skirts with thigh-high boots. That afternoon, she'd been all covered up from her chin to knees like an uptight socialite. Of course, that sweater had just drawn attention to her large breasts, and every man in the room had been wondering what she looked like naked.

Ty lowered the bottle and glanced over at his gym bag. He guessed some of the guys already knew. He set his beer on the coffee table and moved across the room. Looking at her photos wasn't something he would have gone out of his way to do, but they were sitting right there and he was a man. He reached into the bag and pulled out the five-year-old magazine with some woman he didn't recognize on the cover all painted up like Uncle Sam. As he moved back toward the sofa, he flipped to the pictorial in the middle. His feet stopped as he stared down at Faith Duffy standing in a field of wildflowers wearing a sheer yellow dress. The light was behind her and she was nude beneath the loose material. In the next photo, her back was to the camera. Her green eyes looked over one shoulder, and the dress was pulled up her long legs and past her smooth behind.

Ty turned the page and this time she was on her hands and knees on a blanket laid out on a deep green lawn. She wore a pair of pink spike heels, white thigh-high stockings, and a pair of tiny white panties that tied at her hips. Her back was arched and her breasts thrust forward in a thin white bra. Heavy. Round. Perfect. It must have been cold that day. Her nipples puckered against the thin lace. Her wild hair curled about her shoulders and a slight smile curved her pink lips. He flipped to the next photo of her kneeling on the blanket next to a picnic basket, her thumb hooked in one side of her panties, pulling them down one thigh. He tilted his head to the side and a brow lifted up his forehead. She was as bald as a little peach.

He turned to the next photo. 'Holy shit,' he whispered as he eyed the centerfold. Faith lay on the blanket, completely naked except for those thigh-highs and a long strand of pearls looped around her left breast. One of her knees was bent, her back arched off the ground and her skin glowed. Her eyes looked into the camera from beneath heavy lids, and her lips were parted as if she wanted to make love.

What a shame, he thought as he looked at her smooth, round breasts. What a shame that she'd wasted that body on an old man. Because no matter what anyone said, Viagra couldn't turn back time fifty years and give an eighty-one-year-old man what it took to please a thirty-year-old woman.

He flipped to her Playmate Profile and read that she'd been born in Reno, Nevada, and was five foot six. She'd weighed 125 pounds and her measurements were 34D-25-32. He thought of her in that black dress the day of Virgil's funeral and figured she hadn't changed much. Her ambition was to 'be a goodwill ambassador and help orphans in third-world countries.'

Rich laughter poured from Ty's lips. Her *ambition* should have read, 'I want to be a gold digger who ends up with more money than a third-world country.' He supposed *Playboy* wouldn't have printed something like that, but at least it would have been more accurate, and he would have respected her honesty.

Her favorite food was crème brûlée. Her least favorite: hot dogs. Her favorite movie: *Sweet Home Alabama*. She hated social injustice and rude people.

Ty chuckled and flipped back to the centerfold. He knew the photos had been airbrushed, and she really wasn't his type of woman, but damn, she was something. Her hard nipples were perfect little pink berries in the center of her breasts and there wasn't a mole or mark anywhere on her. A woman who looked like that should have at least one love bite somewhere on her perfect body.

He thought of her curled along the side of her old husband. He'd liked Virgil, but the mental image made him a little queasy. Maybe it was just him, but he tended to think he wasn't alone in his belief that an eighty-one-year-old man just didn't have the jump in his junk to keep a thirty-year-old happy in the sack. Virgil might have had decades of practice, and more money than God, but it took more than that. It took a healthy stamina to satisfy a woman like that.

He closed the magazine and thought of the phone call he'd overheard the day of Virgil's wake. Virgil might have had enough money to keep his young wife happy, but he'd bet there'd been someone else putting a satisfied smile on his young wife's face.

From twenty-six stories above the city, Faith looked out the two-story wall of glass at the lights of Seattle and the thick fog covering the waters of Elliott Bay. Through the soupy night, she could almost pinpoint the exact location of Virgil's estate. Not that she could see it, but she'd lived there for five years and knew it well.

She thought of the first time Virgil had brought her to his home after their quickie wedding in Vegas a month after they'd met. She'd taken one look at the big house out on the island and just about had heart failure, wondering if she'd get lost in the big, rambling mansion.

She thought of the first time she'd seen Virgil at a *Playboy* party she'd helped host at the Palms. That night he'd made her an offer she'd refused. He'd made it again after the Playmate of the Year ceremony at the Playboy Mansion. He'd told her he'd show her the world and everything in it, and all she had to do was pretend that she loved him for more than his money. He'd promised her a million dollars for every year that she stayed married to him and she'd said yes.

In the beginning, she'd figured she'd stay married to him for a few years and get out. But after a short time, they became best friends. He'd shown her kindness and respect, and for the first time in her life, she'd known what it felt like to be safe and secure and not have to worry about anything. By the end of the first twelve months, she loved him. Not like a father, but like a man who deserved her love and respect.

He'd been good to his word, and during the first few years of their marriage, they'd traveled all over the world. Hit every continent, and stayed in exclusive hotels. They'd toured the Mediterranean in yachts, gambled in Monte Carlo, and lounged on the white sands of Belize. But shortly after their second year together, Virgil suffered a massive heart attack and they didn't travel out of the country after that. They'd stayed in Seattle and socialized with Virgil's friends, but mostly they stayed at home in the big house on the island. Faith hadn't really minded. She'd cared for him and loved taking care of him.

But they'd never actually made love.

All the money and surgeries and miracle pills in the world hadn't prevented Virgil's old age and diabetes from interfering with and robbing him of the one thing that made him feel like a vital man. Long before he'd met Faith, he hadn't been able to have and sustain an erection. Nothing had worked for him, and his enormous pride and gigantic ego insisted that he settle for the next best thing. The appearance of sex with a much younger woman. A centerfold.

If she were totally honest, she would admit that she hadn't minded. Not just because he was fifty-one years older than herself, although that had been a part of it – especially in the beginning. But mostly Faith just didn't like the uncertainty of sex. You could never tell by looking at a man if he was good in bed or not. There was never any way of knowing until it was too late and your panties were missing.

Before Virgil, she'd had a lot of boyfriends and a lot of sex. Sometimes it had been really good. Sometimes it had been really bad. To her, sex was like a box of chocolates – and yeah, she'd sort of stolen that from Forrest Gump – she never knew what she was going to get. Faith didn't like anything that wasn't a sure thing, and there was nothing worse than craving something wonderful and yummy but getting a horrible orange jelly.

She hadn't had sex since she'd married Virgil. At first it had been difficult, especially since she was young and she'd been fairly active, but after a few years of going without, she really didn't miss it anymore. Now that Virgil was gone, she doubted her sex drive would suddenly come back to slap her in the head. And she just couldn't see herself with another man.

The doorbell brought Faith out of her contemplation of sex and men. She moved through the living room and the travertine tile felt cool beneath her bare feet. She and Virgil had purchased the four-bedroom penthouse last year, but they'd used it only on the rare occasions when it had been easier to stay overnight in the city. It was mostly finished in marble and tile and had an ultramodern feel. Virgil had let her decorate it, and she'd picked out white leather and tons of red and purple pillows. It had a main-level terrace that looked out over Elliott Bay, and a rooftop solarium covered with glass that had an unrestricted 360-degree view of the city, the busy waterways, and Mount Rainier beyond.

She opened the door and a white ball of fur jetted past, its little toenails clicking on the tile. Faith felt an overwhelming urge to punt.

'Mother.' Faith looked behind her own shoulder as a white Pekingese jumped up onto her white leather sofa. 'And Pebbles.' The nastiest dog on the planet. 'You should have called.'

'Why? You would have told us not to come.' Valerie Augustine wheeled her large pink suitcase into the penthouse; her overly painted lips air-kissed Faith's cheeks as she passed.

'It isn't that I don't want to see you,' Faith said and shut the door behind her. 'I'm just swamped.' She followed her mother and pointed to the pile of books open on the glass-and-stainless-steel coffee table.

'What are you studying for?' Her mother shoved the handle down into her suitcase and moved toward the leather couch on her five-inch spike heels. Pink, of course. To match her leather pants. She picked up a book and read, '*Idiot's Guide To Hockey*. Why are you reading this? I thought you sold the team.'

'I decided not to.'

Valerie's big green eyes widened and she shook her head, disturbing her perfectly feathered Farrah 'do. In the seventies, someone had told Valerie that she looked like Farrah Fawcett. She still believed it. 'What happened?'

She didn't want to get into the whole story with her mother. 'I just decided to keep it.' She thought of Landon reaching for her and Ty Savage stepping between them. She was grateful he'd been there. Grateful he'd stepped in. Almost grateful enough to forgive him for calling her 'Miss January' in the press.

'Well, I'm glad. Now that the old bastard is gone, you need something to do.'

'Mother.'

'I'm sorry, but he *was* old.' It wasn't exactly a secret that her mother hadn't liked Virgil. The feeling had been mutual. Virgil had provided a nice monthly income for Valerie, but there had been strings attached that Valerie resented even as she cashed the checks. One of them being that she could not show up whenever she felt like it. 'Too old for a young, beautiful girl,' she added as she tossed the book on the sofa and picked up her dog. Pebbles looked at Faith through beady black eyes and growled and snapped as if Faith had tried to snatch a piece of jerky from her jaws. 'Oh hush,' Valerie said through pursed lips as she raised the dog to lick her face.

'Yuck. That's disgusting.'

'I love Pebbles's kisses.'

'She licks her butt.'

Valerie frowned and tucked the dog under one arm. 'No, she doesn't. She's very clean.'

'She pees the bed.'

'Not my bed. And she just did it that one time because you yelled at her.'

Faith sighed and walked into the kitchen. 'How long are you staying?'

'As long as you need me.'

Faith groaned inwardly and opened the door to the small wine cellar. It wasn't that Faith wasn't happy to see her mother or that she didn't love her, she just didn't want the responsibility right now. Not for Valerie and certainly not for the evil Pebbles.

For as long as Faith could remember, her mother had never really been a mother. They'd been 'friends,' as opposed to child and parent. One of the best days in Valerie's life had been the day Faith got a fake ID and they could party together. And when Faith had turned eighteen, she'd followed in her mother's acrylic-heeled footsteps on the stage.

She pulled a perfectly chilled bottle of Chardonnay from the rack and closed the door behind her. She knew her mother believed anything could be solved with a fine bottle of wine, a good cry, and a new man. While Faith didn't believe that herself anymore, she did believe everything tasted better served in Waterford – something she'd learned from her late husband – and she set a pair of crystal glasses on the black granite countertop.

'I ran into Ricky Clemente at Caesars last weekend. He asked about you,' Valerie said as she ran her pink nails through her dog's fur.

Faith didn't know which was more appalling, that her mother chatted with 'Ricky the Rat,' the guy who'd cheated on her with half the dancers in Vegas, or that she was in Caesars. She glanced at her mother as she uncorked a bottle of Virgil's finest.

'Don't look at me like that. I was meeting Nina at the Mesa Grill for dinner. I stayed away from the slots.'

Faith wanted to believe it, but she didn't. Her mother had relapsed too many times to be trusted in a casino. Her mother was a pleasure seeker. She needed it like oxygen, and playing the slot machines had been pure bliss for her. Thank God she'd never really developed a fondness for cards or dice.

'Ricky said you should call him.'

Faith made a gagging noise as she poured the wine.

'If not Ricky, someone else. You need to jump back on the horse. Take a few rides around the track.' She reached for the glass and held it to her lips. 'Ah, the good stuff. This will make you feel better.'

'I feel fine, and it's too early to date.'

'Who said anything about dating? I'm talking about riding around the track a couple of times with someone fun. A man closer to your age.'

'I don't want to *ride* anyone.'

'It would get rid of that sad look on your face.'

'My husband just died.'

'Yeah. Last week.' She set Pebbles on the floor, and the dog waddled to the pantry door and sniffed around.

'You need to get out. Have fun. I'm here to make sure you do both.'

Most mothers would have come over with a casserole and cautioned their daughters not to jump into anything too quickly. To take it slow.

Not Valerie. Valerie wanted to party.

'Tomorrow we'll go shopping and go somewhere nice for dinner.'

'Tomorrow I have to meet with Virgil's former assistant.' Darby had put her in touch with Julian Garcia and he'd agreed to meet with her the following afternoon. If he also agreed to work for her, and she wanted to hire him, he'd begin working tomorrow night. Starting with the second game against Vancouver. If he didn't agree and she didn't like him, she didn't know what she'd do next.

'After your meeting then.'

'After the meeting, I want to read my hockey books.'

'What's happened to you?' Her mother shook her head, disturbing wisps of fine, blond hair. 'You used to be so full of life. You used to be so fun.'

She used to be a stripper who partied until the sun came up. She used to be a lot of things she wasn't anymore.

'You used to be audacious and sexy. Virgil made you old before your time. You don't dress like yourself anymore, and I could just cry.'

No. She didn't dress like her mother anymore. 'Maybe we can go out to dinner afterward. Tomorrow night's game against the Canucks will be my first as the official owner and I don't want to screw it up.'

'How could you possibly screw it up?'

So, so many ways. 'I'm sure the press will want to talk to me afterward. I just don't want to embarrass the guys.' She took a drink and thought of the pain in Ty Savage's eyes when she'd asked about hiring Terrible Ted. 'Or myself.' Especially herself. 'I don't want to look dumb. I'm terrified they'll ask me questions and I won't know the answers.' And the likelihood of that happening was probable to certain.

Valerie nodded like she understood the dilemma perfectly. 'You need a good outfit,' she said, offering motherly advice. 'Something tight.' She pointed to her large breasts. 'Low cut. Flash any man enough cleavage and he'll forget every intelligent question in his head.'

Julian Garcia was Irish and Hispanic, with the fashion flair of Doctor 90210, a.k.a. Robert Rey, thrown into the mix. To his first meeting with Faith, he wore a gold Saint Christopher necklace visible inside the collar of his purple-and-pink-striped shirt. His black trousers were tight and his hair was spiked with gel. He was one snappy dresser, but the most striking thing about him wasn't his brave use of color or even his green eyes, but his muscles. He was five-six with his boots on and had a neck the size of a tree trunk. The man was serious about his workouts. The kind of serious that made Faith wonder if he was gay. Not that it mattered, but a lot of the muscled-up bouncers who worked in strip clubs were gay.

Faith had met with Jules at a little after noon in Virgil's office – well, hers now – inside the Key Arena. The first question she asked was, 'Did Virgil fire you, or did you quit?'

'I was fired.'

'Why?'

He looked her in the eyes and answered, 'Because he heard me talking about you.'

At least he was honest. He could have lied and she'd have never known. 'What did you say?'

He hesitated. 'Basically, that he'd married a stripper with big boobs and he was a fool.'

Virgil wasn't a fool, but the rest was true. She had a feeling there was more, but she didn't ask. It was ironic that he'd been fired because of her and here she was, offering him his job back five years later. She asked him a few more questions about his relationship and job with Virgil. When he spoke, he looked into her eyes, not her chest. He didn't talk down to her, nor did he act as if her questions were silly or stupid.

'Don't worry about not knowing everything. This organization has somewhere around fifteen different departments and basically runs itself,' he told her. 'Virgil was a shrewd businessman and he treated it like one of his corporations. Because that's really what it is, and one thing he did very well was put smart people into position and let them do their jobs.'

'You make it sound easy.' But she knew it wasn't.

'Not easy, but not hard, either. Virgil didn't micro-manage the organization, and you certainly don't have to.' He paused to straighten the crease in one leg of his pants. 'In fact, I would suggest that you don't. The executive management does that hard work for you.'

By the end of the meeting, she wanted to hire him, but he wasn't so sure he wanted the job. 'The thing is,' he said, 'I like my job at Boeing. I'm not sure I want to come back.'

Faith didn't know if he was holding out for more money or if he was telling the truth. 'Why don't you come to the game tonight?' she offered. 'You can decide then.'

Now, seven hours later, she and Jules were seated on the sofa inside the owner's skybox poring over a stack of files he'd carried up from the office. She'd worn her black Armani suit, white blouse, and black spike heels. She wanted to be taken seriously, and she knew there were people out there just waiting for her to show up someplace wearing a short skirt and bra top.

The first order of business was to learn her players' names and their positions and to look over the schedule. As Jules went over the team roster, cheers and boos from the arena below filtered upward to the luxury box while snippets of music blasted from the sound system.

'Yes!' her mother hollered from the balcony overlooking the arena. 'Faith, come quick. The camera's on me and Pebbles. We're on the big TV.'

Faith glanced over at her mother, clutching her evil dog and blowing kisses like a movie star. Big pink and orange bracelets slid up and down her wrists. She wore a pair of hot-pink stretch leggings and a lace blouse with a pink bra underneath. Her blond hair was layered and sprayed into the perfect shaggy Farrah 'do. 'Oh God,' Faith whispered.

'She's a nice lady,' Jules said and sat back. Obviously, her mother's strange brand of mojo still worked. Not that Faith was surprised. Gay or straight, men liked Valerie.

'She's embarrassing.'

Jules laughed. 'She's having a good time.'

'You can laugh because she's not your mother.'

'I'm the oldest of eight children. My mother doesn't have that kind of energy.' He reached into a file and pulled out a stack of papers. 'This is a game schedule for the first round of the playoffs.' He handed it to her. 'And I printed off a brief bio of each player for you to look at. When you become more familiar with the team, we can go over their contracts so you know who your free agents and unrestricted free agents are.'

Faith pushed her long hair behind one ear and perused the schedule. She'd known they played a lot, but she hadn't realized there were several games a week. 'What is a free agent, an unrestricted free agent, and what is the difference?'

Jules explained that a free agent plays without a contract and can leave anytime before he is renewed. An unrestricted free agent is a player with an expired contract who has been released from his club and hasn't been picked up yet.

'It all came about when the league stopped using restrictive clauses because of collective bargaining.'

Whatever that meant. 'Do we have any free agents?'

she asked as an air horn ripped through the area and music blasted from the ice below.

'Not at the moment. Management got them all locked down before the playoffs.' Jules looked up and called out, 'What's the score, Valerie?'

'Tied at two. Number Twenty-one on your team just scored.'

Number Twenty-one was the captain of the team and Faith flipped to Ty Savage's bio and read his stats. He was thirty-five, born in Saskatchewan, Canada, which explained the accent. He was six foot three and weighed 240 pounds. He shot left, and this was his fifteenth season in the NHL. He'd played for the London Knights in the OHL before being a first-round draft pick and signing with Pittsburgh in the NHL. He'd played for the Penguins, the Blackhawks, Vancouver, and now the Chinooks. The next bit of information made Faith's jaw drop. 'Thirty million,' she wheezed. 'Virgil paid him thirty million? Dollars?'

'For three years,' Jules clarified, as if that made perfect sense.

Faith looked up and reached for a bottle of water sitting on the table. 'Is he worth that much?'

Jules shrugged his big, beefy shoulders covered in a teal-colored silk T-shirt. 'Virgil thought so.'

'What do you think?' She took a drink.

'He's a franchise player and worth every penny.' Jules stood and stretched. 'Let's watch and see what *you* think.'

Faith set the papers on the table, then rose and followed Jules to the balcony. She had so much to learn, it was daunting, and she was too overwhelmed to think. She moved past the three rows of padded stadium seats and joined her mother standing at the railing.

Below on the ice, the action was stopped and the teams were in position. In his dark blue jersey, Ty skated past the face-off circle twice before moving inside. He stopped, planted his feet wide, placed the stick across his thighs, and waited. The puck dropped and the battle was on. Ty shoved his shoulder into his opponent as his stick slapped the ice and he shot the puck behind him. As one, the skaters on each team flew into action, a whirl of organized chaos. The dark blue Chinooks jerseys with their white numbers mixed it up with the white and green of Vancouver.

Number Eleven, Daniel Holstrom, skated toward the Canucks' goal and shot the puck across ice to forward Logan Dumont, who passed off to Ty. With the puck in the middle of the blade, Ty skated behind the goal, came around the other side, and shot. The puck bounced off the goaltender's knee pad and a battle broke out. Faith lost track of the puck in the collision of sticks and bodies. From her position, all she saw was pushing, shoving, and flying elbows.

A ref blew a whistle and the play stopped . . . except for Ty, who shoved a Vancouver player, hard, and nearly knocked him on his butt. The player caught his balance just before he toppled backward. They exchanged words and Ty threw his gloves to the ice. A referee skated between the two and grabbed the front of Ty's jersey. Over the top of the ref's head, Ty pointed to his face and then at the other player. The ref asked him something, and as soon as he nodded, the smaller man let go of his jersey. Ty picked up his gloves and while he skated to the bench, an instant replay flashed on the sports screen. 'Welcome to the Jungle' blasted from the arena speakers, and on the big sports screen suspended above the ice, Faith watched Ty raise a hand before his face and point to his intense blue eyes. Over the ref's head, he stared out from beneath black brows and white helmet. Then he turned his hand and pointed at Number Thirty-three on the opposing team. A menacing smile curved his lips. A shiver ran up Faith's spine and raised goose bumps on her arms. If she were Number Thirty-three, she'd be afraid. Very afraid.

Just in case anyone missed it, it was replayed one more time in slow motion. The crowd below went wild, cheering and stomping their feet, as once more Ty's intense blue eyes locked on his opponent, the scar on his chin slicing through the dark stubble.

'Lord have mercy.' Valerie took a step back and sank into her seat. 'And you own him.' She set Pebbles down and the little dog waddled over to Faith and smelled her shoe. 'You own them all,' she added through a sigh.

'You make it sound like they're slaves.' Pebbles raised her beady black eyes to Faith and yipped. *Stupid dog.* 'I employ them.' But how many women in the world could say they employed twenty or so good-looking, buff men who swung at pucks and pounded on other players?

She was probably the only one, and the thought was both exciting and terrifying. She looked down at the row of men sitting on the Chinooks bench, spitting on the ground between their feet, wiping sweat from their faces, and chewing on their mouth guards. The sight of all that spitting and sweating should have made her feel a little nauseous, but for some reason didn't.

'After the games, Virgil always went to the locker room and talked to the team,' Jules told her.

Yeah, she knew that, but she'd never gone. 'I'm sure they won't expect me to make an appearance in the locker room.' It had been a long time since Faith had been around so many men in a confined space. Not since they'd stuffed money in her G-string. A lot of them had been jocks. As a rule, she generally didn't like jocks. Jocks and rock stars didn't think they had to abide by the rules.

'You have to, Faith,' her mother said, pulling her attention from the ice below. 'Do it for Virgil.'

Do it for Virgil? Was her mother smoking weed again?

'Reporters will be there,' Jules continued. 'So it's important. I'm sure they'll want you to make some sort of statement.'

On the ice below, a whistle blew and the action resumed. 'What kind of statement?' Faith asked as she studied the players, who looked like a swarm of organized blue and white jerseys.

'Something easy. Talk about why you decided not to sell the team.'

She glanced at him then returned her attention to the game. 'I decided not to sell the team because I hate Landon Duffy.'

'Oh.' Jules chuckled. 'When you're asked, you should probably say you love hockey and Virgil would have wanted you to keep his team. Then mention that people should come out and watch Game Four next Wednesday night.'

She could do that. 'What if they ask me something about the game?'

'Like what?'

She thought a moment. 'Like icing. What's an icing call? I read the rules last night and didn't understand it.'

'Don't worry about it. Not many people understand icing.' Jules shook his head. 'We'll go over a few basic answers before you talk to reporters. But if there is a question you don't understand, just say, "I can't comment at this time." It's the standard non-answer.'

She could do that. Maybe. She sat next to her mother and watched the rest of the game. In the last three minutes, Ty knocked an opponent off the puck and raced to the opposite end of the ice. The crowd inside the Key cheered, and just inside the blue line, he pulled back his stick and fired. The puck shot across the ice so fast that Faith didn't know it scored until a horn blasted and the light above the net flashed. The fans jumped to their feet screaming 'Rock and Roll Part 2,' thumping the concrete beneath Faith's pumps, and the Chinooks skated around Ty, slapping him on the back with their big gloves as he skated with his hands in the air as if he was the champion of the world. All except Sam, who punched some player in the head, then threw off his gloves – and the fight was on.

Jules lifted one hand and gave both Faith and Valerie high fives. 'That hat trick is why you pay the Saint thirty million.'

Faith didn't know what a hat trick was and made a mental note to look it up in her *Idiot's Guide*.

He grinned. 'Damn, Virgil put together one hell of a team this season. I'm going to love watching them play.'

'Does that mean you're my assistant?'

Jules nodded. 'Oh yeah.'

In the aftermath of Seattle's 3–2 victory over Vancouver, the post-game media scrum inside the Chinooks locker room was more jovial than the last time they'd played in the Key Arena. The coaches allowed the reporters in after a few minutes, and the players laughed and joked as they toweled off after their showers.

'You're tied in the playoffs. What are you going to do to advance to the next level?' Jim Davidson, the reporter from the *Seattle Times* asked Ty.

'We're going to keep doing what we just did

tonight,' he answered as he zipped up his dress pants. 'After our last loss to the Canucks, we couldn't afford to lose points in our building.'

'Having been the captain of both the Canucks and the Seattle teams, what would you say is the biggest difference?'

'The coaching philosophy in each club is different. The Chinooks give me more freedom to play the kind of hockey I like to play,' he answered, and wondered when they were going to get around to asking about his hat trick.

'Which is?'

He glanced over the reporter's head to Sam, who was being grilled by someone from a Canadian news organization. Ty smiled. 'Coach Nystrom thinks outside the box.'

'The team already has twenty combined penalty minutes. Just last week, Nystrom expressed his desire to keep penalty minutes per game at a minimum. Don't you consider twenty excessive?'

Ty shoved his arms in his shirt and buttoned it. 'Not at all, Jim. We kept Vancouver from taking advantage of the power plays. So, I'd say we did our jobs tonight.'

'You scored your first hat trick of the season on your home ice. How does that feel?'

Finally. 'Real good. The whole team deserves a lot of credit for tonight's win. I just happened to be in the right place when Daniel passed me the puck. Monty's first assist since being called up from—'

'Mrs. Duffy's in the lounge,' someone from the *Post Intelligencer* called out, and Jim turned toward the commotion in the doorway. 'Thanks, Savage,' the reporter said and followed the stampede out of the locker room.

Ty buttoned the front of his blue dress shirt and shoved the tails into his gray wool pants. He glanced around at the guys, who looked as stunned as he was. This was the second game of the playoffs. They'd won in their own house and the coach had granted the press full access to the team. Reporters loved full access. They loved it like a kid loved cake, but the sudden appearance of Faith Duffy prompted an en masse exodus. Like rats bailing from a sinking boat. What the hell?

Ty pulled on his socks and shoved his feet into his shoes. He combed his fingers through his damp hair and moved into the team's lounge. Mrs. Duffy stood in the middle of the huge Chinooks logo woven into the blue carpet, smiling for the cameras and answering questions thrown at her by a knot of sports reporters. She looked almost fragile in the totally male environment. Beneath the bright lights and camera flash, her smooth hair shone, her skin kind of glowed, and her lips were a glistening pink. She wore a black suit that hugged her waist and buttoned beneath her breasts. He and the boys had worked their asses off tonight, and apparently all she had to do was show up all bright and shiny and the guys in the press went ape-shit nuts.

'What made you decide not to sell the team?' someone asked.

'My late husband, Virgil, knew how much I love hockey. He left me this team because he wanted me to be happy. It was only right that I keep it.'

What utter bullshit. Ty moved further into the room and shoved one shoulder into the doorway leading to the workout gym.

'What are your plans for the team?'

A smile curved her lips at the corners and damned if it wasn't innocent and seductive all at the same time. She must have been one hell of a stripper. 'To win the Stanley Cup. Virgil put together some great players, and I plan to do everything I can to make sure we bring the cup home to Seattle.'

'We hear there's no plan to pick up Fetisov for next season.'

The corners of her mouth dipped and Darby Hogue stepped forward and saved her butt. 'I don't know where you're getting your information,' Darby said, 'but we have no plans to trade Vlad.' Then Coach Nystrom stepped forward and answered a few questions concerning trade restrictions while Mrs. Duffy smiled like she knew what he was talking about.

Ty glanced about the room at his teammates, and his gaze stopped on his father, who stood near the coaches offices talking to some woman in a lacy blouse and pink bra, and holding one of those hairy little dogs that yipped a lot. She was definitely the old man's type:

overblown, big blond hair. Not bad looking but a little torn up around the edges. He wondered where the old man had managed to find her in the two hours since Ty had spoken to him.

'When was the last time you were at the Playboy Mansion?' a reporter asked, pulling Ty's attention to the owner of the team.

A frown wrinkled her smooth brow. 'Over five years ago.'

'Do you keep in touch with Hef?'

'No. While I appreciate Mr. Hefner and will always be grateful to him, my life is very different now.'

Ty half expected the reporters to ask for her number now that she was single. He thought of her naked photos in *Playboy* and wondered how many of them had seen her spread out across the pages.

'Tonight, the team had twenty combined penalty minutes. At the beginning of the playoffs, Coach Nystrom expressed his desire to keep penalty minutes per game at a minimum. Don't you consider twenty excessive?' Jim asked the same question he'd asked Ty a few minutes earlier.

She smiled and tilted her head to one side. 'I'm sorry. I'm not at liberty to comment on that at this time.' A man with dark hair and wearing a teal silk T-shirt stepped forward and whispered something in Faith's ear. 'Oh. Okay. Our penalty minutes were up and we never like to see that,' she parroted.

Ty might have laughed if he wasn't so annoyed. The

reporters all glanced at each other and instead of calling her on being such a bonehead, someone asked, 'What did you think of tonight's game?' Totally letting her off the hook.

'It was great. All the guys played very well.'

'Virgil put together a solid team. I know that he'd tried to sign Sean Toews. What happened?'

Toews wanted more money than he was worth. That's what had happened.

'I'm not at liberty to answer that.'

'What did you think of your captain's hat trick?'

Bastards had barely asked him about the hat trick. She smiled, and Ty doubted she even knew what a hat trick was.

'We're ecstatic, of course. My late husband believed in Mr. Savage's talent,' she said, once again pronouncing his name wrong.

'It's Sah-vahge.' He spoke out loud before he gave it much thought.

The press turned and looked at him. He pushed away from the doorjamb. 'Since you're the owner of the team, you should know how to pronounce my name. It's Sah-vahge. Not savage.'

She pushed up her smile. 'Thank you. I apologize, Mr. Sah-vahge. And since I sign your checks, you should know that it's Miss July. Not Miss January.'

The Gloria Thornwell Society met the third Thursday of every month. The Society had been named after founding member Gloria Thornwell in 1928, and it was the most exclusive organization in the state. Much more exclusive than the Junior League, which seemed to let in all manner of new-money riffraff these days.

The Society was filled with rich women whose husbands kept them in designer knits and funded their pet charities. This year it was a school in a *favela* in Rio de Janeiro. Admittedly a very worthy cause, although Faith had put in her vote for a more local charity this year. She'd been vetoed, as always.

She fingered her long strand of antique pearls between the lapels of her raincoat as she moved toward the building near Madison and Fourth. The Society was really strict about their dress code, and Faith adjusted the long sleeves of her cashmere sweater set beneath her slick coat as she reached for the front door. She was met in the lobby by Tabby Rutherford-Longstreet, wife of Frederick Longstreet, president and CEO of *Longstreet Financial* and one of Virgil's longtime friends and business associates.

'Hello, Tabby,' she said as she pulled back her sleeve and checked her Rolex. Lunch always started at noon, and it was ten till. 'Is everyone already here?' She moved toward the elevator and Tabby stepped between her and the buttons.

'Yes. Everyone is here. They sent me down to speak with you.'

'About?'

'We all agreed that Dodie Farnsworth-Noble should be put in charge of the entertainment committee for this year's fund-raiser.'

'That's *my* job.' Faith looked into Tabby's blue eyes surrounded by fine lines and pressed powder. 'I'm the head of the entertainment committee.'

'We think it's best if Dodie takes over that position.'

'Oh.' Before Virgil's death, she'd worked tirelessly on this year's benefit. She'd already spoken to the Seattle Philharmonic, and her heart sank a little. 'Then what's my function?'

Tabby pasted a fake smile on her face. 'We feel that with everything going on in your life right now, you won't have time for your responsibilities.'

Sure, now that she owned a hockey team, she had a lot on her plate, but the Society's work was important. 'I understand your concern, but I assure you that I will make time,' she told Tabby. 'You don't have to worry about that.'

Tabby placed a hand against her own throat and twisted her pearls. 'Don't force me to be unkind.'

'What?'

'We think it would be best if you voluntarily gave up your Society membership.'

She opened her mouth to ask why, but then she closed it again. They weren't concerned that 'with everything going on' in her life that she wouldn't have the time. Virgil had once teased that after he died, all the wives of his friends and associates would kick her out of all their clubs because they couldn't stand to have someone young and beautiful around their husbands. Virgil had been wrong. Most of their husbands had mistresses that the wives knew about. They didn't want her because she hadn't been born with a surname worthy of hyphenation. She'd known from the first meeting that they didn't consider her a worthy member of their society. Somewhere along the way, she'd forgotten that she really wasn't one of them. She was 'riffraff.' No matter how hard she worked or how much money she'd raised.

'I see.' If Tabby thought Faith would cause a scene that the Society could all dine out on for months, she was wrong. 'Best of luck to you,' she said. 'I hope this year's fund-raiser is an unqualified success.' She smiled and turned toward the front of the building as heat rose up her chest and tightened her throat. Her hand shook as she opened the door and walked outside into the cool afternoon air. Tears pinched the backs of her eyes and she fumbled in her purse for her sunglasses. She would not cry. Would not care about people who did not care about her.

She could sic her team of lawyers on their asses and make them sorry. She could ruin their day as much as they'd ruined hers, but what would that solve? Nothing. They would be forced to accept her back into the Society. Back into a world where she wasn't wanted.

Faith shoved her sunglasses onto the bridge of her nose and looked up the street to where she'd parked her car. She had two hours before her meeting with the PR department of the Chinooks. She thought of the short drive to her penthouse where she could curl up in bed and pull the covers over her head. She thought of her mother in the shower when she'd left, and Pebbles snapping and barking as she tried to pull her Valentino peep toe from the dog's mouth.

She didn't feel like dealing with her mother and Evil Pebbles, so she wandered a few blocks without direction. She thought of Tabby's face and cool smile. The gloomy overcast day fit her mood, and she thought of marching right back to the Society and telling them what horrible, supercilious, pretentious bitches they were. Instead, she found herself in front of the Fairmont Hotel and walked into the familiar lobby. Shuckers Oyster Bar had been one of her and Virgil's favorite places to eat lunch. She was shown a table and sank into a chair, finding comfort in the familiar surroundings.

Getting thrown out of the Gloria Thornwell Society was horribly humiliating. They'd meant it as a hot slap across her face, and it stung like hell. It hurt a lot more than she wanted to admit. At one time she wouldn't have let it bother her. Living with Virgil had made her soft.

She'd always known that those women weren't her friends – not really – but she never thought they'd toss her out of a *charitable* organization two weeks after her husband's death. She wished like hell Virgil was at home so she could talk to him about what had happened. Of course, if Virgil were at home, they wouldn't have booted her out on her ass. There was no one at home to whom she could rant or vent or even talk to about it.

The waitress approached with a menu and Faith opened it. She wasn't hungry, but she ordered clam chowder, Dungeness crab, and a glass of Chardonnay, because that's what she always ordered at Shuckers. As she raised her glass to her lips, she glanced about the restaurant. She became suddenly aware of the fact that she was the only person dining alone, which added to her already frazzled nerves and hot humiliation. But this was her life now and she'd better learn how to get used to it. If there was one thing Faith knew how to do, it was how to adapt. Being alone after five years of marriage was something she'd just have to adjust to.

As she sat within the richly carved oak paneling of the oyster bar and ate her chowder, she pretended an interest in the tin ceiling. The restaurant was filled with people, but she had never felt so alone in her life. The last time she'd felt this self-conscious was the first time she'd stripped to her G-string. Sitting there by herself felt a bit like being naked in public.

The people with whom she'd socialized for the past five years were Virgil's friends. As she picked at her crab and ordered a second glass of wine, she wondered how many of those *friends* were going to ostracize her now. Without Virgil, she didn't have friends of her own, and she wasn't quite sure how that had happened. The friends she'd had in Vegas before her marriage lived a lifestyle she'd left behind. Some of them had been really great girls, but these days she couldn't imagine knocking back cherry bombs and partying till the sun came up. She'd lost touch with the few friends she'd made at Playboy.

Somewhere in the last five years, she'd lost herself. Or at least, whom she'd been. She'd become someone else, but if she was no longer a part of Seattle society, where did she belong? She was a former stripper and Playmate. Her mother was a flake, and she hadn't seen her father since 1988. For the past five years she'd played the role of a rich man's wife, but who was she now that he was gone?

As her lunch dishes were cleared away, the waitress recited the dessert menu. It was on the tip of Faith's tongue to refuse. To bolt from the restaurant and the uncomfortable situation, but like the first time she'd reached for a stripper pole, she forced herself to endure it. To get through it until the next time, when it would be easier.

She ordered vanilla-bean crème brûlée, and for good measure, another glass of wine. Which probably wasn't a great idea since she had a meeting in just a bit, but she'd had a very bad day.

She'd been kicked to the curb by the charitable society she'd belonged to for five years. That alone was enough to justify a few drinks. Add to that her sudden identity crisis, and hell, she deserved the whole damn bottle.

After a few minutes, the dessert arrived and she broke the hard sugary top with a spoon. As a child, she'd dreamed of crème brûlée. To a poor kid raised in northeast Reno it had sounded rich. Exotic.

She took a bite and the rich custard tasted smooth on her tongue. She thought of her meeting with the PR and marketing departments. They'd said they had an exciting concept to promote ticket sales. She wondered what they'd come up with.

'Savage,' Coach Nystrom called from the doorway of the locker room. 'You're wanted upstairs in the conference room.'

Ty pulled his practice sweatshirt over his head. 'What's up?'

'Don't know.' The coach glanced at his clipboard. 'The rest of you hit the ice.'

Ty shoved his feet into a pair of Nike flip-flops and walked from the dressing room and through the lounge. The bottoms of the rubber soles slapped his heels as he moved down the hallway to the elevator. He hoped it was important. He had to hop on a flight in the morning and head to Vancouver for Game Five. The Chinooks were ahead 3–1 in the series, but that could easily change, and he needed the ice time with his teammates.

Before he hit the up button for the elevator, the doors slid open and the Widow Duffy stood inside. A pair of sunglasses covered her eyes and her full lips were painted red. Ty placed his hand on one side to keep the door open for her. 'Hello, Mrs. Duffy.'

'Hello.' She had a raincoat thrown over one arm, and she wore some ugly beige sweater set and pearls, like she was an over-fifty socialite on her way to some 'save the starving orphans' meeting. Despite her sedate clothes, she was hot as hell and overblown sexy.

She stood there looking at him through the beige lenses and he was forced to ask, 'Is this your floor?'

'Actually, I'm on my way up.' She pushed the glasses to the top of her windblown hair. 'I'm a little distracted and accidentally hit the wrong button.'

Ty stepped inside and the door closed behind him. He hit the Number Two button and the elevator started to move. 'Have a liquid lunch?'

She looked at him out of the corners of her eyes and clamped her mouth closed. 'I don't know what you're talking about,' she said through pursed lips.

He shoved a shoulder into the mirrored wall and clarified. 'I'm talking about you smelling boozy.'

Her big green eyes widened and she opened her bag to dig around inside. 'I've had a very rough day.' She pulled out a piece of cinnamon gum. 'Very rough.'

She owned a hockey team worth close to 200 million. How rough could it be? 'Break a nail?' He half expected her to check her red fingernails before she stuck the gum in her mouth.

'My life is more complicated than worrying about a broken nail.' She chewed, then added, 'Very complicated, and now that Virgil is gone, everything has changed. I don't know what to do.'

He wondered if she was one of those women who liked to talk about their problems with strangers. Lord, he hoped not, and raised his gaze to the ceiling, purposely breaking eye contact so she wouldn't feel free to unburden herself.

Thankfully, the elevator opened and Ty followed Faith down the hall to the conference room. He stepped ahead of her and opened the door.

She looked up into his eyes as she passed, close enough that her purse brushed the front of his sweatshirt. 'Thank you,' she said, smelling like cinnamon and flowers.

'You're welcome.' His gaze slid down her back to

her behind, covered in a pair of dull beige pants, and he had to admit that the woman's body did amazing things to her boring clothes. Stepping inside the room, he came to a sudden halt. He put his hand on his hip and stared at the billboard mock-ups propped up on easels about the space.

'Hello, everyone,' Faith said, all cheery as she hung her coat over a chair and took a seat beside her assistant at the conference table.

In contrast to Mrs. Duffy's cheerfulness, Ty asked, 'What the hell is this? A joke?'

A woman named Bo something or other from the public relations department shook her head. 'No. We need to capitalize on the coverage we've received and all the media attention we've been getting.' She pointed to a drawing of two people standing back to back with the caption 'Can Beauty Tame the Savage Beast?' 'The media seems to think there's a problem between the two of you, and we want to use that to our advantage.'

The PR director, Tim Cummins, added, 'Of course we know that there is no real problem.'

But there was a problem. A big one. Ty took a seat across from Faith and folded his arms across his chest. He and the boys had worked their asses off the last four game nights and all the press had been able to write about was 'the palpable friction' between him and Mrs. Duffy. In the sports section last Sunday, the *Seattle Times* had devoted a full three paragraphs to the supposed 'sparks' before they'd gotten around to mentioning his hat trick or goalie Marty Darche's impressive thirty-six saves. Frankie Kawczynski had broken a finger mixing it up in the corner with Doug Weight, and all she'd had to do was breeze into the lounge with her blond hair and big boobs and the press corps lost its damn mind. If anything, he wanted her less visible. Less involved with the press. Not more.

Faith looked up from the press clippings in front of her. 'I had no idea they blew that up and made something of it.' Her big green eyes looked up at him. 'Did you?'

'Of course. You didn't read the Chinooks coverage?' What had she been doing?

'Jules has given them to me, but I've been busy.'

With what? Meeting with the lover she'd been talking to the day of Virgil's funeral? Is that what she'd meant by a *rough day*?

'We think this will pack the seats with fans,' Tim continued. 'We're all aware the ticket sales have not yet reached the pre-lockout numbers. If fans think there might be some friction between the team's captain and the female owner, they might turn out to see it for themselves.'

Bo what's-her-name added, 'We think it's a good angle. Sexy, and as everyone knows, sex and contro-versy sells.'

Ty sat back in his chair and frowned. He didn't like it. Not one bit. What were they planning on doing? Sexing up Mrs. Duffy? She didn't need any more help.

Or him? A T-shirt and jeans were as sexy as he got. He just wasn't a hair-gel-wearing, blinging kind of guy.

'I think it's a good idea.' The king of gel and bling, Jules Garcia, pointed to one of the boards with the caption 'Beauty and the Savage Beast.' 'I like the idea of Faith wearing Ty's jersey, while he's bare chested.'

Ty frowned. The guys would never let him live that down. 'Forget it. I'm not going to be some "Savage Beast." '

'I believe it's some Sah-vahge Beast,' the drunk woman across the table pronounced dramatically.

Ty's gaze moved from Tim to Mrs. Duffy. 'That's right, Miss July.'

She twisted the pearls around one long finger and Ty's traitorous brain flashed on the picture of her naked with a string of pearls looped around one of her breasts. 'Perhaps the reporters saw something that I didn't. *Do* you have a problem with me, Mr. Savage?'

Other than she didn't know the difference between a defenseman and a forward, and the press tripped all over themselves to get to her? Other than he'd seen her naked peach and couldn't get it out of his head? 'No. No problem.'

'Excellent.' She smiled as her finger continued to twist those damn pearls, her red nails a bright contrast against all that beige.

'This is all very preliminary,' Tim assured him. 'We want you to feel comfortable.'

That wasn't going to happen. 'Well, Tim, I'm just

never going to feel comfortable being some savage beast in a pair of hockey shorts.'

'Would you feel more comfortable if you were a savage beast in a loincloth?' One corner of Faith's mouth tilted up higher than the other, and he was sure she was just trying to piss him off.

'Christ.' Ty stood and moved toward the door. 'Find some other asshole.'

'She was kidding. I think.' Tim looked at Faith. 'Weren't you?'

'Of course.'

'We can come up with something you like better,' the PR manager said in a rush. 'We really feel this will boost sales!'

Kidding or not, appearing on a billboard half-naked wasn't his style. His style was playing hard and putting points on the board. He reached for the doorknob. 'Forget it.'

'Baby.'

There was a collective gasp as he stopped and turned slowly around. 'What did you say?'

Jules leaned over and spoke in her ear. She shook her head and said, 'I don't particularly like the idea of creating friction to sell tickets, but you don't see me whining and storming out like a baby.'

That was probably because she didn't have to take off her shirt. Although it certainly wouldn't have been her first time. 'Let me make a few things really clear for you, Mrs. Duffy. First, I'm not a baby and I never whine.' Not even when he fractured bones or pulled tendons. Hell, he'd finished a game against the Rangers with a broken foot. 'Second, I play hockey. That's what you pay me to do. Nowhere in my contract does it stipulate that I have to appear shirtless on billboards and the sides of buses.'

'If you don't want to take your shirt off, I think that's fine.' She shrugged a shoulder. 'Some people aren't comfortable with their own sexuality. I understand, but the least you could do is listen to Tim and Bo. They've obviously put a lot of work into this, and in such a short time, too.' She turned her attention to the PR director and his assistant. 'Thank you.'

'Sure.'

'You're welcome.'

'Mr. Savage is just being unreasonable,' she added.

Comfortable with his sexuality? Did she just call him gay?

'Ten minutes,' Tim assured him. 'Give us ten minutes to change your mind.'

To prove her wrong, and that he wasn't *completely* unreasonable, he moved back to his chair and sat. 'Ten minutes.' They could talk until they dropped dead from exhaustion, but they weren't going to change his mind.

'Tilt your chin down just a little, Faith, and look right here.' Faith dipped her chin and raised her gaze to the photographer's hand a few inches above his head. 'Keep your eyes on me, Ty,' he added.

Inside the players' lounge, Faith stood in the center of the big Chinooks logo and slightly behind the captain of her hockey team. Almost a week had passed since she and Ty had sat in the PR meeting. Four days since the Chinooks had beaten Vancouver in game six and advanced to the next round in the playoffs.

It was after 7 p.m., long after the rest of the team had gone home for the day. The lounge had been stripped of furnishings and filled with camera equipment. Faith's mother made herself useful by holding up a white light reflector. For once, Faith had been able to persuade her mother to leave her dog at home. Although she did fear that Pebbles might retaliate by chewing up the furniture.

'A little more to the right, Faith.'

For the shoot, she wore a tight black pencil skirt,

black silk Georgette blouse with a black camisole, and a pair of red crocodile pumps. It had been a while since she'd stepped out of the shadows and into the spotlight. She felt a bit out of practice. It had been a while since she'd had her hair and makeup professionally done, and she felt a bit overdone. Everything from the arch of her brow to her red lips was perfect. In fact, everything in the room was perfect, from the lighting to the photographer. Everything except the 240 pounds of unhappy man standing directly in front of her. Heat and displeasure rolled off Ty in waves. His arms were folded across his chest; a posture she'd seen him take in the past when he was less than pleased about something. Today that something was getting his picture taken with her.

He wore a plain T-shirt that matched the darker blue of his eyes and a pair of worn Levi's. He hadn't allowed them to put makeup on his face or even a little gel in his hair. He was being a complete pain in the ass, but by contrast, he smelled wonderful, like soap and skin, and Faith had an odd little urge to lean forward a bit and smell his shirt or the side of his neck.

The photographer snapped the picture. 'Put your hand on his shoulder,' he said and adjusted the lens. 'Valerie, tilt that up a little. That's it.'

Other than the occasional handshake, Faith hadn't touched another man since she'd agreed to marry Virgil. She lightly rested her hand on Ty's shoulder. The warmth of his hard muscles heated her palm through the soft blue cotton, and for the first time in a very long time, she became acutely aware that she was a woman standing very close to a man. A young, healthy man. Not that she hadn't noticed before. It was impossible not to notice a man like Ty, but she'd never thought of him as anything more than the surly captain of the Chinooks.

'Slide your fingers forward. I want to see your red nails against the blue of his shirt.' She slid her hand over his shoulder and spread her fingers a bit. 'Yeah. Like that.'

Click. Click.

She dropped her hand but could still feel the heat of him in the center of her palm. She hadn't felt anything the least bit sexual for a man in a long time. She paid Ty's salary. He didn't even like her. So why did her stomach suddenly feel light, like she'd swallowed too much air?

'You doing okay, Ty?' Tim asked.

'Are we about done?'

'We just got started.'

'Shit.'

The photographer lowered his camera. 'Faith, if you could just come out in front a bit.'

Faith happily moved so that Ty stood just behind her left shoulder. She took a deep breath and cleared her head of all the hot pheromones he'd been throwing off like a tantalizing mirage.

'Spread your feet a little and put your hands on your

hips.' He raised the camera. 'And Ty, just keep looking belligerent.'

'I'm not belligerent.'

'Yeah. Perfect.' *Click.*

Faith laughed and glanced over her shoulder and up into his face and the furrow between his dark brows. 'If you're not being belligerent, then I'd hate to see you when you're downright hostile.'

He lowered his blue-on-blue gaze to hers. 'I'm never hostile.'

She thought of the last game against Vancouver and chuckled. He'd body-slammed a Canuck into the boards and jabbed him with his elbow. 'You're just a sweetheart.'

One corner of his mouth turned up and the feeling in her stomach got a little lighter. 'I wouldn't go quite that far, Mrs. Duffy.'

'Faith. You can call me Faith.'

His smile fell and he returned his gaze to the photographer. 'That's not a good idea.'

'Perfect.' *Click. Click.* 'Let's move into the locker room.'

'Faith, I have a change of clothes for you in the trainers' room,' Bo Nelson said. 'We want you in your home uniform, Ty.'

As Faith watched Ty leave the room, she wondered why he thought calling her by her given name was a bad idea. She and her mother followed the assistant PR director across the lounge and shut the door behind them. He probably just wanted to stay on professional terms. Which was always best, but she was fairly certain he hadn't called Virgil 'Mr. Duffy' all the time.

A rack of clothes took up the middle of the room. She looked them over and wondered why using her name wasn't the same as calling Virgil by his given name. Had she crossed some line she didn't know about?

'How do you feel?' Bo asked as she straightened the shoes. 'Like your face might crack from smiling?'

Faith pulled out a black sheath, then put it back. 'Being in front of the camera felt a little awkward at first, but I'm getting the hang of it again.'

Her mother pulled a hot-pink Betsey Johnson baby-doll dress off the rack. 'Try this one.'

Faith shook her head. 'I don't think that's appropriate for the owner of a hockey team.'

'We thought this.' Bo pulled a vibrant red dress with a scoop neckline and full silk skirt. It was sleeveless, and except for the silver metallic leather belt, it looked like something from the fifties.

'It's very bright.'

'The colors will look great on you.'

She hadn't worn that color red since she'd married Virgil. 'Who picked these out?' she asked the woman, whose auburn hair was pulled back in a stumpy ponytail.

'Jules worked with a stylist, and they chose that one because it will accent the red in Ty's home uniform.'

Jules? She knew he'd been busy consulting with the PR department, but she'd had no idea he'd helped choose outfits. Despite his unfortunate love of pastels and his ripped muscles, she'd never really gotten the gay vibe from him, but again she had to wonder.

'I'd wondered if he was gay,' Valerie said.

'Me too,' Bo added as she looked through the rack. 'He's very pretty.'

Faith kicked off her pumps as she unbuttoned her blouse. 'Being pretty or not is no indication that a man is gay.' One of the gay bouncers at Aphrodite had looked like a rode-hard biker.

'Not always.' Bo took the black blouse from Faith. 'Ty Savage is a pretty boy, but you'd never even think to question what he prefers.'

'Or his father.'

Faith looked from her skirt zipper to her mother. 'You know his father?'

'I met him the other night after the game.'

'You never mentioned it.'

Valerie shrugged. 'I wasn't impressed.'

Which probably meant he hadn't asked her out. With Bo's help, she pulled the dress over her head and her mother zipped it up in back. It showed a little more cleavage than she was used to, and the hem rested an inch above her knee.

'I *love* these.' Bo handed her a pair of Versace mirror leather sandals with four-inch stiletto heels.

Faith sighed. 'Come to Mama.' She slid her feet

inside and buckled the straps around her ankles. A full-length mirror stood a few feet away and she posed in front of it, adjusted her breasts within the tight bodice, then buckled the belt around her waist.

'It's perfect,' Bo told her.

'I look like an ad from the fifties. Like I should have a martini in one hand, waiting for my husband as he walks through the door.'

'A little *Leave It to Beaver*,' Bo agreed. 'June with more cleavage. I think you look sophisticated and fun.'

'How about these?' Valerie held up a pair of onyx chandelier earrings.

'I like the ones I'm wearing,' she said as someone retouched her hair and makeup. For her twenty-ninth birthday, Virgil had given her three-carat-diamond stud earrings that she loved for their clarity and class. She looked at herself one last time in the mirror. It was a bit shocking to see herself in such a bright color again. She wasn't sure when she'd given up wearing colors. If it had been her idea or Virgil's. Not that it mattered, she decided, as she left the trainers' room and moved through the now empty players' lounge.

Ty was sitting on a bench in front of an open locker filled with hockey sticks while the photographer and his assistant checked the lighting around him. His helmet and street clothes hung on hooks inside the locker, and his name was on a blue-and-red plaque above his head. Except for the helmet, he was dressed in full gear.

Faith had never been in the locker room before, and it smelled a little funky. Like leather and sweat and chemical cleaners. Each open locker was filled with hockey gear and had a plaque with each player's name above it.

Ty looked up as she approached. 'I've been ready for fifteen minutes.'

Lord, what a grouch. 'It doesn't take as long when you refuse to let anyone brush your hair,' she told him.

'I can brush it myself.' To prove his point, he ran his fingers through his hair, but one dark lock sprang forward and fell across his brow.

Before she gave it a thought, Faith raised her hand and pushed it back into place. The fine strands curled over her fingers and the heel of her palm brushed his warm temple. His gaze locked with hers and something flashed behind his eyes. Something hot and needy that turned the lighter color in his eyes a dark sensual blue. It had been a while, but she recognized the heat in his eyes. Her lips parted in alarm and confusion. She dropped her hand to the flutter in her stomach.

'You two ready?' the photographer asked.

Ty pulled his gaze away and looked beyond her. 'Let's get this over with. I have an early-morning practice and a game to win against San Jose tomorrow night.' He glanced back up at Faith and his gaze was clear. 'That's what you pay me for.'

'Yes,' she uttered, and wondered if she'd imagined the hot interest in his eyes.

'How's it going?' Jules asked as he walked into the locker room.

Faith licked her lips and smiled at her assistant. 'I'm doing great,' she assured him and pushed her confusion about what had just happened to the back of her mind. 'I was a little rusty at first, but it's coming back to me. Kind of like riding a bike.'

Jules looked her up and down with a critical eye. 'Well, you look great.'

'Thanks. So do you.' Or at least she tried to push it to the back of her mind. With Ty sitting a foot away, it was impossible. 'I like your sweater,' she added, reaching out to touch the arm of the gray cable-knit cardigan. 'Nice color.' Subtle. 'Cashmere?'

'Cashmere-silk blend.'

'Jesus,' Ty swore. 'Are you two girls finished? I'd like to get out of here sometime tonight.'

'What's wrong with *him*?' Jules gestured to Ty with his thumb. 'Still pissed off about screwing the pooch in Game Five against Vancouver?'

Ty looked at the assistant as if he was going to kill him with his big hands.

Faith's eyes widened and she shook her head. 'Don't poke the bear, Jules.'

Jules laughed. 'Listen, the reason I'm here is because I just got off the phone with an editor from *Sports Illustrated*. They want to interview you.'

The last time she'd appeared in a magazine, she'd been naked and the questions had been easy. The thought of appearing in *Sports Illustrated* and being asked hard questions that she couldn't answer made her want to run and hide. Making uninformed blunders to a room of staff and management was embarrassing enough. The last thing she wanted was to appear ignorant to the world.

'The PR department wants you to do it, but I think you should hold off until you're more comfortable speaking publicly about the team,' Jules suggested, and she could have kissed him.

'Thanks, and you're right. I'm not ready.'

'We're about set,' the photographer announced as he handed Valerie the light reflector. 'Faith, I need you to stand right in front of Ty. Maybe put your foot on the bench.'

She glanced at Ty's big legs covered in his blue-and-green hockey shorts. Long white socks covered his thick shin and knee pads. The tops were taped around his thighs. 'Where on the bench?'

'Between Ty's thighs.'

She looked down into his narrowed gaze and expected him to raise a loud objection and swear until everyone's ears bled. Instead he said, 'Mind your foot, eh? I'm not wearing a cup.'

Carefully, she planted the sole of her Versace sandal on the bench between his widely spread thighs. She purposely stared into his face to keep from lowering her gaze to his crotch. She didn't even want to think about the close proximity of his package to her toes. Of course, trying not to think about it only made her think about it all the more. 'Don't make me jumpy, and I won't hurt you,' she said through a nervous laugh.

'Don't get jumpy and *I* won't hurt *you*. I'm going to need that equipment later.'

She turned her face toward the photographer and curved her lips into a smile. She might be a little rusty, but she knew how to pose for a photo without showing her true emotion. 'So that's why you're in a hurry to leave. Not because you have an early flight.'

The photographer snapped a few pictures. 'Faith, turn your right shoulder slightly toward me. That's it.'

As she smiled for the camera, she asked, 'Got a hot date?' and gave the photographer a slightly different angle of her face.

'Something like that.'

'Wife?'

'Not married.'

'Girlfriend?'

'Not exactly.'

Friend with benefits? It had been a long time since she'd had a friend with benefits or a boyfriend or even a one-night stand. Being here with Ty, surrounded by his toxic testosterone, reminded her exactly how long it had been. Just the deeper timbre of his voice brushed across her skin and reminded her how much she missed being held and touched by a strong, healthy man.

'Lean forward just a tiny bit, Faith. More aggressive, like you're the boss.'

'Do you want my hands on my hips?' Faith leaned and the skirt of the dress slid up her thigh.

'Yep, that's great. And Ty, just continue to look pissed off.'

Ty turned his gaze of doom on the photographer. 'I'm not pissed off.' The intense glare usually reserved to intimidate opponents didn't work on the photographer.

'Perfect. That's exactly what I'm looking for.' He snapped a few more photos. 'Faith, lean in just a bit and turn your shoulders toward me just a little more.' *Click*. 'Yeah, toss your hair. That's it. Beautiful.'

Ty could not recall a time when he'd been so turned on. Not even as a horny sixteen-year-old rolling around in the backseat of his dad's Plymouth with a semi-naked girl named Brigit.

Christ. He stood in the shower in the Chinooks locker room and let the cold water run down his neck, his back and behind. He'd had to wait for half an hour for everyone to clear out of the locker room before stripping out of his gear and walking into the shower. If anyone thought it was odd that he took a shower tonight, no one mentioned it.

He turned and the cold water hit his chest and ran down his stomach to his groin. He hadn't been in this much throbbing pain since he'd broken his thumb on Hedican's helmet last season. Only this time the throbbing pain was lower and hadn't been caused by an aggressive defenseman trying to get at his puck. It had been caused by a living, breathing centerfold trying to drive him insane with her pouty mouth, soft hands, and sizzling-hot body.

The whole thing had been a bad idea. He'd known it going in. Despite what they thought of him, he wasn't a hard-ass, and he'd let them talk him into the promotion for the good of the team. To get fans into the seats.

He placed his palms on the wall and shoved his head under the shower. He'd been doing a pretty good job of ignoring Mrs. Duffy. He'd ignored the scent of perfume on warm skin, the sound of her laugher, and her red, red lips. Then she'd touched him. The weight of her hand and her fingers sliding across his shoulder had sent fire down his spine and straight between his legs.

Rubbing her hand on his shoulder had been bad, but touching his hair and face had made his gut clench, and he'd had to fight like hell to keep from turning his mouth into her palm and sucking her skin. Then she'd put her foot in his crotch, leaned forward, and stuck her breasts in his face. After that, all he'd been able to think about was sliding his palm up the back of her smooth thigh and grabbing a handful of her ass. Pulling her closer and burying his face in the front of her dress. While she'd been smiling and tossing her hair for the camera, he'd been having some wild fantasies about what he wanted to do to her. Things that involved pulling her down on his lap and kissing her red lips.

Tangling his fingers in her hair while she rode him like Smarty Jones in the long stretch. And yeah, he'd been royally pissed off about that. The last thing he wanted and needed in his life was a hard-on for the owner of the hockey team, but for some inexplicable reason, his body didn't care what he wanted and needed.

Ty straightened and rubbed his hands over his face. It wasn't as if she was all that beautiful. He cleared the water from his eyes and shook his head. Okay, that wasn't true. Everything about her was hot as hell, but it wasn't as if he'd never been around beautiful women. He was a hockey player. He'd had his share of beautiful women.

Faith. You can call me Faith, she'd said, like that was a good idea or ever going to happen. He needed a constant reminder of who she was and what she was to him. A reminder that she held his fate in her hands. Even if she was willing, he needed to remember that sex with the owner of the Chinooks was an appallingly bad idea.

Gooseflesh rose on his skin as he tried to clear his head of Faith Duffy. There were a few places he could go before he headed home. A few clubs where there were women who would be happy to share a little one-on-one time with him.

He stayed in the shower a few more minutes, until he was in control and could breathe again. He turned off the water and wrapped a towel around his waist. He grabbed a second towel and dried his hair. His dad was still hanging out at his place. Maybe he'd just go home and see what the old man had going on.

Jules Garcia stood in the middle of the locker room waiting for him. 'What do you want?' he asked Faith's assistant.

'To ask you to stop giving Faith such a hard time.' He had his arms folded across his big chest like he was big, bad trouble.

Ty kind of respected him for that. 'Who says I give Mrs. Duffy a hard time?' As he moved to his locker, he dried his face and wondered if this was a case of an employee sticking up for his employer, or something else. Some of the guys wondered if Jules might be gay. Ty wasn't convinced.

'I do.'

Ty sighed and sat down on the bench. He didn't want to give her a hard time. He just wanted to be around her as little as possible, and her relationship with her assistant wasn't his business.

'She's not just some blonde off the street. She's the owner of the team.'

'That's right,' Ty agreed and ran the towel over his head. 'And she knows nothing about hockey. I was hired by Virgil to win the cup. I'm the captain of the Chinooks and my ultimate responsibility is to get us into the last final round. But I have major concerns about how I'm going to do that with a former Playboy Playmate holding our fate in her hands and making us look like idiots in interviews.'

'Are you talking about *Sports Illustrated*?'

'Yep.'

'Are you jealous because they want to put her on the cover?'

Ty folded his arms over his bare chest. He hadn't known about the cover. 'I've been on the cover three times, and I don't give a flying fuck about the cover. What I do give a fuck about is picking up the magazine and reading softball questions that she can't answer. Or picking up the magazine and reading a recap of her *Playboy* years that makes us all look ridiculous.'

'That's understandable. Everyone is concerned about the team's image. Especially Faith.' He dropped his hands to his sides. 'I admit that when she first called and set up a meeting with me, I was more curious about seeing her than wanting to take the job. Virgil fired me five years ago for talking shit about her.'

'What did you say that got you fired?'

Jules looked him in the eye and answered. 'He overheard me telling the head scouts that he'd married a stripper young enough to be his granddaughter.'

Ty dropped the towel on the bench beside him. 'Doesn't sound like something to get fired over.'

'It wasn't, and if I'd stopped with that, I would have kept my job. But I'd seen her layout and I described her in detail for the guys. Everything from her big boobs to her bald . . . you know.'

Yeah, he did know.

He shrugged a shoulder. 'Anyway, I resented her for

a lot of years, but it wasn't her fault I was fired. Any more than Virgil dying and leaving her the team is her fault. It landed in her lap and she's trying hard to deal with it the best she can.'

'I am aware that it's not her fault.' He reached behind him into his locker and pulled out his sports bag. It wasn't her fault she'd inherited the team, and his hard-on wasn't her fault either. The former was Virgil's doing and the latter was his horny imagination. He had to figure out a better way to deal with both. 'I'll try to be . . .'

'Nicer? Make her happy.'

'More respectful. It's your job to make her happy. Maybe you two can go shopping, buy matching sweaters, and have a girls' night.'

'What?' Jules folded his arms over his big chest, again looking like he was big, bad trouble. 'I'm not gay.'

Ty stood and dropped his towel. 'I don't give a shit if you're gay or straight or somewhere in between.' He knew several gay players who hit like freight trains.

'Why do you think I'm "gay or straight or somewhere in between?"' Jules looked truly baffled. 'Do the other guys think I'm gay?'

Ty shrugged.

'Because I use hair product?'

'No.' He stepped into his underwear. 'Because you *say* "hair product."'

7

A discordant wave of cheers and cowbells rose from the arena below and clashed with the clinking of wineglasses within the skybox inside the Key Arena in Seattle. Faith leaned forward, her fingers gripping the arm of her chair as she gazed down at the scrum in front of the Chinooks net. Sticks and elbows flew in the crease, and of course Ty Savage was right in the center of the action. Goalie Marty Darche went down in a butterfly, stacking his pads while the players on both teams battled it out in the second period.

'Clear the puck,' she whispered, just as the blue light at the back of the cage spun, tying the score at two.

'Shit,' Jules swore as a small contingent of loyal Sharks fans went wild in the stadium below. 'Who Let the Dogs Out' blasted from the speakers, and Faith put a hand over her eyes. Now that she was so invested in the game, it was painful to watch. It made her nerves jump and her stomach knot and had her wishing for something stronger than the Diet Coke she had sitting next to her right foot.

As if she'd read her mind, Valerie took Faith's hand from her eyes and pressed a glass of wine into her palm. 'This will help.' Then she went back to the buffet set up in the box to entertain her girl friend, Sandy, up for a few days from Vegas. Valerie hadn't even asked if Sandy could stay before she'd invited her. Faith had known and liked Sandy all her life and didn't mind, she just wished her mother had asked.

After the game, her mom and Sandy planned to hit some bars and 'raise hell.' Faith wasn't sure who was the most pathetic. Them, for wearing spandex and 'raising hell' at their age, or her, for going home and going to bed early.

Faith took a drink of her Chardonnay as the goal was replayed over and over on the sports timer suspended in the center of the arena.

On the ice at the other end, Marty Darche rose to his feet and grabbed a water bottle from the top of his net. Ty stood in front of him while the goalie shot water into his mouth. Marty nodded and Ty patted the top of the goalie's helmet with his big gloved hand before skating toward the bench.

On the big sports screen, the camera zoomed in on the back of Ty's broad shoulders and the white letters spelling out SAVAGE across his blue jersey. The San Jose Fans booed. The Chinooks fans cheered and Ty moved across the ice with his head down; the hair at the back of his neck curled up around his helmet. Last night in the Chinooks locker room, she'd run her fingers through his hair and a warm little flutter had tickled her stomach. The kind she hadn't felt in years. But later that night after she'd returned home, the little flutter had turned into a burning stab of guilt. Virgil had been dead less than a month and she shouldn't be feeling warm little *any things* with any man, let alone the captain of Virgil's hockey team. Correction: *her* hockey team.

Ty stopped in front of the bench and glanced up over his shoulder. His blue eyes looked out from the sports screen. One corner of his mouth kicked up into a half-assed smile as if he enjoyed both the booing and cheering fans, and that traitorous, horrible warm flutter settled in the middle of her stomach once more. It had been a long time since she'd felt little flutters and tingles for any man. Why Ty Savage? Yeah, he was beautiful and confident and comfortable with his virility. He wore it like an irresistible aura of hotness, but he didn't like her. She wasn't especially fond of him.

The camera switched to the crowd and scanned the rows of Chinooks fans. It stopped on two men with their faces painted green and blue and the little flutter calmed. From her position high above the arena, Faith turned her gaze to the Chinooks bench and the players who'd stopped shaving for the playoffs. Their facial hair ranged from fuzzy and patchy to Miami Vice scruff. Ty was one in only a handful of NHL players who chose to ignore the tradition and shaved.

Ty took a seat next to Vlad Fetisov. He grabbed a bottle from a waiting trainer and sprayed a stream of water into his mouth. He spit it out between his feet, then wiped his face with a towel.

'Do you need anything?' Jules asked as he stood.

She shook her head and looked up at her assistant, who wore a red-and-white argyle sweater that was so tight, it hugged his big muscles like a second skin. 'No thanks.'

Faith settled back into her seat and thought about tomorrow's flight and the game against San Jose the following night. Faith had never planned to travel with the team, but just that morning Jules had convinced her that it was a good idea and it showed support. He'd said it was a good way for her to get to know the twenty-four men who played for her. If they saw her more, they might feel more at ease with her as the new owner. She wasn't sure if her assistant had her best interest in mind, or if he just wanted to catch the second game.

When his health had permitted, Virgil had sometimes traveled with the Chinooks, often catching a game or two before returning home, but Faith had never traveled with him. Never had the urge to live and breathe the game. And although she was just beginning to understand a little about what 'points against' and 'averages' meant, she wondered if she would ever understand it completely. The kind of understanding that came with living and breathing and loving hockey for years.

Jules returned with a Corona and a taquito and sat next to her. 'Tell me something,' he said in a voice just loud enough for her to hear. 'Do you automatically think a guy is gay because he says "hair product"?'

Faith looked into Jules's dark green eyes. 'No,' she answered carefully. 'Did my mother or Sandy say you were gay?'

'No.' He took a bite of his taquito. 'I know you'll find this surprising, but some of the guys on the team think I'm gay.'

'Really?' She kept her face blank. 'Why?'

He shrugged one big shoulder and raised the bottle to his mouth. 'Because I care about my appearance.' He took a drink, then added, 'And apparently straight men don't say "hair product."'

'That's ridiculous.' They suspected he was gay for the way he dressed and his dubious color choices. She turned her attention to the ice as Walker Brookes skated to the face-off circle while Ty watched from the sidelines. The camera panned the Chinooks bench. Some of them were relaxed and watchful like Ty, while others yelled at opposing players as they moved past.

Walker entered the playoffs circle, stopped in the middle, and waited with his stick down. The puck dropped. Game on. 'Who says you can't say "hair product"?' she asked.

'Ty Savage.'

She looked back at Jules. 'Don't listen to Ty.' He had too much testosterone to be any sort of judge. 'Straight men say "hair product" all the time.'

'Name one.'

She had to think about it for a few moments. She snapped her fingers and said, 'That Blow Out guy, Jonathan Antin.' Jules winced as if she'd just proven Ty's point.

'I don't think that's even on TV anymore,' Jules grumbled. 'That guy was kinda gay. I'm not gay.' Something in her face must have betrayed her because his gaze pinched. 'You think so too!'

She shook her head and rounded her eyes.

'Yes, you do.' He made a motion with his hand. 'Why?'

'It doesn't matter.'

'Tell me.'

She shrugged. On the ice below, the whistle blew and Sam Leclaire automatically skated to the sin bin. Sam might not be a great fighter, but that didn't keep him from throwing his gloves and sitting out an average of seven penalty minutes a game.

'It's the way you dress. You wear everything really tight and your color choices are a bit bold for a straight man.'

Jules frowned and folded his arms across his bulky chest. 'At least I'm not afraid of color. You dress in beige and black all the time.' He glanced at the rink below, then back at her. 'A few years ago, I was fat. I got really tired of wearing a size forty-six, so I decided to change my life. I work hard on my body. So why not show it off?'

'Because sometimes less is better,' she answered. As

in showing less skin, and she should know. 'And sometimes loose is more flattering.'

He shrugged. 'Maybe, but everything you wear is so loose it looks like you're trying to hide something under your clothes.'

Faith looked down at her black turtleneck and black pants. Before Virgil, she'd worn tight clothes with cutouts over her cleavage. She'd gone from one extreme to the other to try and fit into his world. Now, she no longer fit in either.

'But I guess it doesn't matter what *you* wear. You're beautiful and don't have to worry about it. Sometimes I worry that some guy is going to think I'm your bodyguard and try and start something with me.'

Faith figured Jules was being weird and just a tad dramatic. 'I won't let anyone hurt you. You might dress like you're experiencing some kind of metrosexual meltdown, but I need to keep you around. Plus,' she said through a smile, 'your hair's *bangin'*.'

He looked at her a moment as 'Are You Ready To Rock?' blasted from the arena speakers. 'That's the first genuine smile I've seen out of you,' he said.

'I smile all the time.'

He raised his beer. 'Yes, but you don't mean it.'

Faith turned her attention to the sports timer and the action below. Long before she'd met Virgil, she'd learned to smile when she didn't mean it. Long before she'd stepped her first acrylic heel onstage and transformed herself into Layla, she'd learned to mask her true feelings with a smile. Life was sometimes easier that way.

But life had a weird way of throwing curveballs, or curved pucks, rather. Never in a million years would she have thought she'd someday own a hockey team. It would never have even occurred to her in a wild fantasy, but here she was, watching her team shoot pucks and throw punches. She wondered what they were going to think when she boarded the jet with them tomorrow.

The next morning she found out as she followed Coach Nystrom into the BAC-111. She couldn't see beyond his wide shoulders, but a low hum of male voices filled the forty-passenger craft. It was seven thirty, and they were still keyed up from their win against the Sharks the night before.

From the back of the plane, someone complained loud enough for everyone to hear, 'The son of a bitch tried to shove his stick up my ass.'

'Wouldn't be the first time you walked around with a stick up your ass,' someone else said. This triggered a lot of deep manly laughter followed by numerous 'up your ass' commentaries and speculations.

'Listen up,' Coach Nystrom said from the front of the plane. 'Mrs. Duffy is traveling with us to San Jose.' As if someone pushed a PAUSE button, all laughter and butt jokes abruptly stopped. 'So keep it clean.'

The coach took his seat and Faith was suddenly the focus of several dozen startled male faces. From one row back, Ty Savage looked up from the USA Today sports section he held in his hands. The light above his head shone in his dark hair, and his eyes locked with her for several long seconds before he lowered his gaze to the paper once more.

Jules waited for her in the third-row window seat and she took her place beside him. 'How long is the flight?' she asked.

'Less than an hour.'

Behind her she heard a few low whispers and a couple of deep chuckles. She buckled herself in and, except for a few bits of conversation too low for Faith to hear, and the rustle of Ty's newspaper, the fuselage remained quiet as they taxied to the runway and took off. Once they punched through the thick, gray clouds, the stabbing rays of morning sun flooded the oval windows. Almost as one, the shades were all pulled down.

Faith wondered if they were quiet because they'd played a grueling game the night before that had ended in a 3–4 win in overtime and it was suddenly catching up to them, or if it was because she was sitting in the front of the jet.

Once the snow-covered summit of Mount Rainier was behind them, Darby Hogue leaned across the aisle and asked, 'How are you doing?'

'Okay. Are they usually this quiet?'

Darby smiled. 'No.'

'Are they uncomfortable flying with me?'

'They're just a little superstitious about traveling

with a woman. A few years ago, a female reporter traveled with the team. They didn't like it at first, but they got used to her. They'll get used to you, too.' He turned and looked into the seat behind him. 'Got that tape, Dan?'

He was handed a DVD that he plugged into his laptop. Then he turned the screen for Faith to see. 'This is Jaroslav Kobasew. We're looking at him to fill the hole in our second-line defense. We need more size in the back, and he's six foot five and two thirty-five.'

She hadn't known they had a hole in the second line or anywhere else. 'I thought we couldn't make any trades.'

'Not until after the season ends, but we're always scouting new talent,' Darby told her.

She looked into the screen across the aisle as a huge man in a red jersey battled for a puck in the corner. The huge guy won by knocking the other player off his skates. 'Good Lord.'

Jules leaned over her. 'How does he hit?'

'Like he has cement in his gloves,' Darby answered.

'How does he skate?'

'Like he has cement in his shorts.'

Normally, Faith would have thought cement in shorts was a bad thing. But this was hockey and she didn't know. Maybe that meant he could take a hit. 'And that's bad. Right?'

Jules nodded and sat back.

'He's just one of the players we're considering,'

Darby said and turned the screen to face him. 'When I narrow it down, I'll let you know.'

'Okay.' She turned to Jules and asked out of one corner of her mouth, 'Do they have to discuss trades with me?'

He nodded and set his briefcase on his lap. 'Did I forget to tell you that?'

'Yeah. You did.' And it was kind of important, although she couldn't complain. If not for Jules, she'd be lost. Well, even more than she already was lost.

He pulled out a stack of *Hockey News* magazines and handed them to her. 'Dig in.'

She flipped past various copies and settled on the February issue, with Ty Savage on the cover, his face beaded with sweat as his vivid blue eyes looked at the camera from beneath his white helmet. He looked intimidating and intense. The caption on the left read 'Can Ty Savage Deliver Lord Stanley to Seattle?'

The magazine had come out a month before Virgil's death, and she thumbed past a story on Jeremy Roenick to the center of the magazine. On the right side was a color photo of Ty appearing bare chested. He had his hands behind his head and his chest was rippled with clearly defined muscles. In black ink, his last name was tattooed down his side from just below his armpit to the waistband of his jeans. She had a Playboy bunny inked in the small of her back. It had hurt like crazy, and she couldn't imagine getting a tattoo the size of Ty's.

Looking at his photo, if she didn't know better, she'd

think she was staring at a 'hunk of the month' calendar. The shot was from the waist up and only the hint of a smile curved his mouth. The left side of the center spread was filled with columns of career stats with the byline 'Saint or Traitor?' superimposed on the impressive list going back to his days in the minors. The article began:

Without a doubt, Ty Savage is one of the NHL's best and toughest players. He's known for laying on the big hits on open ice. As a result, he makes opponents keep their heads up and think twice about going up against this Selke winner.

He is, as everyone who follows the game knows, the son of hockey great, Pavel Savage. A relationship he is reluctant to talk about.

'My father was one of the best players in NHL history,' he says in his best surly Savage.

Faith smiled. She knew exactly what the reporter was talking about. No one did surly better than Ty.

'But I am not my father. We play different games. When I hang up my skates for the last time, I want to be judged by my skill on the ice. Not by my last name.'

   Enough said.

   Unless he commits an unpardonable sin, history will judge this former Art Ross Trophy winner with the same respect it reserves for the likes of Howe, Gretsky, Messier, and dare we say it, Pavel Savage.

   Although there are those in Canada who'd like the younger Savage deleted from their national archives. This stems from Ty's defection from the Vancouver Canucks to the Seattle Chinooks this past month. To many Canadians, the name 'Savage' is sacred, like Macdonald, Trudeau and Molson. Perhaps unfairly, this native son who once was hailed as a hero is now considered a traitor. In the past weeks, the Vancouver media has vilified him, even going so far to burn him in effigy. At which Savage merely shrugs. 'I understand their feelings,' he says. 'Canadians are passionate about hockey. That's what I love about them, but they don't own me.'

   When asked about his reputation for playing a hard physical game, he laughs and responds, 'That's my job.'

Faith looked up from the magazine. Ty laughs? She'd been around him several times in the past few weeks, and the man had barely cracked a smile.

She returned her gaze to the *Hockey News* in her lap and turned the page. She looked at the photos of Ty colliding center ice with a Flyer, and of him scoring a goal against Pittsburgh.

'Some might say your hard physical style hurts people. That you're not a very nice person.'

'I play hard physical hockey. That's my job, but I never go after anyone who doesn't have the puck. If that means I'm not a nice person, I can live with that. I've never been interested in the Lady Byng Trophy, and I'm not going to lose sleep worrying about whether people think I'm 'nice.' If I'm a dick sometimes, no one will ask me for money or want to borrow my truck to move their crap.'

'Has that happened to you?'

'Not so much these days.'

Speaking of money, the Chinooks paid $30 million for their captain, and there were a lot of people, including those in the Chinooks organization, who thought the money would have been better spent on their defense. But owner Virgil Duffy knows the wisdom of acquiring a player the caliber of Savage.

'Every time he steps on the ice,' Duffy is

quoted as saying, 'he increases the value of the Chinooks franchise.'

A few rows behind Faith, she heard the shuffle of newspaper mixed with the low hum of deep male voices. If Virgil had thought Ty was worth thirty million, then he was, and more.

Traitor or Saint doesn't matter much to Ty Savage. He just wants to play hockey his way and win the cup. 'I have no doubt we'll make it into the final round. We've got the talent to get us that far. After that, it's going to come down to who hits harder and puts the most points on the board.' He flashes a rare smile. 'And what a guy's got in his sac.'
   Enough said.

Faith closed the magazine. Somehow she doubted Ty had been talking about those Sac poof chairs.

A warm breeze blew through the San Jose airport, bringing with it the smell of asphalt and jet fuel. Ty climbed down the steps of the BAC-111 and walked across the tarmac. He unbuttoned his team blazer, shoved his hands into the pockets of his wool pants, and made his way to the chartered bus.

'That's my Louie hatbox.'

He glanced toward the cargo hold of the plane,

where Mrs. Duffy stood, the wind whipping the tails of her black coat about her knees.

'And that's the matching wheelie,' she added, pointing into the bay.

Jules took a big Louis Vuitton suitcase and a round case with a loop handle from one of the equipment managers who stood at the cargo bay unloading bags and equipment.

Ty glanced at the faces around him. Through the lenses of his sunglasses, he could see the guy's confusion. He felt it too. Why did a two-day trip require two pieces of luggage? Especially a hatbox? How many hats could one woman wear in forty-eight hours?

He boarded the bus and took an aisle seat toward the front. Until she'd walked onto the plane in Seattle, he and the guys hadn't even known she was traveling with them. Outside the window, Ty watched her move across the tarmac toward Darby. The loop of her hatbox circled one wrist and she shoved a pair of big sunglasses on her face. Her blond hair slid across her cheek and she raised her free hand to push it behind one ear. The flight from Washington had been quiet. Too quiet for a group of guys who excelled at talking trash at 35,000 feet. If she hadn't been on the flight, they would have questioned the paternity of several San Jose players, and they would have broken out the cards for air poker. Frankie was down five hundred bucks, and Ty was sure the Sniper wanted a chance to get some of it back. Little had Ty known that when he'd suggested they all play poker as a way to bond, it would turn into a never-ending game.

'I'd pay a lot of money to see her on a stripper pole again,' Sam said as he slid into the window seat next to Ty. 'Maybe busting out of a short little nurse's outfit.' He sighed like he was in the middle of some porn fantasy. 'And those clear plastic shoes they all wear. And an ankle bracelet. I love a lady in an ankle bracelet.'

'You should probably give up on that dream, Rocky,' Ty said, using Sam's nickname. 'Especially since she owns you, eh?'

Sam unbuttoned his jacket. 'I don't mind that she owns us. Not like some of the guys. She's surrounded by a lot of smart people who won't let her make a huge mistake. I remember Jules from five years ago. He knows a lot about hockey. Back then he was a pudgy guy with a mullet. He hadn't come out of the closet yet.'

More players piled on the bus, and Ty looked out the window as Faith nodded at something Jules said to her. 'He claims he's not gay.'

'Really.' Sam shrugged. 'I had a cousin who dressed like that in the nineties. He wasn't gay either.' Sam shrugged. 'But he was from Long Island,' he added as if that explained it. He turned his face and looked out the window. 'What do you suppose she's got in the box? Handcuffs? Whips? French maid uniform?'

Ty chuckled. 'I'd guess hats.'

'Why would a woman need that many hats?'

Now it was Ty's turn to shrug. 'I've never been married.' In fact, he'd only come close to it once. That is, if he counted the time his old girlfriend, LuAnn, had proposed to *him*. Though he didn't know if that even counted, because he'd run screaming in the other direction. He wasn't against marriage. For other people.

'Well, my ex never carried a hatbox around when she traveled.'

'I didn't know you were married.' He looked up as Coach Nystrom and goalie coach Don Boclair stepped into the bus.

'Yeah. Been divorced five years. I have a little boy. His mamma just couldn't handle the life, ya know.'

He knew. The divorce rate for hockey players was high. They were gone for half of the long season, and it took a strong woman to stay at home while her man was on the road working hard, living large, and fending off puck bunnies.

Or not. Being married to a hockey player had made Ty's mother crazy, or so she'd claimed. Or perhaps she'd already been crazy, as his father claimed. Who knew? The only thing for certain was that she'd died of a toxic cocktail of Klonopin, Xanax, Lexapro, and Ambien. The doctors had called it an accidental overdose. Ty wasn't convinced. His mother's life had always been one long emotional roller coaster, and whether she'd been born with a mental illness or had been driven to it, the result had been the same. Ty's mother had battled depression that had ended her life. He wasn't worried that he'd end up sad and depressed like his mother. He worried that he was too much like his father to care.

Ty pulled back the thick sleeve of his coat and looked at his watch. It was a little after eight o'clock in Seattle and he wondered what his dad was going to do while he was gone. Other than what he always did: drink all Ty's beer and watch ESPN. It had been two weeks now since Pavel had shown up at his door. Over two weeks of his father practicing his backswing or hanging out at strip clubs. Over two weeks, and it didn't seem like his dad was planning on leaving anytime soon.

The door to the bus opened and Jules entered, followed by Faith. The assistant moved to sit by the window, while Faith took a seat across the aisle and two rows up from Ty. She set her hatbox on her lap and placed her hands on the sides. The light caught on her huge platinum and diamond wedding ring and shone on her red nails.

Just as before, when she had stepped on the plane, silence descended like a heavy brick wall. Singly and collectively, every hockey player on the bus had been around a lot of beautiful women. They'd been around a lot of strippers. Some of them had even been to parties at the Playboy Mansion. But for some reason, this former stripper turned Playmate made all those cocky hockey players tongue-tied. Probably it was because she had so much power over them. More than likely it was because she was stunning. Or it was both.

'Listen up, boys.' Coach Nystrom stood at the front of the bus. 'We have practice this afternoon and then you're on your own until light practice tomorrow morning. We have an important game tomorrow night; I don't need to tell you all to stay out of trouble.' He sat in the first row. 'Okay, bussie,' he said. 'Let's move out.' The driver closed the door and the bus rolled across the tarmac.

The San Jose Marriott was in the heart of downtown and not far from the HP Pavilion. On the short drive to the hotel, Ty folded his arms across the front of his wool jacket and watched the sun hitting the buildings and lighting up rows of palm trees. It was still early in the playoffs, but a win against the Sharks tomorrow night was very important. After practice today, he wanted to review game tapes of the San Jose defense and their goalie, Evgeni Nabokov. In last night's game, Nabokov had stopped twenty-three shots on goal. He was cool under pressure and consistent, but even cool, consistent goalies had bad nights. Ty's job was to make him wish they'd sent in the rookie.

A few rows up, Faith slid her hand up the sides of her hatbox, over the top, and then back down. Her long, thin fingers brushed the Louis Vuitton monogram, back and forth, caressing it like a lover. Her shiny red nails scraped the hard surface, and Ty's scalp got tight, as if she'd touched him again.

'Jesus H,' Ty whispered and leaned his head back. He was tired and his right ankle hurt like a bitch. He had a game against the Sharks to think about, and his old man was making him nuts. And thanks to Sam, one prevailing thought pushed everything out of his head: What the hell was in the damned hatbox? Sam might fantasize about nurses, but Ty was a lingerie man. He loved lacy garters and thigh-high stockings on a pair of smooth thighs.

Being a trophy wife had been hard work. It had been more than champagne wishes and caviar dreams. It had been always looking perfect and going to country clubs and parties that you learned to enjoy. It meant sometimes socializing with people you might not like and who might not like you. Although Virgil had become Faith's best friend, he'd always been the boss. There was never any doubt about it, but after being responsible for her own survival for so long, it had been nice to let someone else take care of her. To kick back and not worry about paying her bills. To have her biggest concern of the day involve which dress to wear to the Rainier Club.

Virgil had never made her do anything she'd felt strongly against, but he'd been in charge. The captain of his life, and for the most part, hers. She'd dressed to fit into his life, and she'd learned about perception and image. She'd learned subtlety. That sexy had more to do with what you covered up than what you let hang out. It was more than skin-tight clothes and flashy makeup – something her mother had yet to learn.

For the first time in years, Faith went shopping that afternoon to please herself and no one else. She hit the streets of downtown San Jose and shopped at Burberry and BCBG and Ferragamo. She shopped the more edgy designs by Gucci and a new, up-and-coming French designer. She bought casual clothes from Diesel in colors she hadn't worn in years. She bought soft cotton T-shirts and jeans. She bought hoodies that she intended to wear for occasions other than to work out. By the time she was finished, it was six hours later and her feet hurt.

The sun had set. She waited next to the curb by Cole Haan for a town car to pick her up. Her cell phone rang and she dug it out of the depths of her Fendi tote.

'Some of the guys are at an Irish pub a few blocks from the hotel,' Jules said into her ear. 'You need to go in there and have a drink with them.'

'What?' She'd spent the morning spying on the Sharks' practice with Jules and the afternoon shopping. 'I'm exhausted.'

'It's a good way for the guys to get to know you. In case you didn't notice, they're kind of uptight when you're around.'

Two teenage girls with complicated haircuts, tight black pants, and thick eyeliner walked past. They looked at her mountain of bags with sad emo eyes and shook their sad emo heads at her disgusting display of consumer greed. 'I noticed, but I don't know what to say to them.'

'Just be yourself.'

That was a problem. She wasn't sure who she was anymore.

'I know you can be witty and charming,' he said, clearly lying. 'Let them see a bit of who you are. Other than the owner of the team and a former Playmate and Las Vegas stripper. Which is how they see you now.' He paused and added a quick, 'No offense intended.'

The town car rolled up to the curb and she waved it to a stop. 'None taken.' She was never offended by the truth. And the truth was that the last time she'd been in the same room with that many athletes, they'd been stuffing money in her G-string and trying to cop a feel.

'You need to develop a rapport with them. Make them feel comfortable around you while they keep a healthy respect for you as the owner of the Chinooks.'

Which sounded fairly tricky. 'Could you put these all in the trunk?' she directed the driver. She hooked her pinky finger in the cuff of her light wool jacket and looked at her watch. 'It's almost seven.'

'I know. Happy hour is over soon, so you need to get your butt in there.'

She wanted nothing more than to take a nice, long soak in the spa tub, put on a fluffy hotel bathrobe, and order room service. 'Fine. I'll meet you in the lobby.'

The driver opened the door for her and she climbed inside.

'I'm in the lobby waiting for you. We need to go over a few things before we go to the pub.'

'What? Why?'

'While you spent the afternoon shopping, I went to Chinooks practice and I took some notes.'

'I'm tired. I've hit the wall. I can't absorb any more information. You need to relax a little.' The driver got into the car and she gave him the address of the hotel. 'I'm not paying you by the hour, Jules.'

'You said you don't want to look stupid in front of the guys.'

'Fine,' Faith moaned. 'You can talk to me about it while I change my clothes.' There was a long pause. 'I have to change, Jules. I've been wearing the same clothes since this morning.'

'I told you I'm not gay.'

She frowned as the car pulled out of the huge parking lot. 'I know.'

'You can't change in front of me,' he said, his tone a bit scolding. 'That isn't professional.'

She rolled her eyes. 'I was planning on changing in the bathroom.'

The Irish pub claimed to be the most authentic in San Jose. Ty didn't care about 'authentic' as he sat in a room near the back with ten of his teammates, eating shepherd's pie and drinking a pint of Guinness. The playoffs beards around him ranged from Vlad's outer Siberian scraggle to Logan's baby fuzz. Ty had his share of superstitions; itchy beards just weren't one of them.

'The Sharks' offense is all speed and no seed,' said Ty, while U2's 'With or Without You' wafted from the pub's sound system. He took a drink of the dark ale then licked the corners of his mouth. He'd spent that morning and part of the afternoon practice watching San Jose game tapes, and he was less concerned about their scoring than he was about their defense. 'Speed might entertain the crowd, but it doesn't put pucks in the net. Clowe is their highest scorer, but he's not setting any records with his goals or his points.'

'Defense is good.' Frankie 'Sniper' Kawczynski took a bite of his sirloin. 'If Nabokov is in his zone, he might be hard to score against.'

Sam grinned. 'I like a challenge.'

Ty took one last bite and shoved his plate away. 'If Marty plays like he did the other night,' he said, referring to their own goalie, 'there's no reason why we shouldn't beat 'em with our offense and defense.'

Alexander Devereaux stood and tossed money on the table. 'I'm meeting up with some of the guys at a bar across town. I heard they have good music and hot waitresses in little outfits.' He reached for his leather jacket hanging on the back of his chair. 'Anyone want to catch a cab with me?'

Ty shook his head. Even if his ankle hadn't been aching like a son of a bitch, he wouldn't have gone.

He'd done his time in hundreds of bars in hundreds of cities, and he'd figured out a while ago that he wasn't missing a thing.

Daniel and Logan stood and reached for their wallets. 'I'm in.'

'Me too.' Vlad tossed two twenties on the table. 'Cali-forn-ya girlz need zome Vlad.'

Ty laughed. 'Don't drop your pants on the dance floor and scare the "Cali-forn-ya" girls.' More than one American woman had run screaming from Vlad's uncircumcised impaler.

'I don't do zhat no more.' Vlad's deep Russian laughter mixed with the ending strains of U2. Vladimir Fetisov had been playing in the NHL for ten years and had seen more than his share of action on and off the ice. A few years back, he'd been involved with a little figure skater. She must not have minded the impaler.

She had been Serbian, though.

'You guys be careful,' Ty felt compelled to say. As the captain, he had to look out for his guys. 'You don't want to get busted with an underage rink rat. And don't come to practice with your ass dragging because you drank too much and hooked up with someone you met in a bar. In fact, those late-night hookups can really take it out of you. Maybe it's best to save your energy for the game.'

They all just laughed as they walked away. Two waitresses cleared the table and wiped it down for Ty and the five remaining guys. He ordered another

Guinness and kicked back as Sam and Blake got into the age-old argument over the best game ever played in NHL history.

'1971,' Sam insisted. 'Game Two of the first-round playoffs between Boston and Montreal.'

'U.S. kicking some Soviet ass in the 1980 Olympics,' argued Blake, the all-American boy from Wisconsin.

'Actually,' Jules said as he approached the table, 'it was 1994. New York and New Jersey. Last game in the Eastern Cup finals. Messier's shorthanded goal with less than two minutes on the clock was the best moment in NHL history.'

Ty looked up. '1996,' he said. 'Game Four of the conference quarter finals between Pittsburgh and Washington. That game went into four overtimes, with the Pens finally winning after a hundred and forty minutes of brutal hockey.' He slid his gaze to the woman walking up behind Jules. A pair of black wool pants hugged her butt and fell loosely down her long legs to her red pumps. Tiny pearl buttons closed the black fuzzy sweater covering her large breasts, and her gold hair was pulled back in a ponytail. She wore huge diamonds in her ears and her lips were painted a deep red. She looked gorgeous and classy. Nothing like a stripper. So, why did he have a vision of her ripping the front of her sweater apart and tossing it to him? It was those damn pictures of her naked.

Ty stood. 'Hello, Mrs. Duffy.'

'Hello, Mr. Savage,' she said above the noise and music in the pub. Her gaze rested on him for several moments before she turned her attention to the other men rising to their feet. 'Hello, gentlemen. Do you mind if we join you?'

Ty simply shrugged as he took his seat once more. The other five guys tripped all over themselves to assure her they'd love to have her take a seat, which Ty knew for a fact was complete bullshit.

'What did you do with yourself all day, Mrs. Duffy?' Blake asked in an effort to engage the owner.

'Well, I hit downtown San Jose and ran up my credit cards.' She took a seat next to Ty and reached for the menu. 'I shopped till I dropped. I found the most wonderful sweater at BCBG. It's fuchsia.' Two slim fingers, with those shiny red nails, slid down the menu. 'And the coolest leather coat at Gucci. It's scarlet. Normally I would never wear such bright colors. They're just too bold and scream "look at me." Like waving and jumping up and down in a crowd to get attention.' Her fingers stopped near the bottom of the menu. 'And I haven't bought leather . . . well, except shoes and bags, in years. But . . .' She shrugged. 'I've decided to live dangerously. Which would explain the sheer madness of the thigh-high boots and the matching lambskin hobo. The last thing I need is another hobo.' She looked up at the men staring back at her with varying degrees of stunned faces. 'I'll have the grilled salmon and a Guinness,' she told the waitress who'd approached during her babbling onslaught. Ty didn't know if she was nervous or drunk or both.

Jules ordered a steak and a Harp's from his seat across the table. 'The poor bellman had to cart all that stuff up to your room.'

'I tipped him well.' She handed the menu to the waitress. 'But it wasn't until I spread everything out in the room that I realized that there might not be enough space in the jet's cargo hold for all my bags.'

'Oh. Ah,' Johan Karlsson managed to utter.

She looked at them all, green eyes shining, and flashed a beautiful smile with her straight white teeth and full red lips. Ty could almost hear their collective gulps. 'You-all don't mind if we leave some of your equipment behind. Do you?'

'Like what?' Sam asked as he raised his beer. 'We don't travel with unnecessary baggage.' He took a drink, then added, 'Unless you count Jules over there. Pound for pound, he takes up a lot of wasted space.'

'Pound for pound,' Jules jumped in, 'your ego takes up a lot of wasted space.'

Faith tilted her head and seemed to consider it. 'No, I need Jules. But you-all don't need that many sticks.' She looked at each of them in turn. 'I figure one apiece is good. Am I right?'

There was a collected inhalation of horrified breath. Everyone knew that a man's stick was sacred, honed for hours until the curve was just right. Not even for a former Playmate of the Year who just happened to be the owner of the team would these players willingly leave them behind. Pads and helmets? Yeah. Their sticks, no way.

The hockey players at the table cast uncertain glances at Ty as if they expected the captain to step in and do something. Like maybe give her a glove rub.

Faith laughed. 'I was just kidding, you guys.' She waved away their concerns, flashing the huge rock she still wore on her left finger. 'If there isn't enough room, I'll have the hotel ship everything.'

Ty almost smiled. No one could bullshit and get the uninitiated going like a hockey player. As a bullshitter, Mrs. Duffy wasn't great, but she wasn't bad for a rookie.

'Jules and I watched the Sharks practice,' she said as her beer arrived. 'We were up in the skybox with binoculars. It was all very undercover hush-hush secret-agent stuff.' She took a drink and licked the foam off her top lip. 'They seem to have a lot of speed, but I'm not convinced they can shoot the puck as well as we can.'

Ty felt his brows rise up his forehead.

'I think we have them beat on offense,' she added as she leaned back and folded her arms beneath her breasts. 'We're better delivering tape to tape and capitalizing on turnovers.'

Sam looked at Ty as if an alien had just landed at their table. A sexy-as-hell alien who talked about hockey and sounded like maybe she knew what she was talking about. Just a few weeks ago, she'd wanted to sign Terrible Ted. He wondered if she even had a clue what she'd just said.

'Ah, yeah,' Sam managed. 'We were just talking about how we need to beat them offensively and hammer their goalie.'

Above the smell of food and beer, Ty caught the scent of her perfume. He recognized it from the other night at the photo shoot.

'I don't know a lot about their goalie.' She raised one hand and toyed with the top button of her sweater. 'But I've read that he isn't consistent.'

'Don't believe what you read,' Ty told her. She looked across her shoulder at him and her green eyes stared into his. 'That's where a lot of people make mistakes.'

'Believing what they read?'

'Yeah.'

'I read that you're persona non grata in Canada. Is that true?'

'Pretty much.'

'I also read that you think the Stanley Cup will come down to who wants it more.'

'Where did you read that?'

'*Hockey News*.'

'I don't remember saying that.'

'I'm paraphrasing.' She lowered her voice a fraction and added, 'You actually said it will come down to who has the biggest sac.'

That sounded more like him. 'Which is different

from wanting it enough.' He took a drink of his beer then set it back on the table. He didn't want to talk about his sac. Not with her. Not when his sac had noticed the way she smelled and the way her breasts filled out that sweater.

'How is it different?'

He looked into her big green eyes surrounded by thick black lashes. 'It just is.' Her cheeks were smooth, perfect. He lowered his gaze from her full mouth and chin down to the hollow of her delicate throat just above the top button on her sweater. He wanted to do things to her. Hot, sweaty things that would make their skin stick together. Wild things that would get him into a lot of trouble.

'How's it different?' she pushed.

'Angel of Harlem' poured from the pub's sound system and he wondered how to answer. If she were a man, he wouldn't even hesitate. If she were a man, he wouldn't have a hard-on. 'You can want something, Mrs. Duffy, but that doesn't mean you're going to get it. Sometimes wanting isn't enough.' And because she pushed, he added, 'Sometimes it comes down to what you've got left in your gut and the size of your sac.'

She chuckled as if she wasn't the least bit shocked. 'The article didn't mention the importance of sac *size*, Mr. Savage.'

'Size is always important. Massive sac is almost as important as massive skill.' And because they were sharing what she'd read about him, he leaned toward her a bit and said just above a whisper, 'I read about you too. I read you hate hot dogs and love crème brûlée.'

Her brows lowered in confusion. 'How did you . . . ? Ah.' Her confusion cleared and she smiled. 'That's true. Where'd you get the magazine?'

'One of the guys.'

'Of course.' She turned her face toward him and, to anyone looking, it appeared as if they were speaking closely to be heard over the music. Her mouth just inches from his, she said, 'So, I assume it's been passed around.'

'I got it a couple of weeks ago.'

'What took so long?'

'Sam wasn't finished looking at it.'

She reached for her beer and laughed, not the least embarrassed. 'Those were taken a long time ago.'

Not that long ago. He thought of her with that long string of pearls.

'You're thinking about those pictures, aren't you?' she asked from behind her glass.

He didn't answer.

She smiled. 'Only seems fair.'

'How's that?'

'Because completely against my will, and no matter what else I try to shove into my head, I can't stop thinking about "massive sac." It's very disturbing.'

He chuckled and she looked at him as if he'd sprouted a horn from the middle of his forehead. 'What?'

'I didn't think you ever laughed.'

Of course he laughed.

'Hey, Mrs. Duffy,' Sam called from down the table. 'Do you know *The Girls Next Door*?'

'I don't think that's appropriate,' Jules admonished like a preacher, and Ty had to admit that the assistant probably had a point. Which made the conversation he'd just had with her completely off the scale of appropriate.

Faith smiled. 'It's okay, Jules. I met Holly and Bridget at the mansion. There were other girls there too. But Kendra didn't live there at the time.'

'What's Hef like?'

'He's nice.' Her salmon arrived and she placed her napkin on her lap.

He was also old. Like Virgil. What was it with her and old men? Oh yeah. Money.

'He's also a very smart businessman,' she continued.

'Did you go to a lot of parties?'

'As Playmate of the Year, I hosted several. That's how I met Virgil.' She squeezed lemon on her fish and picked up her fork. 'He and Hef were good friends.'

'Do you still get invited?'

'Occasionally, but the last few years Virgil really couldn't travel very often. So we didn't go.'

For some inexplicable reason, the thought of Virgil's old hands on her smooth, young body made Ty feel uneasy. Why he should give a shit, he didn't know. Maybe it was the Guinness. He was used to

Canadian brew, and rich beer always hit him hard after a few.

'Maybe you can get us all an invite to the mansion,' Sam persisted.

She looked up and smiled. 'Win the Stanley Cup, and I'll see what I can do.'

The heels of Faith's red pumps clicked across the lobby as she made her way to the bank of elevators. She'd just left Jules and Darby Hogue at the pub, talking hockey and acquisitions. It was a little after ten, and Ty and the other hockey players had cleared out of the pub by nine. She didn't know where they'd gone. They hadn't said, but it was Saturday night, and she suspected they'd joined their other teammates at various bars around town.

She pushed the button and the empty elevator opened. The back wall was mirrored and she looked at herself as the doors closed. She pulled the band out of her ponytail and scratched her scalp as the elevator moved upward. It had been a long, exhausting day, and she was tired. She had a slight headache from the Irish beer or the ponytail or both.

A few floors up, the elevator stopped and the doors slowly slid open. Inch by inch, Ty Savage appeared in the mirror. In the glass their gazes met and held as he stepped inside. He still wore the deep blue dress shirt and jeans he'd had on earlier, and a nervous little flutter settled at the bottom of her sternum. She turned and spoke first to cover her nerves. 'We meet in an elevator yet again.' Although why he would make her nervous, she didn't know. Maybe it was his height. Tall men had never made her nervous in the past.

He acknowledged her with a slight nod of his head and pushed the button for the floor above hers.

'I thought you'd be out partying with the guys.'

The doors closed and he leaned a shoulder into the mirrored wall. 'I don't party during the playoffs. I was just in Sam's room talking to his kid on the phone.'

'Sam has a kid?' He seemed so young.

'Yeah. He's five.' As the elevator moved up, Ty's gaze moved down. It started at the top of her head, lowered over her face and throat and paused for a few heartbeats on her breasts. 'Does it bother you,' he said as his gaze slid down her stomach and legs to her shoes, 'that the guys have seen you naked?'

She was used to men looking at her body, but with Ty it was different. The warm little flutter in her chest slid to the pit of her stomach. 'Roughly four and a half million men worldwide have seen my pictures in *Playboy*. If I worried about who's seen me naked, I'd never leave the house.'

Slowly he raised his gaze back up her body and he looked into her eyes. 'So that's a no – eh?'

'That's a no – eh.'

The doors opened and she stepped out.

'How long were you married to Virgil?' he asked as he followed.

'Five years.'

'And you're what? *Aboat* thirty?'

'I just turned thirty.' She looked up at him. 'Don't judge me. You don't know anything about my life. Sometimes you do what you have to do to survive.'

'Not all women would have chosen to get naked or marry an old man to survive.'

He sounded angry. Like it was any of his damn business. 'Not all women have lived my life.' *Judgmental jerk.* She moved down the hall toward her room and he walked beside her. 'Is your room on this floor?'

'No. Yours is.'

'Are you walking me to my room?' she asked and didn't bother to hide her irritation.

'Yes.' But he didn't sound happy about it.

'Why? I don't need you to walk me to my room.'

'I'm a nice guy.'

She laughed without humor and glanced up at him out of the corners of her eyes. 'If you believe that, you're delusional. Maybe you've been punched in the head one too many times.' She stopped at her door at the end of the hall and reached into her big purse. She pulled out the card key. 'You're not nice.'

'Some women think I'm real nice.'

'There are lots of words I'd use to describe you, Mr. Savage.' She shook her head and tapped his chest with the side of her card. '*Nice* isn't one of them.'

He raised his hand and flattened her palm against his chest. 'What is?'

The warmth of his touch curled her fingers against

the hard muscles of his chest. He stood so close she caught the scent of cologne on his heated skin. 'What is what?'

'How would you describe me, Mrs. Duffy?'

She tried to pull her hand back but his grasp tightened. 'The first word that comes to mind is rude.'

'And?'

She licked her lips and stared up into his sexy blue-on-blue eyes. 'Surly.'

'And.'

The warmth of his touch traveled up her arm and across her chest. She swallowed hard and suddenly couldn't think. She didn't know if it was the Guinness or the pheromones. 'Big.'

A slight smile touched the corners of his eyes and she thought he might laugh. Instead his gaze sank to her lips and he asked in a low voice, 'Where?'

She wondered what it would be like if he kissed her. If he pressed his mouth into hers. If she just leaned forward and kissed his neck and tasted his skin against her tongue. 'What?'

'Never mind. What else do you think of me?'

She took a deep breath and forgot to exhale. She wondered what it would be like if she licked him up one side and down the other.

'What are you thinking?'

She suddenly felt kind of hot and dizzy, and accidentally let Layla out. 'That I want to lick your tattoo,' she whispered.

His brows lifted up his forehead and she shocked him into silence. Once again, she tried to pull her hand from his chest, and once again his grasp tightened. *Lick his tattoo?* A mortified hot wave rose up her neck and heated cheek. She was tired and confused, that's why Layla had slipped out. Mrs. Duffy didn't talk about licking things. Especially tattoos. 'I shouldn't have said that.' She took a step back and he took a step closer. 'It's inappropriate. I take it back.'

He tugged her closer as soft laughter touched her cheek. 'You can't take it back. It's already out there.' He slid his free hand up her arm and shoulder to the side of her neck. 'You took your hair down.'

'I was getting a headache.'

'I like it down.' He slid his thumb across her jaw, leaving a warm trail across her skin as he tilted her face up. 'This can't happen, Mrs. Duffy.'

She meant to take another step back but somehow she swayed closer. 'What?'

'You. Me.' He lowered his face and brushed his lips across hers. 'This.' The soft, moist brush of his mouth closed on her throat and curled her toes inside her red pumps. She couldn't swallow or breathe or think beyond the consuming desire for more. She stood perfectly still, afraid to move. Afraid of what she'd do, but mostly afraid he'd stop.

It had been so long, the kiss was a hot rush across her flesh, an overload to her senses that woke up all those lonely places inside her that she'd ignored for the past five years. He touched his tongue to the seam of her lips, and her chest got tight and achy and her knees threatened to buckle. She raised her hands to his shoulders to keep from falling and tilted her head to the side. Her lips parted, and the slick touch and warm glide of his tongue was like dropping a lit match on a pool of gasoline and she went up in flames. She wanted to burn and make him burn along with her. He tasted like beer and liquid sex and she wanted to eat him up. A low moan escaped her chest, her breasts grew heavy, and her nipples tightened into hard points of pleasure.

Ty's hand found the small of her back and slid up her spine, urging her closer. He exerted a gentle pressure, closing the space between them until her breasts pressed against the front of his shirt. She slid one hand up the side of his neck and her fingers combed through his hair. He pressed the full, hot length of his hard body against hers and she felt his erection against her lower abdomen. His solid muscles, warm breath mingling with hers, and long, hard penis poking her belly awakened the hot, achy place between her thighs and the painful need for a man's touch. The touch of his hands and mouth all over her body. She'd always loved this toe-curling part. This buildup to a mindless yearning that made her lose control and forget everything but feeling as much as she could for as long as it lasted. The grasping, greedy part just before clothes came off.

He pulled back, looking at her through heavy blue

eyes and breathing as if he'd just run a marathon. Then he came at her again and the kiss got hotter. Her mouth opened and closed with his as she gave and received long, feeding kisses. A deep groan vibrated his throat and she got a feeling that Ty had what it took to finish what he'd started. That he could give her what she needed to put out the fire rushing across her skin and pooling between her thighs. That he would make love like he played hockey. That he was a guy who'd keep going at it until he got the job done.

A door down the hall opened and closed, and Ty pushed her away. 'This can't happen,' he said, gasping for air.

She nodded and reached for him. She slid one hand to the back of his head and opened her mouth against the side of his throat. 'Mmm,' she moaned as she sucked his warm skin. He tasted yummy. Like a man. Like a man she wanted to kiss all over.

He placed his hands on her shoulders but didn't push her away. His fingers curled into her flesh. 'This is no good, Mrs. Duffy.'

'So good.' She sucked harder.

'Listen to me,' he gasped as his fingers dug into her.

She bit his earlobe and whispered, 'Don't stop. Touch me, Ty. Touch me all over.'

'Oh God,' he groaned as if he was in real pain. 'You're a talker.'

'Please. Touch me. I want to eat you up.'

He took a step back and held her at arm's length.

'This can't happen,' he repeated, and this time he sounded like he meant it.

A frustrated moan escaped her lips. 'Why?'

'I have too much to lose.' He dropped his hands from her shoulders and took another step back. 'You're not worth my career.'

A steady downpour drenched Seattle as the United flight from San Jose landed at Sea-Tac Airport and rolled to the gate. Faith sat in coach with her Fendi purse on her lap. It had been years since she'd flown coach. She'd forgotten how crowded it was. Not that it mattered. If Jules hadn't found her a flight, she would have sprouted wings and flown herself home. She would have rented a car and driven. Hell, she might have even walked. She hadn't cared what it took; she'd had to get out of California.

She was a coward. Running away like she was guilty of some crime and not wanting to face what she'd done. Maybe at some future date, she'd be able to face Ty again. Maybe next week, or next month, or next year, she'd be able to be in the same room with him and not recall the excruciatingly painful details of kissing him and touching him and wanting him more than she could ever recall wanting a man. His pushing her away and his wide shoulders and dark head as he'd left her in the hall, alone and confused.

She would have to see him again, of course. But not today. She just couldn't face seeing him on the flight back from San Jose. Probably not tomorrow either, when her behavior and his rejection would still be so fresh in her head.

She was definitely a coward, but feeling like a coward didn't compare to feeling like she'd betrayed her husband. After she'd kissed Ty and made a fool out of herself, she'd gone to bed and lain awake all night with a horrible churning guilt plaguing her and burning a hole in her stomach. Virgil was dead, but she still felt married. Felt like that kiss – that hot, consuming kiss she'd shared with Ty – was a knife to the back of her dead husband. Not because it had been so bad, but because it had been so good. So good she might have done anything to make it last. To make it burn hotter and longer. To drink him in and suck him up and feel things for him she'd never felt for Virgil. Hot, achy things she wanted to do with a man who did hot, achy things to her.

She gathered her jacket and hatbox from the overhead and moved toward the gangway. It was after noon the next day, but she still was as embarrassed and confused as she had been standing outside her hotel room watching Ty walk away. How could he have left her? He'd been as turned on as she was. She'd felt his extremely hard erection pressed against her, and yet he'd been able to walk away. And as humiliating as that was to face, thank God he had. Waking up naked with one of her hockey players was so extremely wrong. Way beyond acceptable. He worked for her. Good Lord, he could probably sue her for workplace harassment or something. What a disaster.

She shoved her arms through her jacket sleeves and hung her purse on her shoulder. So, how had it happened? With him? Of all people? There was only one possible explanation.

Layla.

The part of her she'd created to deal with the harsher realities of her life as a stripper. The woman she'd created who didn't mind a lap dance because the money was good. The woman who'd partied till the sun came up and loved a good tequila shooter. The part of her that liked good, hot, sweaty sex with a beautiful man.

She was Mrs. Duffy now. She didn't need Layla anymore. Layla was trouble.

Her Louis Vuitton wheelie waited for her at the carousel and she pulled it to long-term parking. Her neck and shoulder ached from the long flight and she had a difficult time shoving the piece of luggage into the trunk of her Bentley. By the time she made it to her condo, she wanted nothing more than to climb into bed and pull the covers over her head.

Pebbles's yippy bark greeted her as she opened the door to her apartment. She picked up her hatbox and wheeled her suitcase inside. The drapes were drawn across the wall of windows overlooking Elliott Bay, casting the great room in inky shadow. The gas fireplace licked the fake logs and Marvin Gaye's smooth 'Let's Get It On' purred from the speakers of her sound system.

'Mom?' she called out as she moved into the room and hit a bank of lights.

'Faith!' Her mom rose to her knees in the middle of the living-room floor. A man knelt behind her, and except for their shocked expressions, they were both completely naked.

'Oh!' She spun around to face a blank wall as *her* shock buzzed her tired brain. 'Oh my God!'

'What are you doing here?'

'I live here!' While Marvin sang about not beating around the bush, her cheeks burned with the horror at what she'd glimpsed. Walking in on her mother was just as disturbing now as when she was fourteen. And ten. And seven. Hell, pick a year. She pointed behind her. 'Who the hell is this?'

'Pavel Savage,' the man said.

Her mouth fell open as she stared at the rough texture and latte-colored paint on the wall in front of her face. 'Ty's father?'

'You weren't supposed to be back until tonight,' her mother accused.

'What does that have to do with anything? You're having sex. In my living room.' Oh God. 'What's *wrong* with you?'

'Nothing's wrong with me.'

'With one of my hockey players' dads!' she continued, placing a hand on her hot cheek. And not just any hockey player's dad. The father of the hockey player she'd made out with the night before.

'We're adults, Faith.'

'I don't care.'

'You can turn around now.'

Slowly, while Marvin purred about 'being sanctified,' she turned as if she didn't trust what she might see. Her mother had slipped into a red silk robe while Pavel zipped up his jeans.

'I thought Sandy was staying with you.'

'She went back home.

Pavel moved toward her and offered his hands. 'It's a pleasure to meet you, Faith.'

She pulled her hands behind her back and shook her head. 'Maybe some other time. You just had your hands . . . You know.'

'Faith!' Her mother gasped as if her daughter had done something to be mortified over.

Pavel tilted his dark head back and creases wrinkled the corners of his blue eyes as he laughed. Except for the creases and the laugher, he looked a lot like his son. 'I understand.' He reached for the black shirt thrown across the back of the couch. 'How was the trip?'

'What?' He wanted to know about her trip? God, these people weren't normal.

'How is his ankle holding up?'

'What?' she asked again. Her mother had been in

town less than two weeks and she was already having sex in Faith's home. Faith had never even had sex in the penthouse.

'How is Ty's ankle holding up?'

'Oh. Uh. I don't know. I had to leave before they played. I felt sick and came home.'

'What's wrong with you?' her mother wanted to know.

'I'm coming down with something.'

Pavel buttoned his shirt. 'I hear the flu is going around. Perhaps you need to rest and drink lots of fluids.'

Was she really standing here talking to Ty's father about the flu? While he got dressed?

'Maybe you should sit down.' Her mother put her hand on Faith's forehead. 'You do feel hot.'

That's because her blood had rushed to her head. She swatted her mother's hand away. 'I'm fine.' Or at least she would be if and when she could get over the last twenty-four hours.

'I'm sorry, Pavel,' Valerie said as she moved to the sound system and turned off Marvin.

She was sorry, *Pavel*? Faith just caught her mom naked on her hands and knees. Something a child should never see, and she wanted to stab out her own eyes. What about I'm sorry, *Faith*?

'Not to worry, Val.' He tucked his shirt into his pants. 'We will have many more enjoyable times together.' He shoved his feet into a pair of boots and grabbed his leather jacket.

'Next time we'll get a hotel,' Valerie promised as she walked Pavel to the door.

'Please do that.' Faith picked up her hatbox and wheeled her suitcase down the hall toward her room. Just before she shut the door to her room, she could swear she heard them kissing. She tossed her hatbox on the bed, unzipped it, and took out her clean underwear. Years ago she'd lost luggage and now she always carried her jewelry and other essentials on a commercial flight with her.

'I can't believe you,' her mother said as she opened the door and walked into the room. 'You embarrassed me in front of Pavel.'

She glanced over her shoulder as she moved across the floor toward her mahogany dresser. 'You were having sex in my living room like a teenager,' she reminded her mother. 'You should be embarrassed. For God's sake, you're fifty.'

'Fifty-year-olds enjoy sex.'

Which wasn't the point at all. She opened a drawer and placed her panties inside. 'Not in their daughter's homes with strangers.'

'You were gone and Pavel isn't a stranger.'

'I know.' She shut the drawer and moved toward her bed, which was covered in a red silk duvet. Her mother and Pavel were just a disaster waiting to happen. And it would happen. It always did. 'He's Ty Savage's father. Couldn't you have found someone other than my captain's father?'

'Did you see Pavel?' she answered as if that explained it all. Sadly, for Valerie, it did.

'Yes. More than I wanted.'

Valerie crossed her arms beneath her large breasts. 'I've never understood how you could be a stripper and a Playmate, yet remain such a prude about sex.'

She'd never been a prude. Far from it; she just wasn't a nympho like her mother. Despite what people thought of her, her former jobs, and the way she'd dressed, she'd never been a very sexual person. She'd always been able to control herself. Except for last night, anyway. And she wasn't so sure that had been about sex as much as satisfying five years of pent-up need. It was just too bad that need had been released all over Ty Savage.

'How could you be in *Playboy* and want to live like a celibate nun? That doesn't make sense to me.'

Stripping and doing *Playboy* had never been about sex. Those things had been about money. Faith had always kept the two separate in her own head. She'd explained it to her mother before and she didn't feel like explaining it again. To her mother, being sexy and sex were one and the same thing, and she'd never understand. Not even if she tried. Which she didn't. 'And I've never understood how you could sleep with men you hardly know.'

'I know Pavel.'

'You've only been in town for two weeks!'

'It only takes an instant to feel chemistry.' Her

mother sat on the edge of the bed and Pebbles jumped up beside her. 'It's this . . .' She snapped her fingers. 'It's a spark that you either feel for a man or you don't.'

'But you don't always have to act on it,' she said as Pebbles jumped inside the hatbox, spun around in a few circles, then made herself cozy.

'If you keep that kind of passion suppressed, it explodes and you do something rash. Before you know it, you're naked and cuffed to the headboard of some guy named Dirk with a ruler tattooed on his penis.'

Faith held up a hand for her mother to stop. 'How about we adopt the military "Don't ask, don't tell" policy. I won't ask and you don't tell.' She really didn't want to hear about her mother's exploding passion. Although after last night, when she'd kind of 'exploded' in the hallway at the Marriott, she really couldn't cast stones from her glass house. But in fairness to herself, she hadn't exploded like that in a very long time. The last time she could recall had been with an old boyfriend on his Harley. Or at least they'd tried to have sex on his Harley. It hadn't really worked out.

'I don't understand you,' Valerie said.

'I know. And I don't understand you. I don't understand how you can keep repeating the same mistakes with men. When I was fifteen, I stopped counting the men that came and went in our lives.'

'I know I made mistakes.' Valerie sighed as if her mistakes were no big deal. 'What parent hasn't made a few mistakes?'

A few? Valerie had been married seven times and engaged at least a dozen.

Faith reached inside the hatbox and had to dig beneath Pebbles's long fur for her jewelry roll. The little dog growled and bared its tiny white teeth. 'You bite me, and I'll drop-kick you off the balcony,' she warned.

'Don't listen to her, Pebs,' Valerie said as she reached over and scratched the dog's head. 'She's just jealous.'

'Of a dog!'

'Not you. Her. It's called sibling rivalry. She views you as a sister competing for my attention. I read about it in a book.'

Since Valerie didn't read books, Faith suspected she was making it up. She wrapped her hand around the jewelry bag and pulled it from beneath the dog.

'I don't think Pebbles likes you lecturing Mama.'

Mama. Faith almost gagged. 'I'm not lecturing you. I just think you need to respect yourself more.'

'I respect myself.' Her mother tied the belt and smoothed the silk over her legs. 'You're not the morality police, Faith. You married an old man for his money. You can hardly lecture me on morality.'

In the beginning of her marriage, that was certainly true. 'You can only feel secure with yourself if there's a man in your life.' She unrolled the silk bag and spilled her diamonds into her palm. 'I find my security with money. Neither of us can claim the moral high ground.'

'Money is a poor substitute for love.'

'I had both with Virgil.'

Her mother sighed and rolled her eyes.

'It was a good marriage.'

'It was a passionless, sexless marriage to a man old enough to be your grandfather.'

She moved into the big walk-in closet stuffed with clothes in varying shades of beige, white, and black. 'You'll never understand my relationship with Virgil. He gave me a great life,' she said as she punched the numbers to the safe and popped it open.

'He gave you money in exchange for five years of your life. Five years of your youth that you can never get back,' Valerie called after her, and Faith refrained from reminding Valerie that Virgil had given *her* money as well. Enough that she didn't have to work. 'You can't have a great life without passion,' her mother added.

Faith swung the safe door open and pulled out one blue velvet tray filled with Tiffany and Cartier earrings. Passion didn't buy your child shoes when the soles wore out or put food in your child's stomach. It didn't keep the repo man from hooking your mother's car to his wrecker and hauling it away from your single wide while the rest of the kids in the trailer court pointed and laughed because at least they were better off than you.

Faith looked down at the glittering stones of all shapes and colors. Passion did not take away the sick feeling in your stomach that you were one paycheck away from living in an alley behind a Dumpster at the Hard Rock.

'Those don't keep you warm at night.'

She looked at her mother standing a few feet away. At the deep lines in the corners of her green eyes and her Farrah hair, messed up by a man's hands. Faith slept beneath a comforter filled with the down of Hungarian white geese to keep her warm at night. She didn't need a man for that.

She placed her diamonds on the blue velvet tray. She didn't need a man for warmth or money. Passion was overrated and never really lasted anyway. Her mother was certainly an example of that.

Faith had everything she needed. She didn't need a man for anything. And yeah, she knew what people would say about that. That she'd used her body instead of her mind to get what she wanted.

So what? She didn't care. All that mattered was that it all belonged to her and no one could take it away.

Monday afternoon, as Faith sat in a meeting with the coach, Darby Hogue, and the scouts from the player development department, her nerves twisted her stomach into knots. A television was set up and they watched clip after clip of free agents and minor-league prospects. Even though all trades and acquisitions were put on hold until the end of the season, the player development department still worked at finding new talent, and Jules had thought it important that she attend the meeting. While the men in the room discussed the prospect on the screen, she felt as nervous as a sinner in church, wondering if Ty would breeze through the door, looking hot and cool at the same time. She wondered if any of the men in the room knew that she'd assaulted the captain of the hockey team with her lips. She was fairly certain Ty wasn't the kind of man to kiss and tell. That he wouldn't want something like that to get around either, but she didn't know him well enough to be certain he wouldn't talk about her with one of the guys. Who might in turn tell other people.

Yes, he'd kissed her first, but she was the one who'd grabbed hold with both hands and hadn't wanted it to end. Not like that. Not until they were both naked.

'Can I get you anything, Mrs. Duffy?' the coach's assistant asked as he popped in another tape.

A Xanax. She smiled and shook her head. 'No. Thank you.' Her hands lay loosely in her lap, appearing relaxed and composed as her nerves pinged through her veins and zapped her every time someone walked past Coach Nystrom's door, but Ty never showed and no one mentioned the unfortunate episode in San Jose.

That night, the Chinooks won their second of three against the Sharks. Faith chose to attend a benefit instead and skipped the game. She and Virgil had bought tickets to the thousand-dollar-a-plate event the previous summer. She decided to go by herself and participate in the silent auction to raise money for Doctors Without Borders.

She dressed in her black Donna Karan sheath and hung a string of opera-length pearls around her neck. When she walked into the ballroom at the Four Seasons, she spotted several women she knew from the Gloria Thornwell Society. They turned their faces as if they didn't know her. The glittering chandeliers shone down on the Seattle elite as she grabbed a glass of Moët from a passing tray. Toward the front of the room, Landon and his wife stood in a circle of Virgil's close friends congratulating each other for one sort of acquisition or another. She raised the champagne to her lips and her gaze slid to the members of the Seattle Symphony, playing on a raised dais. She knew a lot of these people. Now, as she moved to the table displaying the silent auction items, she caught the gazes of the few trophy wives she'd associated with for five years. In their eyes she saw pity and fear as they turned away, afraid to make eye contact with their fate.

'Hello, Faith.'

She looked across her shoulder at the wife of Bruce Parsons, Jennifer Parsons, a trophy wife only slightly older than herself.

'Hi, Jennifer. You braved the crowd, I see.'

Jennifer smiled tightly. 'How are you doing?'

'A little better. I still miss Virgil.'

They talked for a few short minutes, and in the end promised phone calls that would never be placed and lunch that would never happen.

When the dinner bell rang, she found herself at a table with Virgil's empty seat beside her. Sadness at his absence settled next to her heart. He'd been a strong stabilizing influence in her life and she missed him. Now that he was gone, she had to be strong by herself.

Across the table, Landon and his wife, Ester, ignored her completely while silently transmitting their contempt in venomous waves. If Virgil were alive, he'd have expected her to paste a smile on her face and force them all to be civil. But frankly, she was tired of forcing polite behavior from Landon and Ester when they were in polite society. To some of the people in the room, she would always be a woman who took her clothes off for money. But there'd been some freedom in that life which had nothing to do with being naked and everything to do with not caring what people thought. There were only a few rungs lower on the social scale than a stripper.

While she ate a five-course meal that started with a braised short rib and red cabbage salad, she made small talk with those around her. By the time the fourth course was cleared from the table, she realized that she really just didn't care anymore. Not about Landon and his wife, and not about people who would never accept her now that Virgil was gone. Since the funeral, her life had been different. In just one short month, it had drastically changed.

'I heard the Chinooks are still in the playoffs,' one of Virgil's business associates commented from Faith's left side. She leaned slightly forward and looked into Jerome Robinson's kind brown eyes. 'How's the team looking?' he asked.

'We're looking good,' she answered, as a *panna cotta* with fresh berries was set on the table before her. 'Of course there was a huge concern once we lost Bressler, but Savage has stepped in and done a great job of keeping the team focused. Our goal was to give the players a few games before the playoffs to find their legs and adjust before we started shuffling the deck, but they've adjusted so well, there hasn't been much shuffling.' Or so Coach Nystrom had said yesterday.

She shrugged and lifted her dessert spoon. 'Our front line has a combined twenty-three goals and eighty-nine points so far in the playoffs. I think we have a really good shot at the cup this year.' That, she'd figured out on her own.

Jerome smiled. 'Virgil would be proud of you.'

She liked to think so. But more important, for the first time in her life she was proud of herself.

'My father was a senile old man,' Landon said from across the table.

'Your father was many things.' Jerome turned to Landon. 'Senile was never one of them.'

Faith smiled and took a drink of her dessert wine. Once the dishes were cleared, she stayed just long enough to make a few silent bids. As she stood at the coat check, she realized that in the short month since Virgil's death, she'd become more comfortable sitting in an Irish pub with a bunch of hockey players than with the people she'd associated with for the past five years. It wasn't that all the Seattle elite were supercilious snobs. They weren't. A lot of them were like Jerome. Nice people who just happened to have more money than God. It was more like Faith was different now; she was becoming someone else. Someone she didn't know. She wasn't a stripper or Playmate or a rich man's wife anymore. The weirdest part about it was that even though she didn't know the new Faith yet, she liked her.

By the time she got home, Valerie had returned

from the hockey game, where she and Pavel had used the box to watch the Chinooks dominate in a 2–0 victory over the Sharks. Wednesday night's game would be in San Jose, and if the Chinooks won, they would advance to the next round. If not, it was back to Seattle for Game Six.

'Pavel wanted me to thank you for the use of your skybox.'

'When you see him again, tell him he's welcome,' Faith said and headed to her room. She went straight to bed feeling oddly at peace with her life. She slept like a log until around one, when Pebbles jumped on her bed and curled up against her stomach.

'What are you doing?' she asked the dog, her voice a bit sleep-drugged. 'Get out.' Through the darkness Pebbles's beady eyes looked up at her as a deep moan filtered into the room. Faith recognized that moan and the next one too. Obviously, Valerie and Pavel hadn't found a hotel.

The next morning Pavel was gone, and Valerie acted as if he'd never been there. When Faith confronted her mother, Valerie promised to 'be more quiet.'

'I thought you said something about going to a hotel,' she reminded her mother.

'Every night? That could get expensive.'

Every night? 'You could go to his house.'

Valerie shook her head. 'I don't know. He's living with Ty. Maybe when Ty's on the road. I'll talk to him about it tomorrow.' She pulled off her chunky bracelets.

'You don't mind if he comes over Wednesday night and watches the game here with us, do you? I hate to think of him all alone with nothing but his big-screen TV.'

She wondered why her mother couldn't go *there*. 'I don't really mind. Just as long as you don't make out like teenagers and plug in "Sexual Healing."'

Valerie waved away her concern. 'Pavel gets too engrossed in the game and can't manage to pull himself away,' she said.

But the very next night, the two headed to Valerie's bedroom during the first intermission.

'What are they doing?' Jules asked as he walked into the kitchen and reached for a section of the three foot-long sandwiches Faith had picked up at a local deli.

There was a large thump on the wall followed by deep laughter and a little giggle. 'You don't want to know.' Faith shook her head and bit into a deli pickle. 'My mother and I have adopted the "Don't ask, don't tell" policy.' She took a sip of her margarita and moved back into the living room. 'At least I'm *trying* to make her follow it.' Pebbles lay in Faith's spot on the couch with her feet sticking straight up in the air. 'But like her dog, she doesn't follow commands very well.'

Jules sat beside Pebbles and scratched the dog's belly with his free hand. 'You missed a good game the other night.'

She sat on the arm of the couch and looked across her shoulder into his green eyes. 'I was at a benefit.' She thought of Landon and frowned. 'Unfortunately, I won't be going to many charity events. Landon and his friends have made me persona non grata.'

'If you want to participate in a charity event,' Jules said between bites of his sandwich, 'you should play in the Chinooks Foundation charity golf game this summer.'

'I've never heard of the Chinooks Foundation.'

'They have a charity golf game every year. I know they'd welcome you and it would be fun.'

Big boobs and golf didn't go together. 'No thanks. I'm better at chairing events and writing checks.'

'I know the foundation does other things to raise money too. I'll look into it if you want me to.'

She might actually really like that. At least it was something she knew about. 'Okay.'

'Has Darby talked to you?'

'No.' Faith glanced at the television and the remaining few minutes of the second intermission. After the first two periods of the game, the Chinooks were ahead by one goal, but they had the third period to go, and anything could happen. 'Why?' she asked.

'He wants you to do an interview with a local reporter, Jane Martineau,' he said.

Faith had heard of Jane. Had read her columns in the Life section of the *Post Intelligencer*. 'Doesn't she write about life in Seattle?'

'Yeah, but she used to be a sports reporter for the *Seattle Times*. That's how she met her husband, Luc Martineau. I don't know if you remember, but Luc was the Chinooks goalie until he retired a few years ago.'

Faith only had one question. 'When?'

'As soon as Darby can set it up. Probably sometime next week to coincide with the new billboards of you and Ty.'

'Which photo is going to be used?'

'I'm not sure, but we'll find out at tomorrow's PR meeting.'

Pavel and Valerie walked back into the room, and to fill the awkward silence, Jules asked, 'What do you think of Dominik Pisani?'

'Pittsburgh defenseman? He's fast and can feed the puck.' Pavel and Valerie sat in the love seat and Pavel laid his hand across the back of the small sofa and stroked Valerie's hair. 'Why do you ask?'

'If we play Pittsburgh in the final round, he's going to go hard after our offense.'

'True. How do you feel, Faith?' he asked as he looked at her through blue eyes so much like Ty's.

'About Pisani?'

Pavel shook his head. 'The last time I saw you, you had just returned home early from San Jose because you weren't feeling well.'

Oh yeah. The day she'd seen him naked. The morning after she'd made out with his son at the Marriott. 'I'm better. Thank you.'

'Who Let the Dogs Out' blasted from the sound system on the jumbo tran, and Faith turned her attention to the players lumbering out from the tunnel.

Their awkward gaits became smooth and gracefully athletic the second their skates hit the ice.

Ty was one of the last players to step onto the ice. This was the first time she'd seen him since he'd kissed her, and she felt a strange little pinch in her chest and a restless tumble in her stomach. On the sports screen, the camera zoomed in on Ty as he and the Sharks captain faced off at center ice.

The two men glared at each other from beneath their helmets and got into position with their sticks across knees. Their mouths moved as they spoke to each other. Each smiled and nodded, but somehow Faith doubted they were discussing the weather.

She raised her glass to her lips. 'What do you think they're saying?'

'Just exchanging pleasantries,' Pavel answered, and Jules laughed.

'What's the matter?' Ty asked the Sharks captain as he stared into his eyes. 'Got period cramps?'

The other man laughed. 'Shut up and eat me, Savage.'

'Funny. That's exactly what your sister said the last time I saw her.'

The ref skated to the circle and Ty turned his attention to the puck the man held in his hand.

'I hear your new owner has turned you all into pussies,' the other captain taunted.

Now it was Ty's turn to laugh as the ref dropped the

puck. The two captains battled for it and the third frame started with a sprint to the Sharks goal.

Ty played a three-minute shift before he skated to the bench and grabbed his water bottle, and his gaze lifted to the owner boxes inside the HP Pavilion. Faith hadn't traveled with them. Thank God.

He wiped off his face with a towel, then hung it around his neck. It had been four days since he'd kissed Faith and he couldn't stop thinking about her. Couldn't stop remembering every detail. He remembered the pressure of her soft lips and the taste of her in his mouth. She'd tasted good, like beer and hot passion and sweet sex. He'd pulled her body against his, pressed her breasts into his chest, and about lost his damn mind. She must have lost hers, too, because she hadn't exactly protested. She'd kissed his neck and asked him to touch her all over, and God, he'd wanted to. Everything inside him had urged him to take that card key from her hand and push her inside her room. To shove her onto her bed and bury his face in her cleavage. '*I want to lick your tattoo*,' she'd whispered, all hot and sexy, and damn if he hadn't wanted to let her run her warm mouth across his skin.

She was beautiful and he'd wanted her. He was honest with himself enough to admit that he still wanted her, and walking away had been one of the toughest things he'd ever done.

A whistle blew and Ty turned his attention to the game and the icing call. He took his captaincy of the

Chinooks seriously. The twenty-four guys on the team looked to him. He was an example and a leader, both on and off the ice, and he didn't even want to think of the guys' reaction if they ever found out that Faith had given him that sucker bite on his neck. He hadn't even known it was there until Sam had pointed it out during practice Sunday morning. He'd made up some bullshit lie about hooking up with a waitress in San Jose, for the love of Christ. Not that that had never happened before, just not when he'd been captain and had just lectured the guys about hooking up.

Walker Brookes skated to the face-off circle in the Chinooks defensive zone and waited for the puck to drop.

The guys had harassed him about getting drunk and picking up a waitress, but they'd believed him. Of course they'd believed him. It never would have even occurred to any of them to suspect the owner of the team had put her hot mouth on his throat and left a mark. He was still having a hard time believing it himself.

Kissing the owner of the team could seriously impact his chances of winning the Stanley Cup, and he still couldn't believe he'd been such a colossal dumb-ass over a woman. Especially over that woman. No matter how much he wanted to kiss her and touch her and let her kiss him.

The puck dropped and Walker fought it out until the puck shot behind him and into the waiting blade of the

Sharks' offense. San Jose moved the puck across ice, and Coach Nystrom signaled for Ty to change up on the fly. He stuck his rubber guard into his mouth and shoved his hands into his gloves.

Pavel Savage had been notorious for thinking with his dick and making mistakes. He'd ruined families and his chance to put his name on the cup.

Ty grabbed his stick and hopped over the boards. He kept his head up and skated to center ice as Walker took the bench. Ty was not his father. Kissing Mrs. Duffy had been a big fuckup, but a fuckup that would not happen again.

Nothing was going to come between him and his run at the cup. Not the other teams competing for the same prize. Not a defense that needed a little more size and speed, and especially not a former Playmate with big breasts and soft lips.

F aith spent the morning before the PR meeting going through her closet and getting rid of clothes she figured she'd never wear again. She piled all her cashmere sweater sets and sedate suits in boxes and called Goodwill.

She was ready to explode, or collapse, or something, from aggravation and lack of sleep. Not only had the Chinooks lost last night in overtime, but she'd also had to hear her mother make love all night. To add insult to injury, Pebbles took up the whole dang bed. How could one small dog take up so much space? Every time she tried to move Pebbles, the dog seemed to gain ten extra pounds and become dead weight.

And why was she allowing it? she asked herself as she got dressed for the PR and marketing meeting. Any of it? Her mother had apparently decided to move in without asking and was sneaking her boyfriend in at nights like she was sixteen. A dog Faith hated slept with her most nights and hogged the bed. She didn't recognize her life anymore. It wasn't the life she'd had in Vegas before Virgil or her life with him. She'd been cramming her head full of hockey and trying to learn as much as possible. She didn't want to make a mistake and fail, but there was still so much she didn't know. And to be honest, she wasn't so sure she'd ever know more than she *didn't* know.

The clothes she'd had shipped from California had arrived the day before, and she dressed for the meeting in a pair of jeans and a pink Ed Hardy T-shirt with a red heart and wings on it. She'd found a cute pair of shearling Uggs that laced to her knees and she stuffed the straight legs of her jeans inside. It was late April and still chilly and wet in the Emerald City.

The traffic to the Key Arena was heavy and it took her ten minutes longer than she'd expected.

'We think this one is fun,' Bo said as Faith took her seat beside Jules and pointed to one of the photos she'd taken with Ty. 'It's kind of playful yet has an edge to it.'

Faith looked at the photograph with her foot between Ty's thighs. Her face was to the camera, looking all happy and smiling while Ty looked up at her as if he was totally annoyed. Which he had been. The blue of his jersey made his eyes even more startling, and the tight set of his strong jaw brought out the thin white scar on his chin. He was gorgeous, everything good and yummy in one pissed-off package. He was every catch in a girl's breath, every hitch in her heart, and every flutter in her stomach. He didn't need a poster or billboard or silver screen to make him larger than life. All he had to do was breathe.

The last time she'd seen Ty had been on television when the San Jose crowd had booed him for goalie interference. He'd argued with the ref and hit his stick on the ice, but as he'd skated toward the penalty box, the crowd's boos turned to cheers and a little smile twisted one corner of his mouth. Which, for Ty, represented full-blown rapture.

'I think the one on the left is better,' Jules pointed out. While Faith had dressed down for the meeting, Jules wore a bright orange dress shirt with black stripes. He kind of looked like a pumpkin. 'Faith standing in front of Ty gives it more depth. And for billboards, you want something with a bit more dimension.' He shrugged. 'And the Saint is never going to go for the other one.'

'How do you know which one Ty would prefer?' Faith asked. Had the two been bonding when she wasn't around?

'Because it looks like you've got your foot on his nuts.'

Oh. That wasn't good. Was it?

'Well, as a graphic artist with a bachelor's degree in advertising,' Bo stressed as she pointed to her favorite, 'I think this one tells a better story.'

Faith looked at her assistant and then at Bo. The two stared daggers at each other and Faith wondered what she'd missed.

Tim, the PR director, stepped forward. 'I'm leaning toward the one with the more playful edge first. If it gets a good reaction, we'll keep the momentum going and put the other one up in a month.'

Faith was not a graphic artist, nor did she have a degree in anything, but she agreed with Jules. 'If we're going to put these up back to back a few weeks apart, it makes sense to go with the picture of me standing in front and Ty behind me looking mad and belligerent.'

'I wasn't mad,' Ty said as he walked in and the room felt suddenly smaller. He wore jeans and a black turtleneck with a Nike swoop on the throat. Unlike the rest of the guys on the team, who looked shaggy from their good-luck beards, Ty was still clean-shaven. His hair was wet, as if he'd just gotten out of the shower. She really hadn't expected to see him. She'd been told the team was practicing, and she figured Ty would skip the meeting.

His electric-blue gaze met hers for several heart-beats before he moved to stand before the mockups. He folded his arms over his chest and stood with his feet a shoulders' width apart. His shirt fit loosely about his wide back and was tucked into a pair of Levi's so worn the back pockets softly cupped his muscular butt. He pointed to the photo with her foot between his thighs. 'This looks like Mrs. Duffy has her stiletto on my nuts.'

Jules laughed and Faith bit her top lip to keep from laughing.

Bo pulled a rubber band from her stubby ponytail. 'It tells a story.'

'Yeah,' Ty agreed. 'The story of her foot crushing my nuts.'

Bo looked like she wanted to crush him with her clunky Doc Martens.

'Well, we certainly don't want that to be the image we project,' Tim assured the Chinooks captain.

'Oh, I don't know,' Faith said as Ty turned to face her. 'I think there are probably more than a few women who'd like to see that image.' Her gaze landed on his flat stomach and the bulge behind the five buttons of his fly. She ran her gaze up the hard muscles of his chest, over the scar on his chin, to his blue eyes. She thought of last night's game and his time in the sin bin. 'More than a few men, too.'

'Yeah,' Jules jumped in, 'but that isn't the point of this campaign. It's to create an image of conflict, but we don't want it to look like Faith is busting the Saint's balls.'

'Thank you, Jules.'

'You're welcome, Saint.'

Faith ducked her head and hid her smile. Men were so weird about their balls.

'It's too sensuous and playful to convey that,' Bo argued as she gathered up her short auburn hair and stuck it back in the ponytail. And while Bo and Jules argued about the photo and Ty's balls, his gaze locked with hers. Fine lines creased the corners of his beautiful eyes and she thought he just might crack a full-blown smile.

Of course, he didn't, but that didn't keep something hot and sensuous from sliding down her spine and spreading across her skin. 'I guess I don't want to bust the Saint's balls. At least not today,' she said. 'I need him to win me the cup.'

First his sac and now his balls. He was really going to have to stop having these conversations with Faith. Especially with other people in the room. In some sort of sick, twisted way, it turned him on.

'I think we'll go with this one first,' Tim said, pointing to the poster of Faith standing in front of Ty. 'We'll use the locker-room shot at another time. Or choose something else from that shoot,' he added, sounding suddenly exhausted as he headed for the door. 'I need some Tylenol.'

'Tim, wait,' Bo called after him as she followed him out the door. 'You didn't hear my ideas for the captions.'

'I feel sorry for that guy,' Jules said as he stood.

'I like her.'

'She's like an aggressive Chihuahua who thinks she's a pit bull.'

'I think that's what I like about her.' Faith stood and Ty lowered his gaze from her lips to the pink long-sleeved T-shirt with a heart and angel wings covering her breasts. Gone were her black pants or loose beige skirts. She wore a pair of jeans that hugged her waist and thighs, and had on a pair of furry Pocahontas boots. Without her loose, dark clothes, she looked younger. Softer and definitely less uptight.

'She's bitchy.'

Faith grabbed a big leather purse with a gold chain strap. 'She's spunky. Kind of marches to her own beat.'

'Your mom marches to her own beat, but I don't see you embracing her *spunki*ness.'

'My mother's not spunky. She's got problems.' Faith cast a glance at Ty before she headed toward the door. 'The biggest being that she acts like she's sixteen.'

'Mrs. Duffy,' Ty called out to her. 'Can you stay a minute?' He needed to settle things between them.

'Sure,' she said over her shoulder as she stopped just inside the door. 'I'll be right with you.' As she spoke to her assistant, Ty's gaze lowered from her blond hair and back to the metal buttons closing the back pockets of her jeans. Kissing her had been a massive screwup. He could pretend it hadn't happen, but Ty liked to confront potential situations before they became real big problems.

Faith turned and left the door slightly open. 'Is this about the other night?' she asked as she moved toward him.

'Yes.'

'Good. Then you know about it.'

Of course he knew about it. He'd been there while she'd sucked on his neck.

'I've been so disturbed by it all week,' Faith continued.

Ty rested his behind on the edge of the table and folded his arms over his chest. He didn't like the sound of that.

'At first I was horrified.' She shook her head and her hair fell from behind one ear. 'I was just so . . . so grossed out.' She crossed her arms beneath her breasts. 'All I could do was just stand there.'

Grossed out? She hadn't acted grossed out as she'd kissed him like it was her job and she was working on a big, fat bonus. Irritation pulled at his brows. 'You did more than just stand there.'

'I might have said something. I don't know; I was in shock.' She looked down at the toes of her boots and her hair fell over her cheeks and hid her face. 'It's forever etched in my brain.'

His too. That was the problem.

'God, I just want to take an ice pick and dig it out.'

His irritation turned to anger and settled in his belly right next to the aching part of him that liked the way her butt looked in those jeans. 'Maybe you should have thought about that before you gave me a sucker bite and begged me to touch you all over.'

'What?' She looked up. 'What are you talking about?'

He pulled one side of his turtleneck down and exposed the little purple mark she'd left on his neck. 'This.' His hands fell to his sides and gripped the table. 'I didn't even notice it until the next morning when Sam pointed it out at light practice.'

She plopped her purse down on a nearby chair and stepped forward. The cool tips of her fingers brushed his neck as she pulled the side of his turtleneck back down. The cool touch spread heat down his chest and straight to his groin. 'That's hardly noticeable.'

'It's faded since Sunday.' He looked up into her face and his gaze lowered to her mouth just inches from his. 'I had to make up a story about a waitress.'

Her eyes looked into his. 'Did they believe you?'

The last time she'd been this close, her mouth had been on his neck and she'd bitten his earlobe. *Touch me,*' she'd whispered, and God, he'd wanted to touch her and more. 'Yeah. They did.'

'Sorry.' She frowned and stepped back. Her cheeks turned pink and she shrugged. 'I guess I was caught up in the moment and got carried away.'

'Even though you were disgusted, horrified, and grossed out?'

'What? Oh. I wasn't talking about *that.*' She gestured to his neck. 'I was talking about walking into my apartment and finding your father on top of my mother. Naked. Having sex.' She pointed to the ground. 'On the floor in front of the fire.'

Now it was his turn to ask, 'What?'

'Your father and my mother . . . and I walked in on them.'

'Wait.' He held up one hand. 'My father knows your mother?'

'Obviously.'

He thought of the woman he'd met the night of the photo shoot. She hadn't been bad looking, just overblown and a bit tacky. Exactly his father's type. 'And you walked in on them having sex?'

'Yes, and it was disgusting. They were . . .' She lifted her palm as if she could stop the painful memory. 'Doggy. I think.'

'You're kidding?'

'I wish!'

Even though his father dating her mother could only end in complete disaster, Faith looked so distressed, he had to laugh.

'Oh.' She pointed at him. Her short nails were painted a light pink. 'You think that's funny? The man who never laughs?'

'I laugh.'

She turned her slim finger toward her chest. 'At me!'

'Well, you're so freaked out, it's funny.' She also looked a little indignant and cute and sexy, standing there in her pink shirt and boots.

'If you'd seen what I saw, you'd be freaked too.'

'Believe me. I have seen it.' Pavel had never purposely flaunted his sexual exploits, but he'd never been all that discreet. 'The first time was when I was about seven.' He'd walked into the living room and seen his father having sex on his mother's antique credenza. His mother hadn't been home at the time.

Her pink lips parted and she gasped. 'I was five! And she's sneaking him in at night and he leaves before

I get up in the morning. He's like a ghost. If they weren't so loud, I wouldn't know he was there.'

Ah. That explained his father's sudden disappearances and sudden reappearances. Ty hadn't seen much of the old man, and figured it had to have something to do with a woman.

'And they kick Pebbles out and make her sleep with me.'

'Pebbles?'

'My mother's dog.' She pushed her hair behind her ears and dropped her arms to her sides. 'Pebbles hates me and the feeling is mutual. She snaps and snarls at me all the time. Except when she needs something. Like a place to sleep.'

He tilted his head to one side and looked at her. 'Why don't you kick her out?'

'I tried,' she said through a sigh. 'But she looks at me with those beady little eyes and I just can't be that mean. Now every time Pebbles jumps in bed with me, I know that Pavel's in the other room getting naked with my mom.' She made a face and shook her head. 'I probably wouldn't be so disturbed if it wasn't my mother moaning and carrying on like someone is killing her.'

It wasn't the sort of reaction he'd expect out of a former stripper and Playmate. Especially an unrepentant stripper and Playmate. He didn't really know what he'd expected. Maybe someone who thought sex was no big deal, no matter who was having it. At least, that had been the attitude of the strippers he'd known. 'Huh.'

'Huh what?'

'For someone who used to get naked for a living, you seem all uptight about sex.'

'That was a job.' She shook her head as she looked into his eyes. 'Stripping was never about sex.'

Which made no sense at all. A woman getting naked was always about sex. 'Neither was *Playboy*,' she added.

She should tell that to all the guys who looked at her photos, because it sure as hell looked a lot like sex. At least it had to him. It had felt like it too. He thought of her wearing those pearls and felt his sac get tight. 'Bullshit. You sold sex.'

She shrugged. 'That was acting.'

He didn't believe her, but all this talk about sex had him thinking of sliding his hands up the back of her jeans and cupping her smooth, bare behind as she put her hot, moist mouth against his throat again. He needed to get out away from her, but he didn't want to stand up just yet. His jeans were loose, but not that loose. 'Again, I apologize for kissing you the other night.' He looked at his Rolex as if he had somewhere else to go. 'I'd had a few too many beers. That's not an excuse, and I'm sorry.'

She took the hint – thank the Lord – and reached for her purse on the nearby chair. 'It was inappropriate on both our parts,' she said.

'Let's just chalk it up to alcohol and forget it happened.'

'I can do that.' She hung the gold chain strap over one shoulder. 'Can you?'

He was going to try like hell. 'Absolutely. You have my word that it won't happen again.' She stood before him like a sexual buffet that he wanted to dive into headfirst. 'You could run around naked in front of me and I wouldn't do a thing.'

She raised one skeptical brow. 'Really?'

'Yep.' He lowered his gaze down the full curves beneath her shirt then back up again. 'You could go ahead and whip that top off and I'd just sit here kind of bored.'

'You wouldn't move a muscle?'

He shrugged one shoulder. 'I'd probably yawn.'

She dropped her purse to the floor, crossed her arms over her chest, and grasped the bottom of her shirt. 'You sure you won't feel anything?'

Holy shit. 'Yeah.'

Her fingers gathered the edge, pulling it up until a strip of smooth white skin showed just above her jeans resting on her hips. 'Still not feeling anything?'

Ty had been playing in the NHL for more than fifteen years now. He knew a thing or two about putting on his game face. 'Not a thing.' To prove his point, he yawned. Which was difficult considering he had a hard time breathing.

She laughed, a soft, seductive little chuckle as she pulled the shirt up past her little belly button, pierced with a pink jewel. 'Nothing?'

The blood rushed from his head to his crotch and he fought the urge to fall to his knees and press his open mouth against her smooth belly. 'Sorry, Mrs. Duffy.' Then he told the biggest whopper of the day. 'You're just not that attractive.'

She raised the bottom of the T-shirt further up her slim ribs. 'You don't think so?'

'No.'

'A lot of men have told me I'm beautiful.'

'A lot of men lie to get women naked.' The shirt rose a few stingy inches.

'Even women they're not attracted to?'

His gaze took in her smooth belly as she pulled the shirt up just past the pink satin cupping the bottoms of her breasts. 'Depends.'

'On?'

'If it's after midnight and the bar's about to close.' He held his breath, waiting for more. 'A lot of people get more attractive at closing time. But I've never been the kind of guy to go ugly just to get laid. You could probably come over here and give me a lap dance right now and I'd just go ahead and fall asleep.'

Her little chuckle became deeper as if she could read his mind and knew he was lying. 'I haven't given a lap dance since I quit Aphrodite years ago, but I imagine it's like riding a bike.' She gathered the shirt in one hand and slid a slow, deliberate palm across her bare belly. 'I guarantee that you wouldn't fall asleep.' There was something sinful and hot about a woman touching herself. 'Within seconds you'd be whimpering like a baby and begging for mercy.'

'That's a bold statement, Mrs. Duffy.'

'Just stating a fact, Mr. Savage.' Her little finger skimmed the top of her waistband and dipped below the top button. 'You feelin' sleepy yet?'

'Keep going. I'll let you know.'

The tip of her ring finger followed her pinky beneath her waistband. 'Bored?'

'Gettin' there.'

'Wait.' Her hand stopped along with his heart. 'Wouldn't a lap dance be considered inappropriate behavior?'

Hell no!

She laughed and dropped her shirt. 'And just after we said it wouldn't happen anymore.'

His hands grasped the edge of the table to keep from reaching for her. From grabbing the waistband of her jeans and pulling her to him until she stood between his thighs, close enough to touch. He wanted to tell her she could behave inappropriately all she wanted. Anywhere. His bed came to mind, but the look in her clear, almost calculating eyes stopped him. While she'd just turned him inside out and upside down, she felt nothing.

She reached for her purse. 'Are we going to be able to forget this happened, too?'

'Not a problem.' With his dick throbbing against his inner thigh, he said, 'I've already forgotten.'

She moved toward the door but turned and looked

at him over her shoulder. 'Me too. You're not the only one who was bored.' The door swung open before she reached it and her assistant stepped inside. 'What's up, Jules?' she asked.

Jules looked from her to Ty. 'I just came to let you know that I set up a meeting next week with the director of the Chinooks Foundation.'

'Sounds good.' She adjusted the purse on her shoulder and looked at Ty one last time. 'See you around, Mr. Savage.'

Jules watched her leave, then asked, 'Is there something going on between you and Faith?'

'No,' he answered truthfully. There was nothing and there could never be anything either.

'It looked like something.'

'I'm the captain of her hockey team.' He raised his hands and rubbed his face. What the hell had just happened? 'That's it.'

'I hope that's true. She's my boss and I don't allow myself to think of her like that,' Jules said.

He dropped his hands. 'Like what?'

'Like the way you were looking at her. Like she was standing naked in front of you.'

It was so close to the truth, Ty stared at the bastard. 'Even if that's true, why is it your business – eh?'

'Because her husband just died and she's lonely. I'd hate to see her get hurt.'

Ty folded his arms across his chest. 'You seem overly concerned with her feelings.'

'I'm concerned about her, yes, but she's a survivor. I'm more concerned about the Chinooks.' Now it was Jules's turn to fold his arms across his chest. 'What do you think the other guys will say about you making it with the owner of the team?'

'You seem to know. So, why don't you tell me?'

Jules shook his head and stared him in the eyes. And as much as Ty wanted to punch him in the head, he had always admired a guy who didn't back down when he was right. And as much as Ty hated to admit it, Jules was right. 'I don't think I have to list how many ways that would be profoundly stupid. There is no reason why we can't knock out the Sharks in the next game and advance to the third round. Then we're only two teams from winning the cup. I don't think I need to tell you what a distraction that would be for you and everyone else.'

'That's right. You don't.' Ty stood. 'That's why we were talking about my father dating her mother.' Which was true. In between him looking at her like she was naked. 'I like you, Jules. If I didn't like you, I'd just tell you to stay the hell out of my business.' He moved toward the door and stopped to look down into the other man's face. 'So, I'm going to be straight with you. Every man on the team has seen those pictures in *Playboy*. There's no point in even denying that. Hell, you've seen them, and Mrs. Duffy doesn't seem at all worried about it. But there's a world of difference between thinking about her in those pictures and taking it a step further. Let me assure you that nothing is going to get in my way of making it all the way to the finals.

'Not winning the cup has been a monkey on my back for fifteen years. I've been one overtime shot away from having my name engraved on the cup, and the last thing I'm going to do is fuck that up.' He gave Jules one last hard look and walked from the room.

He'd parked his BMW in the lower level of the parking garage, and on his way home, he thought about what he needed to do in tomorrow night's game. They needed to shut down San Jose's defense, clinch the second round, and move on to the third. He thought about Faith and Jules. And he thought about his dad and Faith's mother. Of all the women in Seattle, why did the old man have to screw around with her? Ty didn't get it. It was like Pavel was the Pied Piper of penis and women followed him anywhere.

He drove across the floating bridge of Lake Washington to Mercer Island. He parked the BMW in between his Bugatti Veyron and his father's Cadillac.

'Jesus, Dad,' Ty said as he walked into the kitchen and tossed his keys on the deep brown granite countertop. 'You didn't tell me that Faith Duffy walked in on you having sex with her mother.'

Pavel shrugged as he turned from the refrigerator and shut the door. 'She was supposed to be in California.' He popped the top on a can of Molson and shrugged as if that said it all. 'But she got sick and came home early.'

Ty doubted she'd been sick and suspected her sudden departure from San Jose had more to do with that kiss in the hall than bad fish or the flu bug. 'Why didn't you tell me?'

'You are judgmental.' Pavel raised the can to his lips and took a drink.

'No. You didn't tell me because you knew I wouldn't like it.' He sighed and shook his head. 'Seattle is a big city, Dad. Couldn't you find another woman besides Faith Duffy's mother to bang?'

Slowly Pavel lowered his beer. 'Don't talk disrespectful, Tyson.'

That was the weird paradox about Pavel. You could treat women like shit, and that was okay. But you couldn't talk disrespectfully. 'What's going to happen when you break up with her?' There wasn't a doubt in Ty's mind that he would, too. 'I don't want to have to deal with a hysterical woman showing up here.' Like when women always discovered that Pavel was married, or wasn't going to marry them, or he had dumped them for someone else.

'Val isn't the type to get too attached. She's only in town for a short time to help her daughter through a difficult time. She's a devoted mother.'

Which brought up a subject Ty had been meaning to talk about. He couldn't come right out and ask the old man when he was going back to his house. 'What are your plans?' he asked instead as he moved toward the refrigerator and opened the stainless-steel door.

Pavel shrugged and raised his can. 'Just having a beer. Later Valerie invited me over for dinner. I'm sure the two ladies wouldn't mind if you joined us.'

After his latest conversation with Faith and the enormous wood she'd given him, that wasn't going to happen. 'I'm meeting some of the guys at Conte's for poker and Cubans.' He was definitely in the mood to kick some ass on the poker table.

'You spend too much time in the company of men and it makes you bad-tempered.'

'I'm not bad-tempered! Jesus, I wish people would lay off about that.'

Pavel shook his head. 'You've always been so sensitive. Like your mother.'

His father was talking out of his ass again. Sensitive? Like his mother? Ty was nothing like his mother. His mother had spent her life loving the wrong man. Ty had never been in love at all.

'You need to find a woman,' Pavel suggested. 'A woman to take care of you.'

That just proved how well the old man knew him. The last thing Ty needed was a woman in his life. A down-and-dirty hookup was a different matter, but even that was too big a distraction. And right now, he couldn't even afford a quick, wham-bam distraction.

12

On Monday morning Jane Martineau walked into Faith's office at the Key. A petite little package with dark hair and glasses, Jane wore very little makeup and was dressed in black from head to toe. She was cute rather than pretty, and not what Faith expected in either a lifestyle reporter or the wife of former elite goaltender Luc Martineau.

'Thank you for meeting with me,' she said as she shook Faith's hand. She put a black leather briefcase on the desk and reached inside. 'I had to threaten Darby with physical harm if he didn't at least approach you for the interview. I also sicced his wife on him.'

'I didn't know he was married.' For the interview, Faith hadn't known what to wear and had dressed in a white blouse, her black pencil skirt, and black patent leather T-strap pumps. Clearly, she'd overdressed.

Jane took out a pad of paper and a pen. 'To my best friend since grade school, Caroline. I introduced them.'

'Wow. You still see your friend from grade school.' Faith didn't know why she found that unusual, other than she hadn't seen her friends from grade school for about fifteen years or so.

'I talk to her almost every day.'

'That must be nice. To have a friend for that long.' She shook her head. 'I didn't mean to sound pathetic.'

Jane looked at her through the lenses of her glasses as she dug around in the briefcase. 'You didn't. People come and go. Caroline and I are fortunate to still be in each other's lives.'

Faith eyed the small tape recorder Jane pulled out of her briefcase and asked, 'Do you have to use that?' God forbid she said something pathetic and it ended up in the newspaper.

'It's as much for your protection as mine.' She set it on the desk and put the briefcase on the floor. 'Don't worry. I won't ask you any embarrassing questions. This isn't an exposé or a hit piece. Seattle hockey fans are excited about the playoffs and curious about you. They want to know a little bit about Faith Duffy. You don't have to answer anything that makes you feel uncomfortable. Fair enough?'

Faith relaxed a bit. 'Fair enough.'

Jane sat and started the interview with simple questions about where Faith had been born and how she'd met Virgil. Then she asked, 'You're only thirty years old; how does it feel to own an NHL franchise?'

'Shocking. Unbelievable. I still can't believe it.'

'You didn't know you were going to inherit the team?'

'No. Virgil never mentioned it. I found out the day his will was read.'

'Wow. That's a nice inheritance. There are probably a lot of women who'd love to be in your shoes.'

True. She had a great life. 'It's a lot of work.'

'What do you know about running an entire organization like the Chinooks?'

'Admittedly not a lot, but I'm learning every day. I'm getting on-the-job training, and I'm actually starting to understand hockey and how the organization runs. It's not as scary as it was a few weeks ago. Of course, Virgil was smart enough to hire good people and to let them do their jobs. So that makes my job easier.'

Jane asked about goals and points and the Chinooks' chances of winning the Stanley cup. In a 4–2 win the previous Saturday, the Chinooks had beaten the Sharks in Game Six and were set to play the Red Wings in the third round Thursday in Detroit. 'Zetterberg and Datsyuk were both top scorers in their division during the regular season,' Jane said, referring to two Detroit players. 'What's the plan to slow down the momentum of Zetterberg and Datsyuk?'

'We just need to keep playing hockey the way we like to play it. We had thirty-two shots on goal last Saturday night, compared to the Sharks' seventeen.'

The two of them left the office and headed down to the arena, where the team was practicing. 'Everyone thinks we should be afraid of Detroit,' Faith said, and the closer they moved to the tunnel, the more the air thickened with testosterone. 'They've got some great talent, but so do we. I think it will come down to . . .' she thought of Ty and smiled '. . . what's in a player's gut.'

'Hey, Mrs. Duffy,' the 'Sniper,' Frankie Kawczynski, called out as Faith and Jane approached. He stood in the tunnel in front of a blowtorch heating the curve of his stick.

'Hello, Mr. Kawczynski,' she said, her heels sinking into the thick mats. Frankie was in his late twenties and built like a tank. At the moment, he stood in a pair of sweatpants, low around his hips, and a pair of flip-flops. He had a pit bull tattoo on his bare back. Her attention was drawn to the play of muscles as he heated his stick. 'How are you?'

'Great.' His dark beard had gone full Mountain Man, and he flashed a brash, cocky smile. Faith was suddenly very aware that she was surrounded by men. Big, tough men who towered over her and Jane. Some of them were half-naked. 'Are you going to practice with us this morning?' Frankie asked.

Walker Brookes walked from the locker room and grabbed his skates off the sharpening rack. She fought the urge to whip her head around for a better look. 'I forgot my gear.' Within her soul, Layla fought to get out. She kicked and screamed for just one little peek. Just one, but Mrs. Duffy did not stare at men's asses. At least not when a reporter was around. 'Perhaps some other time.' And she kept her gaze glued to Frankie's face.

Vlad Fetisov walked out of the locker room with his

helmet in one hand and stick in the other. A wide smile curved his mouth as he moved toward them on his skates.

'Hi, little Sharky,' the Russian greeted Jane.

'Hi, Vlad,' Jane said. 'How's it going?'

'Life iz good. How iz Lucky?' he asked, referring to Jane's husband.

'He's good.'

As soon as Vlad moved onto the ice Faith asked, 'Why did he call you "Sharky"?'

'That's the name the guys gave me because I beat them all at darts. They're very competitive at everything they do.'

They stopped at the end of the tunnel and Faith looked out across the rink. The men on the ice were divided into two groups. Offense practiced at one end; defense drilled at the other. They appeared even more scruffy and unkempt, but they skated with well-timed precision and skill, weaving in and out and passing the puck. There were about fifteen men on the ice, all dressed in dark blue practice sweats and white helmets, but as if pulled by an invisible force, her gaze landed on a pair of broad shoulders and dark hair curling up from beneath the white helmet of the man standing with his back to her at center ice. She didn't need to see his face to know it was Ty. Something warm in the pit of her stomach recognized him.

'Vlad is a little warped,' Jane said, thankfully pulling Faith's attention from center ice.

Faith had never gotten a creepy vibe from the Russian. Still she asked, 'Is he a perv?'

'No. He's just never been shy about dropping his towel in front of women. He used to like to shock me, I think. They all liked to shock me.' Jane shook her head and adjusted the strap of her briefcase. 'They didn't want me traveling with the team. A woman on the jet is considered bad luck.'

Perhaps that's why they'd been so quiet when she'd traveled with them. 'That's stupid and sexist.'

'Exactly.' Jane laughed. 'They're hockey players.' The two of them watched the assistant coach lay a series of pucks on the red line and Jane said, 'Tell me about Ty Savage.'

She thought about the morning she'd stood in the conference room pulling up her shirt. Of his hot blue eyes and the day she'd lost her mind and let Layla out for the second time. The day she'd pulled up her shirt like a stripper, slow and deliberate just to prove him wrong. The day she'd slid her hand across her belly toward the button of her jeans, just to see the heat in his eyes burn a little hotter. 'What would you like to know?'

'Do you think he has what it takes to lead this team to the final round?'

'Well, I think the numbers he puts up speak for him.' She watched Ty take off from one end of the ice, skating like he was on fire. Wind flattened the Chinooks logo on his sweatshirt against his chest as he raced toward the red line. With the blade of his stick on the ice, he turned at the center line and one-timed the row of pucks at the goalie. The goalie twisted and contorted to stop each shot. He caught one puck while the others hit his pads with loud thwaps. One of the pucks got through and hit the inside of the net. 'He's a very intense, serious guy.' Except when he was trying to use reverse psychology to get her to give him a lap dance. 'Very disciplined and in control. I wonder what he would be like if he ever let go.' What she hadn't anticipated that day in the conference room, while he'd sat there acting like he was bored, was the way his hot, steamy gaze on her body had turned her all hot and steamy inside.

With the wind still flattening his sweatshirt, he shoved his stick beneath one arm and looked at the laces on his glove. 'Really let go,' she added, thinking of him walking away from her at the Marriott. 'Maybe he wouldn't be so rude and surly.'

'He makes rude and surly look good,' Jane said.

That was an understatement.

'He's a very good-looking man.'

Faith smiled. 'I hadn't noticed.'

As if he'd heard them, Ty looked up as he came to a hockey stop near the goal. From half the length of the rink, she felt his gaze as cool as the ice on which he stood. It froze her in place even as it heated her up inside.

'A lot has been made out of the fact that you have a contentious relationship with your captain. Is that true?'

As his eyes stared into hers, he grabbed a water bottle from the top of the net and lifted it to his mouth. The water shot between his lips and then stopped. He swallowed then rubbed one big gloved hand across his mouth. For the past month her life had been a whirlwind of activity and change. Sometimes she couldn't recall what she'd done from day to day, but she remembered every hot detail of Ty's mouth on hers. 'I wouldn't call it contentious.'

'What would you call it?'

What did you call a hot, overwhelming attraction to the one guy on the planet for whom it was completely inappropriate to lust after? 'Complicated.' Impossible. A disaster waiting to happen.

'There you are,' Jules said as he moved through the tunnel toward Faith. A man with red hair and a mustache walked beside him.

'We need to get a photograph of Faith with the team,' Jane said.

'Now?' She looked at the shorter woman.

'Yeah.'

'We have a whole PR campaign with Ty, so why don't we shoot with some of the other players?' Jules suggested.

'Faith, this is Brad Marsh.' Jane introduced the stranger. 'Staff photographer for the *Post Intelligencer*. Brad, this is Faith Duffy.'

'Pleased to meet you, Faith.' He took her hand in his. 'I'm a huge Chinooks fan.'

'I'm thrilled to meet you. Especially since you love my team.'

Jules stepped out onto the ice and pointed to the defenders. 'I need some of you guys to volunteer to take a photograph with Mrs. Duffy for the *Post Intelligencer*.'

Sam and Alexander Devereaux were the first to skate toward her, but the rest followed close behind.

'I'll do it.'

'Count me in.'

Soon eight big defensemen, including Vlad, had volunteered.

'Let's take the picture at center ice,' Brad suggested. 'I'll try and get some of the logo in the shot.'

Faith carefully stepped onto the ice, and Blake Conte offered his arm. 'Be careful, Mrs. Duffy,' he said. 'You wouldn't want to fall and hurt yourself.'

Sam offered his arm on her other side. 'Someone might have to give you CPR.'

'I know mouth-to-mouth,' Blake added, and Faith sincerely hoped she would never have to take him up on the offer. For some bizarre reason, he'd shaved his playoffs beard into a reddish-blond strip of hair beneath his nose. It ran down his chin, too. Kind of like he'd gone in for a wax and come out with a Brazilian on his face.

'And chest compressions,' Sam said, whose playoffs beard was blond and kind of patchy.

Faith placed her hands on their forearms and smiled. 'It's good to know you boys are worth more to me than just looking good, shooting pucks, and spitting.' Being the female owner of a hockey team had a few nice perks. Being escorted by two very hot hockey players was a good one.

'Look at those bastards,' Ty said from his position halfway across the ice from Faith. 'You'd think they'd never been around a woman before.' The last time he'd seen Faith, she'd pulled up her shirt, then told him she was bored. Sure, he'd said it first, but he'd been lying.

First-string goaltender Marty Darche pushed the front of his helmet up and revealed his impressive facial hair. 'You've got to admit, Saint, there aren't a lot of women around who look like her.' He leaned back against the pipes and shook his head. 'Damn.'

The photographer pointed to a few of the guys and called out, 'Why don't one of you men give Mrs. Duffy your stick?' The whole blue line rushed forward.

'I wouldn't mind giving her my stick,' Marty said through a chuckle.

Ty liked Marty. Usually, he'd laugh at the stupid shit that came out of Marty's mouth. Most of the time he'd add his own stupid shit and say something about eight to ten inches of good wood. Today he didn't find any of it amusing, for some unknown reason. Maybe he was tired or dehydrated or something. He tended to lose his sense of humor when he was tired or dehydrated.

'Have you seen the pictures of her?'

'Yeah.' The damn pictures. But today he didn't see

the damn pictures when he looked at her. He saw her teasing smile and her smooth belly. He saw her eyes as she'd looked back over her shoulder and said she was bored.

The defense crowded around her for the photo and she laughed. The sound rippled across the ice. It brushed across his skin and tightened his chest. Surrounded by big, hulking men wearing skates and shoulder pads, she looked small and so beautifully female.

When he looked at her across the ice, he didn't see the Playmate. He saw the woman he'd kissed in a hotel in San Jose. He could almost feel her sexy mouth beneath his and her hands in his hair. He could see the lust in her eyes and feel the need in her kiss. He'd kissed and been kissed by a lot of women in his life, but he'd never been kissed like that. Like an all-consuming desperation that was so hot, it made his gut clench.

'Some of you guys come out a bit,' the photographer said. 'That's good.'

Pavel was on a kick about Ty meeting Valerie, but Ty had no interest in meeting his father's latest. Especially when chances were good that he'd have a different girlfriend in a month or two. Especially if it meant hanging out with the woman across the ice who was having a great old time laughing and giggling and turning a bunch of hockey players into slobbering idiots.

He'd rather be fed his lunch by a 250-pound enforcer with something to prove. He might walk away from that encounter bruised and bloody, but a few cuts and a black eye was a hell of a lot better than another set of painful blue balls.

'Oysters are a natural aphrodisiac of the gods.' Valerie reached for an oyster from the iced plate in the middle of the table and slurped it down. 'You should have at least one, Faith. It wouldn't hurt. Might even help.'

'No thanks, Mom. More bread?' She picked up the white plate and held it across the table. Could her mother be any more embarrassing? Sadly, the answer was yes.

'No, thank you.'

'Pavel?' Within the booth of the Brooklyn Seafood Steak and Oyster House in downtown Seattle, Faith's stomach rolled as she held the small plate for her mother's boyfriend.

'No. Thank you,' he answered as he held a rough shell to his mouth. He tipped it up and an oyster slid into his mouth and down his throat.

Faith turned her face away and swallowed hard.

'More than your eyes look a little green,' Ty said next to her ear.

She set the plate on the table, which was covered in white linen. 'I hate oysters.'

'Then why are we here?'

'Because my mother wanted to come.' It had been Valerie's big idea that they should all go out to dinner together, and Faith had reluctantly agreed. If she'd known she'd have to watch her mother and Pavel slurp down oysters, she would have stayed at home with her feet up. Even if it meant spending time with the evil Pebbles.

'I notice you're not eating any,' she pointed out to Ty.

'I don't eat anything that looks like that.' One corner of his mouth lifted in an actual smile. He lowered his voice and said next to her ear, 'At least not in public.'

'Was that some sort of inappropriate sexist comment?'

His eyes met hers. 'That depends. Were you offended?'

'I probably should be.'

He let his gaze slowly lower from her face, down her bare throat to the top button of her pink shirtdress. 'But you're not – eh?'

'No. You seem to bring out inappropriate behavior in me.' She licked her lips and shook her head. 'We should stick to safe subjects.'

'Too late.' He raised his gaze to hers. 'I'm having some inappropriate thoughts.'

'You are?'

'Oh yeah.'

'What?'

'Kissing your mouth like I did a few weeks ago and working my way south.'

He was thinking all that? She squeezed her legs together against the tight ache pooling between her thighs.

'What are you talking about?' her mother wanted to know.

'The weather.' Faith looked across the table as the waiter cleared the oyster plate. 'I just asked Ty how he likes Seattle.'

He reached for his glass of wine, and the sleeve of his dark blue dress shirt brushed her bare arm. 'It's not that much different from Vancouver.' He took a drink, then set the glass back on the table. 'Scheduling a round of golf is dicey.'

'I don't play golf, but the summer is much drier,' she answered, trying like hell to ignore the flush of lust warming up her skin. 'Jules told me that there's a Chinooks celebrity golf tournament some time this summer. The money goes to help injured players, like Mark Bressler.'

'That was tragic.' Pavel shook his head. 'Such a loss to the team. Losing a captain is like cutting out the heart of the team.'

Ty's jaw tightened. 'Captains are traded all the time, Dad. It's not like when you played.'

An almost imperceptible tension settled over the booth. 'That's true,' Pavel conceded. 'Now there is no loyalty.'

The salad course arrived and Faith waited until fresh pepper was ground on everyone's salad before she said, 'Well, I know that everyone in the Chinooks organization is thrilled to have Ty. If that upsets our neighbors to the North . . .' She shrugged and tried to take her mind off the man sitting next to her. 'They'll get over it. I mean, they got over the defection of Jim Carrey.' She reached for her linen napkin on her lap. 'Although Canada should probably give us a big, fat thanks for taking Jim off their hands. Did you see *The Cable Guy*?' She speared a bite of her roasted beet and butter lettuce. She looked across her shoulder at Ty, who was almost smiling. 'What?'

'*Cable Guy*?'

'It sucked.'

He shook his head. 'No more than *Me, Myself and Irene*.'

'It might be a toss-up.'

'I like Jim Carrey,' her mother confessed. 'He was on that *In Living Color* show with J.Lo.'

'I used to love *The Rockford Files*,' Pavel added.

'Oh, *The Rockford Files*,' Valerie cooed. 'I loved Jim Rockford's Firebird. My third husband had a Firebird. Do you remember Merlyn, Faith?'

'He drove too fast.'

'You've been married three times?' Ty asked as he spread his napkin across the lap of his dark wool pants. The back of his hand brushed Faith's hip and she would have scooted over if there'd been room.

Valerie paused with a bite of salad halfway to her lips. She looked at Faith and then at her boyfriend. 'Five times, but only because I was young and vulnerable.'

It had been seven times, but who was counting. Obviously, not Valerie. 'Are you going to join us in the

skybox tomorrow night for the game against Detroit?'
Faith asked to change the subject.

'I would love to. Thank you, Faith.' Pavel ate a few
bites and said, 'The Chinooks are going in as
underdogs, but sometimes that is the best position to be
in. If our guys can get them to draw penalties, I think
there's a very good chance we'll advance to the final
round. Which I predict will be against Pittsburgh.'

'I don't know, Dad.' Ty grabbed his fork and planted
his free hand on the seat beside Faith's thigh.
'Pittsburgh's playing without two of their power
forwards.'

Father and son talked and argued about everything
from power plays to penalty killers. Well into the main
course, they talked about the best games ever played
and Pavel's glory days. Several times during their conversations, Ty's hand accidentally brushed her hip. His
touch spread fuzzy tingles to the back of her knee and
tightened the hot, liquid knot in the pit of her stomach.

'Once I fired that puck into traffic, I lost sight of it,'
Pavel said as he cut into his steak. 'I didn't know I'd
scored until I heard it hit the back pipe.'

'I wish I could have seen you play. I bet you were
something,' Valerie gushed and took a bite of chicken.

'My mom used to love to watch my dad play.' Ty
raised his wine to his lips and his free hand slid to the
top of Faith's thigh. 'She used to buy me a hot dog, and
we'd sit in the middle row behind the goal because she
thought those were the best seats. The old Montreal

Forum had the best hot dogs.'

Faith's eyes widened and she gasped at the heat of his palm spread across her lap. This time his touch was no accident. 'I hate hot dogs,' she said.

He looked at her and his grasp tightened a bit. 'How could you hate hot dogs? You're American.'

'I ate too many of them growing up.'

'Faith was crazy for hot dogs back then.'

Faith's breath caught in her chest and she couldn't respond. She took a bite of salmon but had a hard time swallowing. Especially when his thumb brushed across her leg back and forth. She gave up trying to eat and reached for her wine.

'Is something wrong with your food?' he asked her.

'No.' She looked into his eyes, at the fiery blue lust and need staring back at her, and she wanted more. More of the hot flush and warmth pooling in her belly. She wanted to fall headfirst into more. Into him. She was a thirty-year-old woman who hadn't felt the irresistible tangle of lust and need pulling her under in a very long time and she wanted to go. She wanted him to take her there, and she slipped her hand beneath the table. She ran her fingers down his forearm, over his rolled-up sleeve until her palm rested on the back of his hand. His grasp tightened, but instead of removing it, she licked her dry lips and slid his hand between her thighs.

'I think we should all go dancing after dinner,' her mother suggested. 'Faith was always a good dancer.'

Through the linen of her dress, Ty squeezed and she closed her legs around his warm hand. 'I have an early morning,' he said.

'I'm tired.' Faith looked at her mother and yawned. 'But you two can go ahead. I can take a taxi home.'

'I'll take you.'

She looked at Ty and said, just above a whisper, 'That might be inappropriate.'

'The things I'm going to do to you are very inappropriate.' He lowered his mouth to her ear. 'You should probably be afraid.'

'Are you planning anything illegal?'

'Not the first two or three times.' He shrugged. 'I'm not sure *aboat* the rest.'

13

'It's kind of empty,' Faith said as she stood in the center of the darkened solarium. Overhead, stars crammed the clear night sky, and she felt like she was floating twenty-eight stories above Seattle. 'Virgil and I didn't stay in the city very often, so I never got around to doing anything up here. I always pictured lots of plants and cane furniture. Maybe a tiger, like in *Who's That Girl*, with Madonna. Hated that movie, but I loved that big garden and the tiger.'

'Are you nervous?'

The heels of her hot-pink Chanel pumps tapped across the tile floor as she moved to the edge and looked out. 'Can you tell?'

'You talk a lot more when you're nervous.'

She put her hands against the glass and gazed at the Space Needle, all lit up like a giant flying saucer. On the way home from the restaurant, they'd stopped at a pharmacy and he'd run in and bought condoms. Magnums. 'You make me nervous.'

He moved close behind her. 'Why?'

Several reasons. Starting with, 'Were those magnums necessary?'

'I like 'em snug.'

Oh God. And ending with, 'It's been a long time for me.'

He bent his head and asked close to her ear, 'A long time since . . . ?'

'I was with anyone.'

He placed his hands on her hips and pulled her back against his chest, nestling her behind against his erection. 'Anyone but Virgil?'

She looked into the shadowy outline of his watery reflection. So tall and powerful and ready. 'Virgil was good to me and I loved him, but we never . . .' She couldn't say it. She couldn't betray him even though he was gone. 'Our marriage wasn't about that.'

His hands touching her hips and stomach stilled. 'You never had sex?'

She didn't answer.

His barely visible gaze met hers in the glass. 'Not even with someone who could?'

'Of course not.'

'How long were you married?' He sounded incredulous.

She turned her head and looked back over her shoulder into the variegating light touching his face. 'Five years.'

He was silent for several heartbeats. 'You haven't had sex in five years? A woman who looks like you?'

'Why's that hard to believe?' Quiet laughter escaped her lips and whispered across his chin. 'You said I was ugly.'

'I think I said unattractive.'

'That's right. You don't go ugly just to get laid.' She lifted her face and kissed his jaw. 'Should I stop?'

'No. Tonight I'll take one for the team.' He slid his palm up her stomach and he said next to her ear, 'Sometimes being the captain is a burden.' His hands slipped up the slopes of her breasts and he cupped her through the pink linen dress and her white lace balconnet bra. 'I've had a hard-on for you since that night of the photo shoot.'

Her nipples tightened beneath the brush of his fingers. 'That night you made me feel things too.' She arched her back and pressed her bottom into him. 'Things I haven't felt in several years.'

'Then it's past time to do those things,' he said as his mouth came down and opened against hers. Against her behind he was hard as a club. He fed her hot kisses as he rocked his hips and slowly thrust against her. She didn't think she'd ever wanted anything in her life like she wanted this. This warm, inviting flush tightening her chest and flooding the apex of her thighs with aching need. He softly squeezed and kneaded her breasts. She opened her mouth and devoured his kiss. Everything about her life was chaotic, but this wild, forbidden moment felt right. Like something she needed and wanted and desperately had to have. She stood on top of the world surrounded by stars and light and thin air, and Ty was the only thing that felt solid.

She raised one hand behind his head and held his mouth to hers, and the heat of his kiss spread outward, across her shoulder, and down her chest. Her heart pounded and swelled, and she leaned back into the solid, warm comfort of his embrace. Breathing the scent of him into her lungs as his fingers worked the buttons closing the front of her dress until it lay open to her waist.

He raised his head; his heavy lids were lowered to half-mast, and even in the darkness, there was no mistaking the desire burning in his eyes. No mistaking the long, hard length of it pressed into her behind. He slipped his big hands inside the collar of her dress, his fingers slid across her shoulders, and he pushed it down.

She lowered her hand from the back of his head, and her dress slid down her sensitive skin and fell to her waist, and she stood in front of him in her white bra, matching thong, and her pink pumps. His fingers brushed across her stomach and she placed her hands on top of his and moved them back to her breasts. 'Touch me,' she whispered and pressed her smooth behind into the rougher texture of his wool pants and his huge erection.

'Here.' Through the stretch lace of her bra, his thumbs brushed across her nipples until they got tighter, harder, more painfully sweet. 'You like it when I touch you here?'

She moaned, 'Yes.'

'I've thought a lot about touching you here.' His right hand slid down her stomach to the top of her panties. 'And here. Do you want me to touch you here?'

She nodded. 'All over.'

His fingers slipped beneath the lace underwear. 'You still shave.'

'Does that bother you?'

He shook his head and lowered his mouth to the side of her throat. 'It's all I think about.' His fingers slid lower and parted her flesh, touching her where she craved it the most.

Her knees buckled and he tightened his hold to keep her from falling to his feet. The heavy ache between her thighs became razor sharp and his touch was the only thing that satisfied it.

'You're wet for me.'

'Does that bother you?'

He shook his head and brushed his lips across her shoulder. 'I love that I make you this wet.' He shoved his erection into her.

She felt hot and itching and it would be so easy to orgasm while he played with her, but she wanted more. She wanted something she hadn't had in more than five years. She wanted all of him.

Faith turned to face Ty, and his wet fingers trailed across her pelvis to her behind. She raised her mouth to his and unbuttoned his shirt. She pulled it from his pants and pushed until it fell to the floor. Then she was on him. Pressing her breasts into his warm, hard chest and running her hands over as much of his tight skin as she could. She wanted to devour him for as long as possible, and at the same time, her body throbbed and ached for immediate release. The hair on his chest brushed the tops of her breasts and his happy trail tickled her belly. She kissed him like he was her last meal, and her skin felt hot and tight. His hands caressed her bare butt as her hand slid to the front of his pants and she pressed her palm to his erection. She felt the heat of him through the wool. She wanted every long, hard inch of his penis, and she squeezed.

Ty lifted his head and stared down at her, his breathing rough and choppy. 'I can't wait any longer.'

'Yes,' she managed through her labored breath. Lust, hot and liquid, rushed through her veins, burning away everything but the need for him.

He stepped out of his shoes and reached for his wallet as she unbuttoned his pants and pushed them down his muscular thighs. His boxer briefs went next, and she reached for him and ran her palm up the long, heated shaft. A drop of moisture rested in the cleft of the plump, succulent head and she spread it with her thumb. 'You're a beautiful man, Mr. Savage. Don't finish before the race is over.'

'I'm a professional.' He sucked in a breath and pushed her hands away. 'I don't pull the trigger early.' He unrolled the condom down to the base of his penis.

'Slide those panties down. Unless you want them ripped off.' He looked up. 'Keep the shoes on.'

She pushed the thong down her legs and kicked it aside. Then he reached for her and ran his hands down her bottom to the backs of her thighs. He lifted and she automatically wrapped her legs around his waist. He pinned her back against the cool glass.

Faith ran her hands through his hair and kissed his mouth as he lowered her onto his erection. A stitch of pain brought her head up as he entered her. She sucked in her breath and held it, the big head of his penis slid up into her, stretching her tight flesh.

'Ty.'

'It's okay. I'll make it good for you. Just stay with me, Faith. Don't stop me now.' And then he was buried to the hilt and he was true to his word, he made it good for her. Her bare stomach stuck to his as he ground his pelvis into hers. He pulled out, then plunged deep inside, touching her cervix and all the hot, tingling places inside.

'Mmmm, yes,' she whispered. 'That feels good.' He moved again. 'Like that. Right there. Don't stop. You make it good, Ty.' In and out he thrust, and her breathing grew choppy, her skin tight as he pushed her faster and harder toward release.

'How good?' he asked, his voice a low growl.

'It's so hot. So good. Don't stop. Faster. Yes.' She sucked in a deep breath as he thrust into her harder and harder. His powerful muscles tightened, flexed, with each drive of his hips.

Her whole world narrowed and centered on Ty and where his body joined hers, stroking her inside and teasing her G-spot. Liquid fire poured through her body and burned her up from the inside out. Hot tingles spread across her flesh and she couldn't remember sex ever being this good. This intense. Maybe it had, but she didn't think she'd ever been so absolutely consumed with the intense pleasure, wanting it so much that nothing else mattered. She opened her mouth to tell him not to stop. Before she managed to get the words from her throat, the first wave of orgasm hit. She moaned or screamed or something as it pulled her down and the scalding flames licked her body. Her heart pounded in her ears as Ty pounded into her body, untamed and unleashed in a hot sexual storm of hands and mouths and Ty's enormous hard-on. Beautiful and intense and painfully sweet. Over and over, and it seemed to last forever and not nearly long enough. Her legs tightened around his waist as she rode out the last throbbing pulsations.

'Faith.' His breathing was heavy and strained. 'You're beautiful. Tight. Jesus.' Then he gave one long groan as if he'd pushed a boulder up a hill and heaved it over the other side.

When it was over and the night air began to cool her skin, Ty kissed the crook of her neck and she said, 'Thank you. That was wonderful.'

He lifted his head and looked into her face. 'This isn't over,' he said.

She smiled. 'No?'

'I'm sure we'll probably regret this in the morning.' He lifted her off his still-hard penis and set her on her feet. 'We have a box of condoms and about six hours of really inappropriate sex to get busy on before sunup.' He pushed a strand of hair from the corner of her mouth. 'If we're going to regret it, let's do something to really be ashamed *aboat*.'

Several hours later, Faith stood on the small putting green in Ty's media room, wearing nothing but his blue dress shirt and red toenail polish. Her blond hair fell down her back and she looked stunning and beautiful, especially for a woman who'd already made love three times that night. The last in his spa tub while little bubbles of air brushed their skin in interesting places.

'I remember now why I hate golf.' She held his club in her hands and gave an irritated shrug of her shoulders as his dress shirt rode up her thighs.

She was every fantasy that he'd ever had of her. Only much more, because she was softer and hotter and better in bed. It had been hard enough to keep his hands to himself before he'd made love to her. In a few hours he was going to give her up, and he didn't fool himself that it would be easy. Perhaps if he just saw her as Playmate. As great tits and ass, but he didn't. Somehow in the past few weeks, he'd grown to like her. Quite a lot.

'My boobs get in the way.'

Ty stepped behind her. 'Let me help you with that.' He slid his hand beneath her arms and cupped her breasts. The back of his dress shirt brushed his bare chest. 'Now try.'

She laughed as she swung and the ball flew toward the net. The radar registered twenty-five. 'That's worse than last time. There's no help. My boobs are too big.'

'You're not too big.' Round and white with tight pink nipples that fit perfectly into his mouth. 'You're perfect.' He wore a pair of old Levi's and she nestled her behind into him. Like she had at the solarium, when he'd had incredible sex with her against the glass, a million stars about her head and the Seattle skyline around her body. It was the wildest lay he'd ever had, and he'd had a lot of wild lays in his thirty-five years. 'You just need a man with big hands.'

She chuckled and lined up another ball. 'Okay, but no distractions.'

'I'll behave.'

'I saw *Caddy Shack*. There's no talking in golf.'

She swung back and he whispered next to her ear, 'I want to eat your bald peach.' The club flew out of her hands and landed across the room.

She turned and looked up at him. 'I thought you were going to behave.'

'I am.'

'There's no talking while someone is swinging.'

'I was whispering. That's allowed on some courses.'

He pointed at the ground. 'My putting green. My rules.'

'You didn't mention any rules.' She folded her arms beneath her breasts and looked up at him through her sparkling green eyes. 'What are your other rules?'

'Women have to play naked.'

She tilted her head to one side and tried not to smile up at him. 'How many women have played on your stupid little putting green?'

'I'm going to let the "stupid" comment slide 'cause I like you.'

'How many women have had to get naked, Savage?'

'Just you.' He grabbed the front of his shirt and pulled her close. 'You're special.'

She slid her fingers up his arms to his shoulders and the diamonds on her wedding ring sparkled in the light. 'What time is it?'

He wished she'd take the damn thing off. It sort of made him feel like he was doing a married woman. 'Around three.'

'I better go. You have a practice and a hockey game to win tonight.'

'The practice isn't for twelve hours.' He dropped his hands to her hips and he pulled the shirt up. 'I have plenty of time to sleep and only about an hour left to have sex.' He patted her bare behind. 'You need to get busy.'

She shook her head as she ran her fingers through the sides of his hair. 'I don't want to deplete all your strength. You're going to need it against Detroit's blue line.'

'I have untapped reserves. I'm like Superman. Just when I think I'm spent, I tap into it and kick ass and take names.'

She laughed like he was joking. 'Well, I don't want to jinx you. I know all you hockey players are superstitious.'

Ty wasn't as superstitious as some of the guys. He just didn't need any distractions. Detroit was going to bring their A-game, and he had to be ready. Physically and mentally. 'Once I get my head in the game, I'm hard to knock off the puck,' he said as he pulled her against the front of his jeans.

She lifted a brow. 'You're hard again.'

'Watching you play golf turned me on.'

'Was it my brilliant backswing?'

'Your swing sucks.' He shook his head and lowered his face to hers. 'It was your brilliant back*side*,' he said against the corner of her pouty mouth.

'When does your father usually get home?'

'He's here by six. We have time.'

She ran her hand down his side, over his tattoo. 'Did this hurt?'

He sucked in a breath as her palm slid to his belly. 'Not as bad as a broken ankle.'

'You broke your ankle?' she asked as she placed little kisses along his jaw. 'When?'

'2001. Third round, Game Two against the Devils.'

'What happened here?' She kissed his chin and slipped her hand down the front of his pants.

'I got hard watching you play golf.'

She laughed and wrapped her palm around the head of his dick. 'I know that. I'm asking about your scar.'

That had happened so long ago, he never thought about it these days. 'High stick. Claude Lemieux. 1998. Post-season game against Colorado. Twenty stitches.'

'Ouch.' She slid her mouth to the side of his throat as her free hand unbuttoned his pants. 'I've never broken a bone or had stitches.' His pants slid from his hips and pooled about his bare feet. 'Just have the one tattoo,' she said.

He'd noticed the Playboy bunny in the small of her back. 'And it's sexy as hell,' he managed as she sucked his neck.

'Virgil hated it.' She kissed her way across his shoulder and down his chest. 'He didn't want anyone to know about it. He said classy girls don't get tattoos.'

'Virgil was old and didn't know what the hell he was talking about.'

She knelt in front of him and slipped her hand up and down his shaft. 'It's been a long time since I've done this,' she said as she looked up at him through her beautiful green eyes. 'If it doesn't feel good, tell me and I'll stop.'

Jesus. She pressed her soft lips to the head of his cock and he about went off. 'Yeah, I'll be sure and do that.' After this, he should be good for a while. She'd be out of his system, he thought as she took him into her hot, wet mouth. He ran his finger in her hair as she moved. Yeah, getting off four times in one night should last him for some time. Then she moaned, a sweet little sound that vibrated her throat and he gave up thinking at all.

Giant billboards of a towering Faith and Ty hung about the city of Seattle and dominated the front of the Key Arena. Beneath the shot of the owner standing in front of the team captain, the words simply said, CHINOOKS HOCKEY. GET HOOKED. To Bo's utter disappointment and Jules's unabashed pleasure, there was no mention of beauty and savages and no appearance of nuts-stomping at all.

In the days leading up to the game, excitement buzzed the city, and that Thursday evening the Key was packed for Game One in the semifinal against the Detroit Red Wings. From the drop of the first puck, everything went Seattle's way. The team scored two goals in the first frame. In the second period, the Detroit offense rallied with one goal and held the Chinooks at 2–1 going into the third set. For fifteen minutes each team defended their goals, passing the puck from coast to coast without a clear shot at the crease. With five minutes left, Ty passed the puck across ice to the Sniper, Frankie Kawczynski, who made a shot through traffic. Goalie Chris Osgood got a tip of his glove on it as it sailed behind him into the net, and the Chinooks sewed up the first game 3–1.

Faith walked into the players' lounge fifteen minutes after the game ended with Jules by her side. He wore a Chinooks T-shirt beneath a dark blue suit jacket and a pair of jeans. He would have looked unusually subtle if the T-shirt hadn't been two sizes too small.

'What did you think of the game?' a reporter asked as Faith walked into the room.

'I'm pleased, of course. But I'm not surprised.' She wore her new red leather jacket over her blue-and-red Chinooks T-shirt. 'The team worked really hard to get here.'

'Will you be traveling with the team to Detroit?'

She opened her mouth to answer and got out, 'I don't th—' when Ty walked out of the dressing room. Her brain froze and she lost track of all thought. He wore a pair of loose shorts around his hips and that was it. A few hours ago he'd worn even less. A few hours ago she'd touched all that smooth skin and hard muscles. A few hours ago his pants had been around his ankles and she'd had him in her mouth. She raised her gaze from the defined muscles of his hairy chest to his face. His blue eyes stared into hers and he raised one brow.

'Will you be traveling with the team to Detroit?'

Heat crept up her chest and she tore her gaze from Ty. 'No.'

He'd made her feel so good that she fought the urge

to sprint across the room and attach herself to him. She thought she'd feel regret for sleeping with the captain of her team. It was unacceptable and unprofessional, and she should feel regret. But she didn't. At least not for the reasons she thought she should. What she felt mostly was a big lump of guilt in the pit of her stomach. Her husband had been dead for a month and a half, and last night she'd had wild, amazing sex with a man who'd made her feel things she'd never felt before. She'd been a stripper, a Playmate, and a rich man's wife, but she'd never craved a man's touch like she did Ty's. Or had craved, rather. It was over, but for those few short hours while she'd been with Ty, she hadn't thought of her dead husband. Not really, and not at all while he'd kissed and touched her. The man who'd given her a great life and provided for her in death had been the furthest thing from her mind.

The reporters asked her more questions about the game and the future of the team. More players poured out of the locker room. The excitement in the room was electric; it buzzed the air and elevated voices. Faith answered questions or gave ambiguous responses or deferred to Jules, who knew specifics, and through it all, she was completely aware of Ty.

The sound of his voice cut through the noise and a warm, tingling awareness brushed across her skin and tickled her stomach. Ty had given her that one thing Virgil had always wished he could give but hadn't been able to. A connection that could only happen through physical intimacy. The passion her mother was always talking about. The one thing she hadn't had with her husband. Something so much bigger than her ability to stop it. Something so all consuming it had swept her up and knocked her flat like a hot, black hurricane.

Her gaze moved across the room to Ty and the knot of reporters around him. Through the other voices in the room, she heard him say, 'My quick transition from Vancouver has been very easy. Coach Nystrom knows how to inspire great hockey and the players all bring their best to every game.'

'Are you getting along better with the owner of the team?'

He lifted his gaze to Faith's and one corner of his mouth lifted in an honest-to-God smile. 'She's okay.'

Faith's heart felt like it lifted a little too. Right in her chest. Right there in the locker room in front of players and coaches and journalists.

'Although,' he added as he continued to look across at her, 'I read in the paper this morning that she thinks I'm a control nut, and if I let go, I might not be so rude and surly all the time.'

'I didn't say all the time,' she muttered.

'What?' Jim from the *Seattle Times* asked her. 'What did you say, Mrs. Duffy?'

'That I didn't say he was rude and surly *all* the time.'

One of the journalists laughed. 'Savage is notoriously cranky. I'd like to know when he isn't scowling.'

He watched her, still smiling like he was amused, waiting for her answer. *When he's having sex*, she thought to herself. He hadn't been cranky or rude last night. He'd been wonderful and charming. He'd made her laugh and, incredible as it seemed, relax with him. Something she hadn't done in a while with anyone, and he certainly wasn't being surly tonight. 'When he wins important games,' she answered.

'What is your strategy for Saturday night's game in Detroit?' someone asked Ty.

He gave Faith one last look before he turned his attention to the man in front of him. 'Hockey is a game of one-on-one battles. We just need to keep that in mind and win every battle.'

Faith turned to Jules. 'Are you still going to be able to make the Chinooks Foundation meeting tomorrow?' she asked.

He gazed at her, then looked across the room at Ty. He opened his mouth, then closed it. A wrinkle appeared between his dark brows. 'I hadn't planned on it, but I can if you want me to,' he answered, but she had a feeling something was bothering him.

She shook her head and moved toward the door. 'No. I can take my own notes.' As she stepped out into the hall, she couldn't resist one last look at Ty, standing a head taller than the other men. She remembered every detail of the night before. His face in the dark solarium and the touch of his hands and mouth. She'd like to blame last night on Layla, but she couldn't. Not if she was honest with herself. Last night had been all her. There'd been no teasing. No ulterior motive. No making a man want her when she just wanted his money. She couldn't blame Layla for last night's behavior. Not when Faith had been in complete control.

She turned away and headed toward the elevators. Last night had been all about giving in to what *she* wanted. About sitting in the Brooklyn Seafood Steak and Oyster House and letting Ty touch her under the table. Of putting her hand over his and taking it a step further. She'd done that. Not Layla. Not the wild, shameless person she'd created to hide behind. Last night had been about Faith letting go and being shameless all on her own.

On the drive home, she thought about her life since Virgil's death. One moment she'd been living a nice, comfortable life. A life where her biggest decision on most days was what she was going to wear. That person, that Faith, would not have let go and moved a man's big, warm hand to her crotch.

She pulled her Bentley into the parking garage and rode the elevator to the top floor. Her life had changed so much in such a short period of time. It had gone from a slow, easy pace to a whirlwind of meetings and activity. Her decisions had gone from what to wear to how much to pay a first-round draft pick for the next season. And while she had a lot of help with the latter decision, it was such a huge responsibility that she probably would have buckled under the pressure if she were ever allowed to stop and rest long enough to think about it.

She opened the door to the penthouse, and nothing but Pebbles's yipping and the light in the kitchen greeted her. No 'Sexual Healing' on the stereo or giggling from her mother's room.

Faith moved through the kitchen and down the hall to her own bedroom. She took off her jacket and tossed it on a chair. She couldn't recall the last time Virgil had stayed in the penthouse, but it had been so long ago that there was no trace of him anywhere. No clothes or ties. No shoes or combs. His toothbrush wasn't in the marble tile bathroom.

The only thing that belonged to him was his copy of *David Copperfield*, which Faith had taken from the big house the day she'd left. She sat on the bed and turned on a lamp. Pebbles jumped up beside her as she took the book from the nightstand and ran her hand over the dark brown cover. She lifted it to her nose and smelled the old paper and worn leather. Virgil had always smelled like expensive cologne, but the book held no lingering trace of him.

Pebbles walked in three tight circles next to Faith's hip, then stretched out alongside her thigh. Faith dug her fingers into the dog's thick fur as tears filled her eyes. She missed Virgil. She missed his friendship and his wisdom, but it wasn't her deceased husband she saw when she closed her eyes. It was another man. A man who didn't smile easily, but who did other, wonderful things with his mouth. A beautiful, strong man who had made her feel safe within his arms as he'd held her against the solarium glass and made love to her. A man who looked at her from across the room and made her stomach go light and heavy and tingly all at the same time. A man who made her want to walk over to him and lay her head on his bare chest.

Faith opened her eyes and brushed a tear from her cheek. She'd just buried her husband and she couldn't stop thinking about another man. What did that say about her? That she was a horrible person? As horrible and without morals as Landon had always accused her of being?

A book she'd read about grieving said that a person should wait a full year before dating or getting involved. Although could she really call what had happened with Ty the other night 'dating or getting involved'? No. Not really. It had been about having sex. About scratching an itch. About letting go and finding release.

But if that's all it was about, why the warm little tingles tonight? Why the urge to walk across the room and lay her head on his bare chest? After scratching that particular itch four times in one night, shouldn't she be all scratched out? Shouldn't she be over letting go? If it had been just about sex, shouldn't she be good for a while? Especially considering how long she'd gone without?

She ran her hand down Pebbles's fur and the dog

turned over and exposed her belly. There was something deeper than the sex. Something else going on that scared her. It wasn't love. She did not love Ty Savage. She'd been in love a few times and knew what it felt like. Love felt nice and warm and comfortable – like the love she'd had with Virgil. Or it was hot and consuming – like the love she'd felt for previous boyfriends. It didn't feel wrong. As if one false move and the bottom might fall out of your life.

That wasn't love. That was a disaster waiting to happen.

The next morning, Faith met with the director of the Chinooks Foundation. Her name was Miranda Snow, and she seemed genuinely happy to be meeting with Faith. 'My assistant is out of the office today,' she said as she handed Faith several brochures. 'These are the Chinooks Foundation's different charities.'

Faith looked them over and was impressed. Every year, the Chinooks held a celebrity golf tournament to raise money for players and former players who'd suffered injury and needed extensive rehabilitation beyond their personal medical coverage.

'We're currently paying Mark Bressler's hospital bills that aren't covered by Blue Cross,' she explained. 'And for any additional rehabilitation he might need.'

'How's he doing?' Faith asked about the former captain, whom she'd met a few times at the Chinooks Christmas parties.

'Well, he broke half the bones in his body and he's lucky he isn't paralyzed.' Miranda tossed a pen on her desk. 'His caregivers say he's being a real pain.'

The second charity Miranda told her about was a scholarship program to send eligible children to ice hockey camps. It was based on three criteria. Eligible children had to maintain a 3.0 grade average in school, play above-average hockey, and be of a low income.

The third charity, the Hope and Wishes Foundation, raised money to aid children's hospitals throughout the state of Washington with a three-pronged approach: research, financial aid, and community awareness of childhood diseases. Faith read the assembled press clippings and promotional notes about each charity event and had several questions and a comment. She wanted to know how much money each charity raised. She wanted to know how much money was spent on overhead and administrative costs, and what the foundation had planned for the near future.

'I think the PR on this is overboard,' she commented as she read some of the clippings. 'We should give back to the community because they support us. Not because we get good PR out of it and might sell more hockey tickets.' It was something she'd learned from the Gloria Thornwell Society and something she just happened to agree with. A person or charity should give for the right reasons and not for the glory. There were those who would argue that it didn't matter as long as the result was the same. Faith could understand that argument, but she'd known too many socialites who chaired events or donated money to get their photos on the society pages.

Miranda looked shocked. 'I agree, but I've been the lone voice around here. There's a little girl in that department who is very aggressive about promotion.'

Bo. Faith smiled. 'I'll take care of it.'

The following night, she met Bo and Jules at a sports pub to watch the Chinooks play in Detroit. The first period started off fairly even, with ten shots on goal for the Chinooks, twelve for the Red Wings. With two minutes left on the clock, the Red Wings scored on a 5-on-4 goal.

During the first intermission, Faith told Bo and Jules about her meeting with Miranda and her intention to become more involved with the organization charities.

'You getting more involved will be good PR,' Bo said as she raised a bottle of Beck's to her lips. 'I'll get on it.'

'I don't want to be part of the PR for the charities.' Faith smiled. 'I'm sure we'll need some promotion and advertising for each event, but I think we want really targeted campaigns. I'll get together with you and Jim when we've got something more tangible.'

Bo shrugged. 'The celebrity golf tournament is in July, so let me know how much you're going to be involved in that.'

Jules tore his gaze from the big screen above the bar as the second period began. 'Do you play golf?'

She thought of the putting green in Ty's house.

Of the night she'd worn his shirt. The cotton against her bare skin and scent of his cologne on the collar beneath her chin. Of him standing behind her while she'd swung at the ball. 'No, but I can drive one of those golf cars,' she answered and took a drink of her merlot. On the screen above the bar, she watched Ty skate across ice with the puck in the curve of his stick. He passed off to Sam, then he skated behind the net to the other side and Sam passed the puck back to him as a Detroit defenseman collided with him just inside the blue line. The two fought for possession, shoving and throwing elbows. Ty's head snapped back and the whistle blew. The ref pointed at the defenseman as Ty raised one gloved hand and covered his face.

'He was hit with the butt end of a stick,' Jules said, leaning across the table toward the bar.

Ty lowered his glove and blood ran down his cheek from the outside corner of his left brow.

'Not his face!' Faith yelled before she even realized she'd spoken out loud. 'Don't hurt his face.' She felt as if someone had hit her in the stomach. The Red Wing fans simultaneously cheered and booed as Ty skated from the ice and the Detroit defender skated to the penalty box. One of the Chinooks trainers handed Ty a white towel and he held it to his eye as he turned and watched the replay on the big screens suspended high above mid-ice.

'Shouldn't he go to the hospital?' Faith asked.

Bo and Jules both looked at her like she was nuts. 'It's just a cut,' Jules pointed out.

Ty pulled the bloody towel away as the trainer looked at the corner of his eye and Faith's stomach tilted a little more.

'Gee.' Bo shook her head and took a drink of beer. 'It's bleeding like he hit an aorta.'

'Your aorta is in your heart. Not your head,' Jules pointed out.

'Yeah. I know that, numb nuts.' Bo set her beer back on the table. 'It's called overstating something to make a point.'

'It's called stupid.'

'Stop it! How old are you two, for God's sake?' Faith put her hands flat on the table. 'Ty has just sustained a gash to his head. This could be serious.'

Bo shook her head again. 'It's not that bad.'

'They'll have him fixed up and on the ice by the third frame,' Jules added as Ty and the trainer stepped from the ice and headed into the tunnel.

'I don't think so.' If she'd been hit like that, she'd need a full night's stay in a hospital and lots of pain-killers. Ty wasn't as big a baby as she was, but there was no way he could come back after receiving such a gash.

But Jules was right. When the front-line offense took the ice in the third period, Ty was with them. The corner of his eye was only slightly swollen and was taped with white strips. Blood stained the front of his white jersey, but he skated his shifts.

In the closing minutes of the game, the score was 4–3 in favor of Detroit. Coach Nystrom pulled the goalie and loaded the ice with his first-line players, but despite a hard effort, it was Detroit's night, and they won 5–3, scoring on an empty net in the last ten seconds of the game.

'We'll beat 'em in our building Monday night,' Jules predicted as they all three left the bar.

The drive from the bar to the penthouse took about fifteen minutes. Pebbles wasn't around, which meant her mother was already in bed. Faith brushed her teeth, washed her face, threw on a Looney Tunes T-shirt, and went to bed herself. The wine and excitement of the game had taken its toll and she went out minutes after her head hit the pillow. She wasn't sure how long she'd been asleep when the telephone beside her bed rang and woke her up. She reached for the receiver in the dark and hit herself in the forehead. 'Ouch. Crap. Hello?'

'Did I wake you?'

She blinked. 'Ty?'

'Yeah. Are you alone or is that dog in your bed?'

'What?' She felt around and her fingers touched fur. 'Pebbles is here.'

His soft laughter filled her ear. So rare it poured through her and woke her up inside. 'That must mean my dad's there.'

'He must have snuck in after I went to sleep. Did you want to talk to Pavel?'

'God no.'

She licked her lips. 'Then why are you calling?'

'I'm not quite sure.'

She turned her head and looked at the glowing numbers on her bedside clock. 'Do you know what time it is?'

There was a pause and then, 'Three fifteen.'

'Where are you?'

'I'm in my car. Sitting in front of your building.'

She sat up and pushed the cover aside. 'You're kidding.'

'No. We just landed a half-hour ago. Did you watch the game?'

'Yeah.' She swung her legs over the side of the bed. 'How's your eyebrow?'

'I got five stitches.'

'It looked like it hurt.'

'Like a son of a bitch. You should come down and kiss it better.'

'Right now?'

'Yeah.'

'I'm not dressed.'

'At all?'

Through the darkness, she glanced down at her Looney Tunes T-shirt. 'Completely naked.'

He cleared his throat. 'Throw on a coat. I promise I won't look.'

She smiled and shook her head. 'Looking isn't what gets us into trouble.'

His voice lowered and he said, 'You like trouble. Apparently, so do I.'

She did. She liked it a lot. 'What kind of trouble were you thinking we should get into?'

'The kind that has you naked and in my bed. Since you're already naked, maybe you should just come on down and go the rest of the way.'

She shouldn't. Really shouldn't. 'That would be inappropriate.'

'Very.'

'And you don't regret what happened the other night?'

'Not yet, but I've got a few twisted positions with your name on 'em. I figure that after tonight, we'll be filled with enough shame and regret to last a while.'

'It sounds like you've been thinking about me.'

'A lot.'

She'd thought about him, too. She shouldn't have, but she couldn't help herself. And while he might not regret what had happened, she should. But at that moment, listening to his voice and knowing he was parked outside wanting her, she didn't feel anything but a hot curl of lust tugging at the pit of her stomach. 'Me too,' she answered just above a whisper. 'There's a golf tournament this summer. I think I need to practice.'

'Honey, you can practice with my nine iron all you want.'

'I'll grab my coat.' She hung up the phone, then stepped out of her panties and pulled her T-shirt over her head. Right now, wanting to get into trouble with Ty won out over the guilt she would feel in a few hours.

She hurriedly brushed her teeth and hair and grabbed her slick black raincoat from her closet. She shoved her feet into a pair of red pumps and dropped her keys into her coat pocket on the way out the door.

Ty stood next to his black BMW parked heading the wrong way next to the curb. Darkness surrounded him, and a cool breeze blew off Elliott Bay, tossing several strands of Faith's hair in front of her face.

'Mrs. Duffy.'

'Mr. Savage.'

He opened the passenger door. 'Nice coat.'

She stepped in front of him and looked through the darkness into his face. Stark white bandage strips were taped at the corner of his left eye. The same breeze that tossed her hair about her head brought the scent of his skin to her nose and she breathed him in. She placed her hands on his chest and raised her face to his. Beneath the cotton of his dress shirt, his muscles bunched and turned hard.

Ty lowered his mouth and kissed her. His lips pressed into hers and something hot and intense flooded her senses and her fingers curled into the fabric warmed by his flesh. His tongue touched hers as his hand slid between the lapels of her raincoat. His warm hand cupped her breast and he fanned his thumb over her nipple.

Just when she gave serious thought to grabbing his

wrist and leading him upstairs, he lifted his head and pulled his hand from her coat. 'Get in,' he ordered, his voice a bit gravelly from exhaustion or lust or both.

He opened the door and she sat in the passenger seat and looked up at him. 'What sort of twisted positions do you have planned for me?' she asked.

'Working our way from one end of my mattress to the other.'

She pulled her feet inside and remembered his king-sized bed. 'That could take a while.'

'Exactly.'

15

The brush of something warm across Faith's shoulder brought her out of a sound sleep. Her lids fluttered open and she turned to stare into a pair of brilliant blue eyes a few inches from her face. Smile lines appeared in the corners, wrinkling the white strips covering Ty's stitches as he lightly bit her shoulder.

'Good morning,' he said against her skin.

'What time is it?'

'A little before noon.'

'Oh my God!' She sat up and the white sheet slid to her waist. 'It's late.' A sudden knot of panic kicked up the beat of her heart and tightened her stomach. She hadn't woken up in a man's bed in . . . she didn't know how long. She pulled the sheet up to cover her breasts and glanced back over her shoulder at him. He looked at ease and relaxed in a gray T-shirt and a pair of loose shorts. 'You're dressed.'

'I ran five miles on the treadmill.'

'And you didn't wake me?'

He rolled onto his back on top of the thick black paisley comforter and stacked his hands behind his head. 'You were out.' His gaze ran down her bare back. 'You didn't get to sleep until around five.'

'Neither did you.'

'I don't need a lot of sleep.'

With one hand she held the sheet to her chest and rubbed her face with the other. Her heart pounded in her throat as she looked around the room at the sparse oak furniture and the blinds closed across the huge, arching window. 'Don't you have practice?' She was twenty minutes from home – if the traffic was good – with nothing but a raincoat. What had seemed like such a fine idea last night felt like a horrible mistake in the harsh light of day.

'Not for a while.' He sat up and pushed her hair behind her shoulder. 'I thought I'd drop you off on my way and pick you back up afterward.'

Her heart pounded in her ears. She didn't even have a pair of panties. There was a time in her life when that wouldn't have bothered her, but that was a long time ago. A different time and a whole different life. She'd been a different person, and that wasn't her anymore. Anxiety tightened her forehead and she feared she was going to have a panic attack. She'd worked hard to put that kind of life behind her.

'Faith?'

She looked at him. 'Yes.'

'Did you hear what I said?'

'You have to go to practice.'

He lowered his mouth to her shoulder and softly bit her skin. 'I want to pick you up afterward. Maybe take you to a little Italian restaurant I discovered in Bellevue. Service sucks, but the food is great.'

'No!'

His head snapped up and he looked into her eyes. She had to think. Had to get control of her life and herself. She couldn't *date* her hockey player. Her husband had just died. She couldn't *date* anyone.

After several heartbeats, he said slowly, 'Okay.'

'I meant . . .' What did she mean? She was so confused. She didn't know. 'I didn't mean that the way it came out. I just meant . . .'

'I know what you meant. You just want to have sex and that's it.'

Is that what she meant? No. Yes. She couldn't think beyond the confusion tightening her skull.

He shrugged and took off his shoes and socks. 'I'm cool with that. A lot of women want to fuck hockey players.' He pulled his T-shirt over his head but he didn't look cool. He looked a little angry. The T-shirt flew across the room and he yanked the sheet from her grasp.

'Ty!'

'Now we know where things stand.' He pushed her shoulders until she lay back looking up at him.

'You're mad.'

He shook his head and leaned over to plant his

hands beside her head on the pillow. 'I was just trying to be nice before. Now I don't have to worry about it.'

Faith raised her hand to the hard muscles of his chest. 'I like it when you're nice.'

'Too bad.' He lowered his face to the side of her neck.

Before she'd fallen asleep in his bed, they'd had sex twice. The last time had been in his shower that had body jets and could easily accommodate a party of six. Which meant her hair was probably a horrible mess. A frown wrinkled her brow as he kissed her throat. Her life was in crisis and she was worried about her hair?

'I don't want to play nice anymore.' His warm breath fanned across her neck and down her chest and she felt a slight easing of her tension.

'How do you want to play?' she asked.

'Rough,' he answered, as his mouth moved across her neck, pausing to bite the side of her throat. He slid down her body to her right breast and looked up at her, his gaze a volatile mix of anger and lust as he opened his mouth and sucked her nipple inside. He drew her hard into his hot, wet mouth while he palmed her other breast. Gone was her lover of the night before. The man who used his big hands to tease and stroke a response wherever he touched. Gone was the man who took his time and paid attention to her response as he made love to her body.

He turned his attention to her other breast and stabbed at her stiff nipple with his tongue. His rough hands kneaded her soft flesh and God help her, but it turned her on. She grabbed handfuls of sheet and comforter and arched her back. She moaned deep in her throat and he laughed.

'If I'd known you like it rough,' he said as he kissed and bit his way down her body, 'I wouldn't have wasted my time playing nice.' He kissed her belly before continuing to her hip and stopping at her inner thigh. He looked at her beneath heavy lids, his beautiful eyes a shining turmoil as he sucked the sensitive skin just below the crease of her thigh, teasing her and driving her crazy with need. Just when she was ready to scream with frustration, he ordered, 'Put your feet on my shoulders.' Then he parted her thighs and took her into his hot mouth. He didn't show her any more gentleness now than he had to her breasts a moment ago. He ate her like she was strictly there for his pleasure alone. He ravished her with his mouth and tongue, and God help her if she didn't love that too. She blamed Layla.

Within a few short minutes, a hot, violent orgasm clenched her belly and burned her from the inside out. It shook her and left her gasping for air. Ty stayed with her until the last wave and then he rose to his knees. His heavy gaze stared into hers and he wiped the back of his hand across his mouth. His eyes looked into hers as he unrolled a condom down the length of his erection.

She opened her mouth to speak, but couldn't think of one thing to say besides, 'Thanks. I think.'

'Don't thank me. It's not over yet.'

Then he lowered himself and shoved his hard penis into her body. The force of his thrust pushed her up the mattress, and the oxygen whooshed from his lungs. 'It's not over until I say it's over.'

She looked up into the harsh angles of his face and ran her hands around his shoulders to the sides of his head. Ty might be mad at her, but she couldn't be mad at him. Not after the intense orgasm he'd just given her, and not while the head of his hot penis stroked her inside and started another fire only he could put out. 'Okay,' she whispered and rocked her pelvis, contracting and releasing her muscles around his thick shaft.

His breath hissed from his lips and he swore as he pulled out and drove into her. Over and over he plunged deep inside, stroking her, pushing her toward orgasm, making the air around her thick and hard to breathe. She wrapped her legs around his waist and met him thrust for thrust until a fiery climax rushed through her veins as he pounded into her body. She arched her back and held on as he rode out his own storm.

When it was over, they dressed in silence. He in his T-shirt and shorts. She in her raincoat. Neither spoke on the drive home. Ty stuck Linkin Park into the CD player and flooded the rich interior with heavy metal, relieving them both of awkward conversation. He seemed lost in his own thoughts, and she was still so confused she didn't know what to say anyway. Even though he'd denied it, he was angry. Like she'd hurt his feelings, which, given his hard exterior and surly nature, seemed bizarre.

As he drove into the parking garage and pulled to a stop next to the elevator, he turned off the music. 'I'm sorry if I hurt you.'

'You didn't.' She felt a little tender in certain areas, but she wasn't hurt. Quite the contrary. 'I'm sorry if I hurt your feelings.'

'Faith, I'm not a girl.' His blue eyes looked at her through the deeper shadows of the car. 'I don't get my feelings hurt when a gorgeous woman tells me she just wants to use me for sex.' He laughed without humor. 'Although you're the first. It's never happened before. It's always the other way around.'

'Aren't you just using me for sex too?'

He ran his gaze across her face and pushed the button to unlock her door. 'Yeah. I am. Thanks.'

Monday night, Ty taped his socks just below his knees as Coach Nystrom pointed to the marker board. The rest of the Chinooks sat or stood around, waiting for the game to begin. The sound of ripping tape competed with Coach Nystrom's last-minute instructions.

'Block the shots. Get in front of our goal,' he said as he drew *O*'s on the board.

In the arena beyond the tunnel, the Chinooks announcer warmed up the crowd as Queen blasted from the sound system.

'Keep your heads up and eyes on the puck,' Nystrom said one last time before the team followed the coaches out of the locker room and into the tunnel. They walked across the mats covering the floor. As the announcer read each number, position, and name, the player skated onto the ice. Ty stood at the back of the line and glanced up at the owner's box. Several people sat in the red stadium seats, but Faith wasn't one of them.

Air horns split the air as the announcer called Sam's number and name and Ty stepped closer to the opening. Yesterday he'd told her that he wanted to take her to dinner. No big deal. He'd just spent several hours having sex with her. She'd had her hands and hot mouth all over his body, and he wanted to take her out for some great Italian food. It wasn't exactly unheard of. Any other woman would have expected it and more, but she'd acted like he'd asked her to have his baby. Her reaction had pissed him off, and he'd retaliated by having rough sex with her. Only it had backfired on him, because she'd loved it. He couldn't stop thinking about the bite he'd left on her thigh, and that just made him madder.

The next player was called and Ty stepped forward.

He'd thought he'd regret having sex with Faith. He didn't. He thought it would create complications for him. It hadn't, and wouldn't as long as no one found out. Physically, Faith was the perfect woman. Stunningly gorgeous from the top of her blond head to her little red toenails, she was more than great tits and a nice ass. She had a brain and a sense of humor, but the most attractive thing about her was her determination and the strength of her will. To stand up and appear confident even when she didn't feel it at all. Ty admired guts and grit and balls.

Blake was called onto the ice next, and Ty moved closer. The one thing about her that used to annoy the shit right out of him now attracted him like a bee to a sweet pot of honey. Ironic as hell. Or maybe it was karma. Whatever it was, it needed to stop. Here he was, about to be called out onto the ice to play one of the most important games of his life, and he couldn't stop thinking about Faith. He needed his head in the game. Not turned around because a beautiful blonde just wanted to have sex with him and nothing more. Not even dinner.

Vlad was announced and Ty stepped to the edge of the ice. With another woman, that might be the perfect arrangement, but Faith wasn't any other woman. She owned the Chinooks. Something he kept forgetting with alarming frequency.

'Number Twenty-one,' the announcer said, his booming voice almost drowned out by the screaming crowd, stomping their feet and blowing horns. 'Playing the center position. The captain of the Chinooks, *Ty S-a-a-v-a-a-a-ge!*'

With his head down, Ty took off like he was shot from the tunnel. The glassy surface of the ice sped past as he sprinted around the long line of his teammates and then turned his skates to the side, sending up a fine spray of ice and coming to an abrupt stop at the end of the line. The fans went wild and he glanced up at the owner's box. Faith stood at the rail looking down at the ice. He could not see her face clearly, but he knew she was looking back at him, and anger tightened his chest. An anger that was out of proportion burned a hole in his stomach. Even though he knew his anger was over the top given the true nature of his relationship with Faith, it still lowered his brows and shot sparks from his eyes. Sparks that did not bode well for the Red Wings' defensive line.

16

Early-morning sun shone through the windows like oval spotlights as the BAC-111 punched through the cloud cover and headed east.

Faith opened the latest copy of *Hockey News* and tried to ignore Ty seated directly in front of her. Like the rest of the players, he wore a dark blue suit jacket, and his big shoulder filled the crack in the seats. In his hands he held the *Seattle Times* sports page. No doubt reading about the 4–1 trouncing the Chinooks had given Detroit the night before at the Key, and loving himself. Ty had been unstoppable on the ice last night. The Detroit defense had failed to contain him, and he'd scored early in the first period and followed it with up two assists in the second and third.

After last night, he had nine goals so far in the playoff season, with fourteen assists, for a total of twenty-three points. It was the highest game-point average on his team and third-highest in the NHL.

This morning as she'd boarded the plane, he'd hardly looked at her. In her head she knew that everyone was supposed to believe they didn't like each other. After the last time they'd been together, she wasn't sure it was an act on his part.

The other players had acknowledged her. A quick hello wouldn't have killed Ty. Unless she'd made him so angry he didn't want to be with her anymore.

She took one of the high-protein bran muffins from the tray being passed around and handed one to Jules sitting next to her. 'Where is the real butter?' she asked as she gave him a pad of Promise Buttery Spread. And why did the thought of never being with Ty again make her want to cry even as it made her want to kick the back of his seat? Hard. 'I read that hockey players are supposed to eat an obscene thirty-five hundred calories a day,' she rambled. 'Can you imagine *trying* to eat that many calories? Gee, you'd think they'd have butter around.' She lowered her tray and put her muffin on it. Had she done something? Other than not wanting to have dinner with him in public? 'If I could have that many calories, you'd better believe my muffin would have butter. And chocolate chips in it. Or better yet, I'd have a banana-walnut muffin.' Ty's newspaper rustled and something in her chest pinched. How was she going to face him now if he didn't want to be with her? 'Oh, and I'd wash it all down with a real latte. No more fat-free, sugar-free skinny lattes with no whip, either.'

Jules looked at her. 'Are you okay?'

'Yeah.' She wished she'd stayed home. 'Why?'

'You seem irrationally upset about a muffin.'

Faith tore off a piece and shoved it into her mouth. No, she wasn't irrationally upset about a muffin. She was irrationally upset because the man sitting in front of her, flipping through the paper, hadn't talked to her since he'd dumped her in her parking garage wearing nothing but her raincoat. Yeah, okay. So she'd kind of made it plain that she only wanted sex, but he still should have called. He could have said hello this morning.

'*I was just trying to be nice. Now I don't have to worry about it,*' he'd said, and she guessed he was serious. She was *irrationally* angry because, while she was extremely aware of Ty, aware of the texture of his suit and the back of his dark head, she wasn't sure he even knew she existed.

As she chewed her muffin, she tore the top off a little bottle of organic orange juice. She shouldn't have let Jules talk her into accompanying the team to Detroit. Although in fairness, he hadn't had to do much talking.

The rustle of newspaper in front of her drew her attention to the aisle and Ty's elbow on the armrest. She raised the plastic bottle to her lips and took a drink. The excitement of last night's game had gone straight to her head. The Chinooks' smackdown of Detroit had sent an electric buzz through the arena that had raised the hair on Faith's arms. Instead of watching organized chaos, she saw the skill and training. The perfectly executed plays and precision. The control that looked so out of control. For the first time, she understood Virgil's love of the game.

Last night, as the clock had run out and the arena went wild, Jules had mentioned that she'd only traveled with the team once and that she should consider traveling more.

Now in the light of day, sitting behind Ty while he ignored her completely, it didn't seem like one of her better ideas. More rash than thought out. Kind of like running out of her penthouse at three in the morning wearing nothing but a slick raincoat.

She set the juice back on the tray and the light above her head caught on her wedding ring. The three brilliant diamonds sparkled on her hand. The ring had always made her feel important, classy, rich. Now as she looked at it, she just felt conflicted. Like she was being pulled in several different directions and didn't know which way to go. She wasn't the same person she had been two months ago. Her life was completely different. It was filled with more than dinner plans and taking care of her elderly husband's needs. She was actually beginning to understand how the Chinooks organization worked and even how the game was played. She was looking forward to working with the charitable foundations.

While parts of her life were feeling more stable, other parts were completely out of control, and she had a pink love bite in the crease of her thigh to prove it. If she hadn't just turned thirty, she'd think she was having a midlife crisis. Layla was in control of her sex life. Which was insane. Faith felt as guilty as hell about even having a sex life. But apparently not enough to stop, because she was freaked out at the thought of never being with Ty again.

The movie screens in the jet's ceiling lowered and the latest James Bond movie started. In front of her, Ty folded his newspaper, and Faith took a drink of her organic juice. Having sex with Ty had always been a bad idea. She'd known that from the beginning. If they were discovered, she would suffer huge embarrassment. The team would also suffer, but it had the potential to ruin Ty's career. The fallout would be horrible for him. In her head she knew that it would be best if Ty wanted to end things with her. Best for her and him and the team. Too bad the rest of her body didn't want what was best.

Faith closed the red frog buttons on the black *cheongsam* Virgil had bought for her when they'd visited China the first year of their marriage. A red dragon was embroidered on the back of the dress and she wore a pair of red Valentino peep toes with five-inch heels. She'd secured her hair with red jade sticks and lined her eyes in black. She grabbed a tissue and blotted her deep red lips. A chocolate-chip muffin sat next to the sink and she tore a piece off the top and stuck it into her mouth, careful not to smear her lipstick. When she'd returned to her hotel room after a day spent at a local spa getting a whole body massage, a facial, and a manicure and pedicure, the muffin had been waiting for her. It sat on the coffee table in a pink-and-white-striped box with the name of a local bakery on the top.

She smiled at the thought of Jules phoning around town for a muffin, thinking she'd been freaking out about bran versus chocolate chips when she'd really been freaking out for a totally different reason.

She shoved the tube of Rogue Red lipstick into her little black purse as someone knocked on her door. She glanced at herself in the mirror, then moved through the sitting room.

'You look good,' Jules said as she opened the door and he took in her dress.

Jules wore a pair of black trousers and a red silk shirt. Tame, for him. 'We match.' The two of them walked to the elevators and she asked, 'Who's going to be at dinner?'

'Most of the team.' Jules hit the up button and the two stepped inside. 'The travel office reserved the private wine room inside the Coach Insignia.'

The Coach Insignia restaurant was located on top of the seventy-three-story Detroit Marriott. The restaurant had breath-stealing panoramic views of Detroit and its Canadian neighbors. By the time Faith and Jules arrived, most everyone was seated and munching on appetizers. They all wore designer suits and ties, and if not for the scruffy playoff beards and numerous cuts and black eyes, they would have looked like regular businessmen.

Ty stood at the far end of a long table, one hand on the back of Daniel's chair, the other drawing invisible patterns on the white tablecloth as he talked to the younger man. He wore a blue-and-white-striped dress shirt, open at the throat. His gaze lifted to hers as he spoke and his finger stopped. His blue eyes watched her as she and Jules took their seats in the middle of the long table between Darby and Coach Nystrom and across from Sam and Blake.

'You look beautiful tonight, Mrs. Duffy.' Blake complimented her and she got another good look at his facial hair. He still wore the unfortunate Hitler mustache with the matching stripe on his chin.

'Thank you, Mr. Conte.' She smiled and opened the wine list. Out of the corners of her eyes, she watched Ty straighten and move to the last empty seat a few chairs down from Sam. 'I spent the day getting a whole-body massage. The masseuse had the hands of a god. He used hot oil and warmed stones on me. I thought I had died and gone to heaven. I was so relaxed, I was practically drooling.' Her gaze lifted and she looked at the faces staring back at her. 'Are we going to order a red and a white wine?'

Coach Nystrom adjusted his tie. 'Sure.'

'Most of the players don't drink the night before a game,' Darby told her, which Faith knew for a fact wasn't true.

'Whole-grain muffins. Organic orange juice. You boys don't live dangerously.' She placed her hand on Jules's arm. 'Oh, I forgot to thank you for the muffin.'

'What muffin?'

'The chocolate-chip muffin in my room. That was really sweet. Thanks.'

Jules opened his menu. 'I set you up at the day spa. I don't know anything about a muffin. Maybe the hotel gave it to you. Kind of like getting a cookie at a Doubletree.'

Faith sat back and glanced down the table at Ty. He absently raised a glass of ice water to his lips as he read his menu.

'I didn't get a muffin,' Blake said as the waitress took his order. 'Did you, Sam?'

Sam shook his head and ordered chop-chop salad and pan-seared sea bass. 'No.'

'Did you send me a chocolate-chip muffin?' she asked Darby.

'I didn't know you wanted one.'

'That's weird.' For a split second she thought of Ty but quickly dismissed the idea of the muffin coming from him. He'd been so wrapped up in his newspaper, she doubted he'd even known she was sitting behind him, let alone paying the slightest attention to anything she said. She pushed the mystery from her head and ordered a Caesar salad, chicken, and a 1987 German chablis.

Tomorrow night's game dominated the conversation

around Faith. The coaches and players talked about containing Zetterberg and Datsyuk, the dual threat that had proved lethal to the Penguins in the final playoffs the year before. Faith ate her chicken and drank her wine and answered an occasional question. Several times during dinner, she caught herself watching Ty. The way he talked and joked with the other men around him, and his hands as he cut into his huge steak or reached for his water.

'What are you going to do before the game?' Darby asked her.

She tore her gaze from Ty's fingers, which were brushing beads of condensation on his glass. 'I don't know. I'm sure there's some great shopping around here. Although I'm kind of shopped out.'

'There's a new casino,' Daniel suggested.

'When you are born and raised in Nevada, gambling kind of loses its appeal.'

'I saw some people rollerblading along the Riverwalk,' Coach Nystrom said.

Faith shook her head. 'I don't skate.' Twenty-two stunned faces stared at her as if she'd just said something unimaginable. Like she was putting salary caps at fifty grand. 'Right *now*. I plan to take lessons,' she lied before things got ugly. 'Maybe I'll go swimming tomorrow.'

'When are you going swimming?' Sam wanted to know. 'I always try and hit the pool in the morning. I was on my high-school swim team and took state in the butterfly.'

'Last year you injured your rotator cuff showing off and were out half the season,' Coach Nystrom reminded him. 'Stay out of the pool.'

Sam smiled. 'That's because I was freestyling.'

'That's your problem on the ice, too,' someone down the table commented in a slight Swedish accent. 'Too much freestyling and you end up in the penalty box.'

'At least I have style, Karlsson.'

Faith glanced down the table at Johan Karlsson, who was dressed worse than Jules, in a bumblebee-yellow-and-black-striped shirt. He had a thick blond beard and an unfortunate Will Ferrell 'fro.

'Yeah, an eggbeater style,' Logan Dumont joined in the razzing.

'Shut your donut, rookie. You're barely out of the shinny league.'

Faith had no idea what an eggbeater or a shinny league was, but apparently it wasn't good.

'Not here, guys,' the assistant coach warned.

'Logan's just got his equipment in a tangle because he can only manage to grow a scraggly patch of hair on his chin,' Blake told Sam.

Faith wondered if Logan's 'equipment' was a euphemism for something else. Knowing the guys at the table, she would bet it did. She took one last bite of her chicken and set her fork across the edge of her plate.

'At least my patch doesn't look like Jenna Jameson's crotch,' Logan fired back.

Faith felt her eyes round and she raised her napkin to her mouth to hide her inappropriate smile.

'Jesus, Dumont. Mrs. Duffy is sitting here,' the coach admonished.

'I beg your pardon,' the rookie apologized.

Faith lowered her napkin. 'Apology accepted,' she said, and as she glanced away from Logan, her gaze met Ty's. From the length of half the table he simply looked at her. His blue eyes gave nothing away. Not the anger she'd seen in them the last time they'd been together, nor the lust. Nothing, and she felt a little pinch near her heart.

They weren't a couple. They weren't even dating. Their relationship, if it wasn't over, was purely physical. So why did it bother her that he looked at her as if she meant nothing to him?

Faith reached for her purse next to her plate. 'I'm tired,' she told Jules. 'I'm going to skip dessert.'

Jules looked at her across his shoulder and put his cloth napkin next to his plate. 'I'll walk you to your room.'

'No. You stay.' She stood. 'Good night, gentlemen. I had a lovely time. I'll see you all tomorrow night at the arena.' She left the restaurant and forced herself not to look back. Within a few minutes, she was back in her suite and tossed her bag on the table. She turned on the television and pushed the up button on the remote until she stopped on TCM and *Gentlemen Prefer Blondes*. Virgil had been a big fan of classic movies and starlets like Marilyn Monroe and Sophia Loren. Faith had never really been all that interested in old movies and continued flipping the channels.

There was a knock on the door and she tossed the remote on the couch. She expected to see Jules, but wasn't all that surprised that Ty stood on the other side.

'Who is it?' she called out as she stared at him through the peephole.

He raised a brow and folded his arms across his chest.

She was irritated with him. Maybe irrationally so, but she was still annoyed and didn't feel like letting him in right away.

'I know you're staring at me. You might as well open up,' he said.

'What?' she asked as she opened the door.

Instead of answering, he stepped inside and forced her to move backward.

'I'm tired and not—' His mouth on her stopped her flow of words as he brought his hands to the sides of her face. The door shut behind him with a soft click, and his thumbs brushed her cheeks. His lips slid over hers with the promise of passion rather than a full-out kiss.

'No skating with Sam,' he said against her lips. 'I'll teach you.'

She hadn't been serious about learning to skate. 'I don't want to fall and hurt myself.'

'I won't let that happen. And the next time you need

a whole-body massage,' he said as he kissed the corner of her mouth, 'call me.'

She almost smiled. 'How? When you're so good at pretending I don't even exist.'

He brushed his lips across hers. 'I should get an award for that.'

She put her hands on his chest and pushed. 'You could at least say hello.'

'No, I couldn't.' He dropped his hands and leaned his back against the door. 'I can't risk it.'

Faith moved across the room and turned off the television. 'What does that mean?'

'It means that when I look at you, I'm afraid everyone within ten miles can see that I have sex with you.'

She tossed the remote on the table. 'Oh.'

'And it means,' he continued as he moved toward her, 'that I'm afraid everyone within ten miles can see that I'm remembering the last time I saw you naked. That I got a little rough with you and I wish I was truly sorry about that, but it was so good I'm not. Every time with you is good, and I'm afraid that anyone within ten miles will look at me and know I'm thinking about how to get you naked again.'

She bit the side of her lip. All he had to do was show up and she'd be more than willing to get naked. 'You took a big risk in coming here.'

He reached for her hands and brushed his thumb over the backs of her knuckles. 'Everyone is still in the restaurant. Besides, none of us are on this floor.' He pulled her toward him. 'So you got the muffin.'

'You sent me the muffin?'

'Can't have you wasting away on bran and Promise spread. I need you full of energy.'

She owned a penthouse in downtown Seattle and an elite hockey team. She had more money than she knew what to do with, yet she couldn't help smiling like a fool over a two-dollar muffin. 'Thank you.'

He reached for the frog buttons closing her dress. 'I have an ulterior motive.'

Faith reached up and pulled the jade sticks from her hair. 'Shocking.'

'Monday, I played some of the best hockey of my life. I'm not usually superstitious, but I gotta believe it had something to do with the night before.'

She tossed the sticks on the table and her hair fell down her back.

'You have to have lucky sex with me before each game or I could be jinxed.' He popped the buttons closing the dress over her breasts. 'I know you want to do the right thing.'

'Take one for the team?' She pulled the tails of his shirt from his waistband.

'It's your turn.'

'Yeah, but what if . . .' she raised one hand. 'And I'm not saying this is going to happen, but what if we have sex and you lose? Then you're not lucky.'

He looked up from the frog buttons as if he hadn't

thought of that. 'Honey, having sex with you makes me one lucky son of a bitch.'

'Thank you. I think.'

He shrugged and continued with the buttons. 'If we lose, it just means that someone else on the team fucked up. Not our fault. We did our part.'

She laughed. 'And we have to do "our part" before each game?'

He nodded. 'At least once.' He pushed the dress down her arms and it pooled at her feet.

She pushed at his chest as she took a step back and kicked her dress aside. 'Don't go anywhere.' Wearing nothing but her black lace bra, matching thong, and red Valentino pumps, she left the room, only to return a moment later with an armless vanity chair. She set it in the middle of the room and said, 'Sit down, Mr. Savage.'

'What are you planning?'

'My part to make sure the captain of my hockey team isn't jinxed.' She walked to the sound system and tuned the radio to a hard rock station. A perennial favorite of every strip club across the country poured from the speakers. Faith had danced to 'Pour Some Sugar on Me' more times than she could recall. This time, she didn't have to slip into character. She wanted to please him and herself. She wanted to spin his head around and leaving him gasping for breath. Just as he'd done to her. She turned to look across the room at Ty, still standing by the chair, watching her.

'I told you to sit.' She ran one hand behind her neck

and lifted her hair as she slid her other hand across her stomach. It had been years since she'd danced for a man, but she hadn't forgotten. She moved toward him, *step step pause . . . step step pause*, touching her body as she looked him up and down, and letting her gaze turn all hot and sensual.

His gaze slid down her body, stopping at her hands before continuing to her feet. 'I like the shoes.'

'Thank you.' *Step step pause . . . step step pause*. 'I'm sure you are well aware of the rules.'

'There are no rules,' he said as he sat.

A sexy smile touched her lips. 'No touching,' she informed him as her fingers slid upward and she cupped her breasts. 'I can touch you. You can't touch me.'

His brilliant blue eyes stared up at her. 'Ah. Those rules.'

She grinned as she walked around him, trailing a hand across his shoulders. From behind, she leaned forward and ran her hands down his chest, whispering the words of the song seductively into his ear in time with the music. She continued around him, then straddled his lap, facing him.

He ran his hands up the backs of her legs to her bare behind and pressed his face into her cleavage.

'No touching,' she reminded him and removed his hands from her behind. She sat with the skimpy crotch of her G-string inches away from the zipper of his pants. She ran her hands over his chest, rocking her hips, coming close to touching the bulge in the front of his pants, but always pulling back.

He groaned deep in his chest and sucked in an agonizing breath. 'Touch me, Faith.'

'I am.'

'Lower.'

Instead of doing as he asked, she stood and teased him with her hands and body. She took off his tie and shirt and rubbed against him, turning up the heat and turning them both on, her hard nipples grazing his chest through the thin lace of her bra.

He reached for her and she danced out of his grasp. 'This is killing me,' he said, his voice a lusty gravel. 'Come slide your little hand into my pants, and I'll slide my hand into yours.'

'That's real tempting, but I'm pretty sure that's against the rules.' She turned with her back to him and sat, grinding her bare behind into him. His palms slipped up her back and he unhooked her bra.

'That's definitely against the rules.'

'Fuck the rules.' He kissed her spine and slid his hand up her stomach to cover her naked breasts. 'We don't play by the rules.'

17

'You'd be surprised at the number of men who slipped their number in my G-string.'

Ty wouldn't be surprised at all. Faith lay with her head on his bare chest, brushing her fingers across his stomach. The tips of her short nails spread fire to his belly and groin and if he had the time, he'd make love to her again. If he had time, he'd damn sure have her dance for him again. She'd been beautiful and erotic and he'd loved it. 'Did you call any of them?'

She looked up at him and rolled her eyes. 'Sure. Like I would ever date a man I met in a strip club.'

'I've hung out in a strip club a time or two.'

'I'm not surprised. Strip clubs attract jocks and musicians like ants to a picnic.'

'I haven't been in a few years,' he defended himself, although he wasn't quite sure why he felt the need to. He ran his hand down the smooth skin of her back. 'My father still loves the strippers.'

'Which explains his attraction to my mother.'

'Your mother was a stripper?' Again, no big surprise.

'Yep. She was a stripper and sometimes a cocktail waitress.'

'Sounds like she worked hard.'

'She did. She played hard too. I was alone a lot.'

'Where is your father?' She rubbed her foot on the inside of his calf and came dangerously close to kneeing him in the nuts.

'I haven't seen him since I was little.'

He rolled her onto her back and looked down into her face. 'You've never tried to find him?'

'Why? He didn't want to know me. Why would I want to know him?'

Good point.

She pushed a piece of blond hair from her face. 'What about your mother?'

He fell onto his back and looked up at the ceiling. He didn't like to talk about his mother. 'What about her?'

'Where does she live?'

'She died about five years ago.'

'I'm sorry.'

He looked across the pillow at her. 'Don't be. She wasn't.' He ran his gaze across her beautiful face. Her green eyes and long lashes. Her perfect nose and the bow of her full pink lips. 'My father has always said that she was crazy, but that's because he never tried to understand her.'

She turned on her side. 'Did you?'

He shrugged. 'She was very emotional. Laughing

one minute, crying the next. She never got over the divorce, and I don't think she had a real interest in living after that.'

'When did your parents divorce?'

'I was ten.'

She looked into his face and her smile was sad when she said, 'I think my mother was on her third divorce when I was ten. I used to ride my bike to dance classes at the Y so that I didn't have to think about it.'

He pictured a little girl on a pink Schwinn, her blond ponytail flying behind her. 'I played hockey twelve months out of the year.'

'Well, all that hard work paid off.'

He'd had great coaches to fill the voids in his life. Good men and mentors. He wondered if she'd ever had anyone. He bet not. 'So did your dance classes.'

She laughed. 'Yeah, but not with the moves I learned as a kid. I had to learn all new moves.'

He liked her moves. Especially tonight. While it was true that he'd played great hockey Monday night, he really didn't believe it had anything to do with sex. He'd just used it as an excuse to be with her. He loved the touch of her skin beneath his hands and the look of pleasure in her eyes when he was buried deep inside her. He was quickly becoming addicted to the sound of her pleasure and knowing he was the one giving it to her. Even on days when he told himself he didn't have time for her, he managed to hook up with her anyway.

Ty sat on the edge of the bed and scrubbed his face

with his hands. She was an addiction. Why else would he risk everything to be with her? How else could he explain it to himself?

'Are you leaving so soon?' she asked as she moved behind him and wrapped her arms around his shoulders. Her breasts pressed into his bare back and he fought the urge to turn and push her back down on the mattress.

'I have to go before I'm missed.' He wanted to ask more questions about the little girl on the bike. To spend all night discovering all the moves she'd learned.

She softly kissed the side of his neck. 'I'll miss you.'

'I'll see you tomorrow night after work.' He looked into her eyes a few inches from his and wondered how much she'd miss him. 'I have a game to win. And a few more after that.'

She sat back on her behind and wrapped her arms around her knees. She looked up at him as he stood and got dressed. 'What are you going to do after you win the cup? Are you going to take a long vacation?'

'I never think that far ahead.' He stepped into his boxer briefs and adjusted his package.

'You never think about what you're going to do after you win?'

'Sure. After I win, I'm going to skate around with the cup over my head.' He pulled up his trousers and looked at her, sitting in the middle of the bed, naked and perfect. 'My focus has always been on winning. For as long as I can remember, that's been my goal.' He'd never really thought beyond that. 'I'll work out and keep the body in shape so I won't show up at camp fat and out of shape like some of the guys.' He reached for his dress shirt on the end of the bed and shoved his arms inside. But as he worked the buttons, he thought about Faith in a bikini, lounging on a sandy beach beside him. The sun warming her smooth skin. Maybe she'd have on a floppy hat and big sunglasses.

A frown settled between his brows. She didn't even want to have dinner with him at a secluded restaurant in Bellevue. She'd made it real clear what she did want, and she was right. There could never be more between them than clandestine sex. And really good lap dances. Especially now with those billboards plastered all over Seattle. He'd never been featured in a tabloid, but he imagined that a photo of him lounging on the beaches of Mazatlan with the owner of the Chinooks might make it into the pages. So why was he even thinking about it?

Faith watched Ty's big hands close his shirt over his hard abs and defined pecs and wondered what had put the frown on his face. 'I understand about single-minded goals,' she said as she rose from the bed and grabbed a hotel robe from the closet. 'My whole goal in life was to have so much money that I didn't ever have to worry about how I was going to pay the bills.'

'I'd say you pretty much exceeded your goal.' He closed the last button, then tucked the tails into his trousers.

'Yeah. I did, and once I reached it, I was kind of aimless. I didn't realize how aimless until now.' She slid her arms into the rich terry-cloth robe and tied the belt around her waist. 'Now I have a new goal. A better goal, and one that I never even dreamed I'd ever have in a million years. It's really scary, but I'm enjoying it. Which is kind of scary too.'

He glanced up, then returned his attention to his black leather belt. 'What's that?'

'The Chinooks. I certainly never thought I'd own a hockey team. And if I'd ever even given it a thought, I wouldn't have ever thought I'd actually come to like it.' She folded her arms beneath her breasts. 'It's a huge responsibility, and for the past few years I've been all about letting someone else take care of everything. Now, I'm learning to like the responsibility. I like owning the Chinooks so much, that I'm actually looking forward to the drafts.'

He looked up at her. 'Who are you looking at?'

'A few top prospects. When I get back, Darby and I are viewing some tapes of two-way defenders.'

He chuckled as he gazed across the room. 'Do you know what a two-way defender is?'

'Someone who can defend and score.' She shrugged. 'At least that's what I *think* it means.'

'You're right. That's pretty much what it means.' He moved toward her. 'Keep your eyes open for a big, hard-nosed checker. Don't worry so much about the kid's speed. Skating can be improved.' He wrapped his hand around the robe's belt and pulled her against him. 'If I don't talk to you again until we get back to Seattle, don't get bent out of shape again.' He pressed his lips to her forehead.

'You'll be thinking about me?'

He shook his head and his lips brushed across her skin. 'I'm going to try like hell not to think about you.'

The different tones and pitches of more than thirty snoring men filled the cabin of the BAC-111 as it circled Boeing Field and prepared to land. Hours earlier, the Chinooks had suffered a crushing 3–4 loss to Detroit. Game Five of the series was two days away and Faith figured Ty would need the full two days to recover from a brutal hit he'd taken at center ice from Detroit enforcer Darren McCarty.

A few plays later, Ty had put a hit on McCarty in the corner that had crumpled the Red Wing to the ice. 'McCarty caught me with my head down,' Ty had told the press later that night. 'Then I caught him with the puck.'

Later that night, Faith saw firsthand the extent of Ty's bruises. He was black and blue on his right side and red across his back and hard stomach. It looked like he'd been hit by a baseball bat instead of a hockey enforcer. Ty was sore and battered and when they made love over the next few days, Faith was thoughtful enough to climb on top.

By Game Five Ty had healed somewhat, and the

Chinooks managed a 3–1 win in their own house. Game Six was back in Detroit at the Joe Louis Arena and went into double overtime. With three seconds left on the clock, Daniel scored and the Chinooks advanced to the final round to face off against the Pittsburgh Penguins in their battle for the cup.

High from the win and advancement into the final round of the playoffs, the team boarded the BAC-111 and celebrated by popping Bollinger champagne. Once the jet reached cruising speed, Coach Nystrom stood, slightly bowed forward to accommodate his height. 'Two months ago when Virgil Duffy died,' he began when everyone had quieted, 'we all worried how the new ownership of the team would affect our run at the cup. Any time there is a change, there is cause for concern. After tonight, I think we can safely say that Mrs. Duffy has successfully filled Virgil's shoes. I think he would be proud of her, and we want to officially welcome her to the team.' He turned to his left and Darby handed him a dark blue jersey. He turned it to show her name, DUFFY, written across the shoulders and the number one on the back in dark green. 'We officially want to welcome the newest Chinook.'

Faith stood and stepped into the aisle. She took the jersey and the backs of her eyes stung. 'Thank you, Coach.' She turned and looked at the scruffy faces looking back at her, at their beards that now ranged from Geico cavemen to patchy fuzz. She met Ty's gaze and both corners of his mouth slid up in a rare smile.

Her heart pinched and her eyes stung and she didn't want to cry like a girl. 'When I discovered that Virgil had left me his hockey team, I was as stunned as all of you. I was just as worried as everyone else that the responsibility would be too much for me and I'd mess things up.' She swallowed and folded the jersey across her arm. 'With the help of my assistant, and everyone else, I'm proud to say I've done all right. I'm proud of all you guys, and I know that Virgil is proud of us too.' She thought she should give some sort of inspiring speech, but her vision blurred. 'Thank you,' she said before she embarrassed herself by crying in front of her guys. She sat next to Jules for the remainder of the flight home and wished she could curl up in Ty's lap and bury her face in his neck.

At three in the morning, when a black Beemer pulled up to the curb in front of her penthouse, she wore the new jersey beneath her raincoat. This time, however, she packed her Louis Vuitton hatbox with extra lingerie and a change of clothes.

Over the next five days, until the first game against the Penguins, their lives fell into a comfortable pattern, as if they were a real couple. Ty practiced during the day while Faith viewed rookie tapes or met with Miranda Snow of the Chinooks Foundation. She had lunch with Jules or her mother, and at night she either drove to Ty's or he came to her home, depending on Valerie and Pavel's plans. The only creature on the planet aware of Ty and Faith's covert relationship was Pebbles. The second the dog set her beady eyes on Ty, she instantly fell in love, much to the 240-pound hockey player's discomfort. The second he would walk in the door, Pebbles circled his legs so he could hardly walk and jumped in his lap when he sat. Ty would give Faith a look, expecting her to do something, but when she tried, the dog snapped at her. Pebbles was a total slut for Ty, but Faith supposed she couldn't blame the evil little mutt.

The one and only time she and Ty argued, it was about Virgil. It happened at his house during a golf lesson when he was teaching her to 'waggle.' She wore a red corset and little panties that tied at the sides, and instead of getting turned on like she'd planned, he'd just gotten irritated.

'When are you going to stop wearing that ring?' he asked as she lined up a shot.

'Does it bother you?'

He shrugged and placed his beer on the bar. He wore a pair of worn Levi's and a ripped-up tank top. His hair was disheveled from her fingers and he looked good enough to lick up one side and down the other. 'It's a constant reminder that you're Virgil's wife.'

She set the club in a rack and turned to face him. 'Obviously, that bothers you.'

'I think it would bother most men. I'm having sex with you, and you're wearing another man's ring.'

She looked into his blue eyes, brittle with anger, and she didn't understand it. 'Virgil's only been dead two months.'

'Exactly. You can come here and have sex but you can't take off that damn ring?'

'I already feel guilty about the sex, Ty.' Suddenly she felt naked and exposed and she moved past him toward her dress, lying on his couch. 'He was my husband for five years.'

'He was your roommate.'

'He took care of me.'

'He bought you because he could.'

'Well, I sold myself to him.' She grabbed the dress and turned to face him. 'Which makes me no better than him.'

'You weren't the one in the relationship with all the power. He was.'

Which was true. She and Virgil had been friends and gotten along very well, but he'd always been in charge. 'He was good to me. Better than any man I've ever known.'

'Then the men in your life must have sucked.' He folded his arms across his chest.

That was true too.

'He's gone, Faith.'

'I know.' She pulled her dress over her head and shoved her arms in the short sleeves.

'You don't owe him anything.'

'That's easy for you to say.' Her hands rose to the buttons on the front. 'He left me enough money to take care of me for the rest of my life. He left me his hockey team, for God's sake. And every time I'm with you, I feel like I'm betraying my husband.' Her fingers fumbled with the button. 'I feel guilty as hell, but I feel the most guilty those times when I'm not feeling guilty at all.' She looked up at him. 'Maybe Landon was right about me. I am a shameless gold digger. But I don't even mind being called a gold digger. It's the truth, but I thought I'd outgrown being shameless.'

'If you were shameless you wouldn't be standing here freaking out.' He shook his head. 'You're thirty years old. You're young and beautiful, and you've been living on a shelf. Jesus, you've been celibate for five years. You shouldn't feel guilty about wanting to live again.'

'I was living. It's just not a life you approve of.' She looked into his still angry eyes. 'Most of my life I've avoided feeling bad about the things I do. Most of my life I was shameless. I always did whatever it took to survive, and most of the time, I didn't feel bad. But being with you isn't about survival. It's about feeling good. It's about risking my reputation, what little I have, and your career, and being so selfish I do it anyway.'

He took a few steps toward her and grabbed her wrists. 'Don't go.'

'Tell me why I should stay.'

'Because despite the possible damage to my career and your reputation, I'm selfish as hell and want you here. It would be easier if I didn't, but I stopped fighting it weeks ago.'

She dropped her hands to her sides and looked up into his face. The stitches had been taken from his brow, and he was left with an angry red line at the corner of his right eye. For how long would he want her? How long could it all last? she wanted to ask him. Instead she wrapped her arms around his waist and laid her head on his solid chest. His heart beat strong and steady against her cheek as his hand moved up and down her back. And it felt so good standing there, her body pressed to his, feeling his warm, soothing touch. She could almost make herself believe that it wouldn't end in disaster.

Tomorrow night was the first game against the Penguins. She would think about that and not the ache in her chest and the clog in her throat. She would worry about their defensemen and not about the fear twisting her stomach. The truly horrifying feeling in the bottom of her soul that the unacceptable had happened. Despite all good reason and sense, despite everything they had against them, she'd fallen completely in love with Ty Savage.

For the first time in five years, her wedding ring felt like a heavy weight on her finger. Suddenly it didn't feel right that she should wear one man's ring when she was in love with another.

When she returned home early the next morning, she took it off and placed it in her safe next to the other jewelry Virgil had bought for her. The beautiful stones in the safe glittered in the light, but failed to give her the warmth and comfort they'd always provided. Her hand looked naked without the heavy diamonds, but it felt lighter, freer, and right. As if it was truly time to let go of the past and Virgil.

The rest of the day, she tried not to think about her situation with Ty. She was just going to live in the moment. It would last as long as it lasted. Yet, in a small corner of her heart, she hoped that everything would work out somehow. That they would find some way to be together, but in her head she knew that wasn't realistic. This relationship was doomed to end in heartache, but perhaps if she was careful, maybe she wouldn't lose her whole heart to him. If she was careful, maybe she could guard one last piece.

But later that afternoon, a package arrived at the penthouse that stole any remaining piece of her heart that didn't already firmly belong to Ty.

The box was wrapped in white paper with a big pink-and-white-striped bow. Inside the polka-dot tissue paper lay a pair of pink patent-leather ice skates with gold blades. Size seven. The same size as her red Valentino pumps.

The card simply read *I'll catch you when you fall.* It wasn't signed but she knew who'd sent the skates. She sat on the couch with the box in her lap. Her eyes filled with tears and the back of her throat felt hot and scratchy. She tried unsuccessfully to blink back the moisture in her eyes, but she was no more successful at that than she was holding back the swell of her heart.

She was in love with Ty. It was impossible. Inappropriate, and she didn't feel good about it. Not the kind of good that falling should feel like.

'What's that?' her mother asked as she walked into the living room.

Faith ducked her head. 'Nothing.'

'It's obviously not nothing.'

She brushed her wet cheek against the shoulder of her BCBG T-shirt. 'Someone sent me skates.'

'Who?'

'I don't know.'

'Really? How long do you think you can keep this up?'

'What?'

'Your secret relationship with Tyson.'

Faith looked up and stared at her mother, a vision of blurry zebra-print pants and black tube top.

'I'm not stupid, Faith. Neither is Pavel. We know you two sneak around and meet each other in private. We've been trying to stay out of your way.' She handed Faith a tissue from the box on the end table. 'Dry your eyes. Your mascara will smear.'

Faith took the tissue and dabbed at the corners of her eyes.

'I've been waiting for you to come to me and talk to me about it.' Valerie sat on the couch and Pebbles jumped up beside her. 'I could help. Maybe give you motherly advice.'

'No offense, Mom, but you've been married seven

times. What advice could you give about relationships?'

Pebbles curled up by Valerie's side as if to say that she was the favored daughter. 'Well, I could tell you what mistakes *not* to make. Like never get involved with a married man. They rarely leave their wives. Despite what they say.'

'That really doesn't apply here, Mother.'

'That's true.' Her hand dropped to Pebbles's fur and she stroked the dog. 'Or sailors. Those men dock at different ports around the world and they all seem to just *love* the hookers. Nasty bastards.'

'Again, Mom. Doesn't apply.'

Valerie sighed as if she were the one suffering. 'I guess my point is that your relationship with Ty is difficult but not impossible.'

'It feels impossible.'

'Do you love him?'

What she felt was so new, so raw, she didn't want to talk about it. 'I don't want to love him.'

'Well, I don't want age spots, but it's something I can't help.'

'Are you equating Ty and age spots?'

Valerie shrugged a bare shoulder. 'Your body is going to react a certain way and there is nothing you can do about it. You can't control who you're attracted to. And you can't control who your heart wants.'

A few weeks ago she would have told her mom that was a load of crap. And she would have believed it too. 'But I don't want my heart to want him. I don't want to fall for any man right now. It's too soon.' And she especially didn't want a relationship that was so complicated.

'I know you loved Virgil. He was your husband but he was never *your man*.'

She looked into her mother's green eyes surrounded by heavy mascara. 'What does that mean?'

'It means that he wasn't the man who drew your attention across the room or made your stomach go squishy at the sight of him. Virgil may have been nice to you, but he didn't make you want to lie beside his body, next to his heart, for an entire afternoon.'

Curling up alongside Ty was one of her favorite things to do. 'Is that how you feel about Pavel?'

Valerie shook her head. 'Pavel is not the kind of man a woman should ever fall in love with. He's a heart-breaker, and I am old enough, with enough experience under my belt, to see him for what he is. But he's great company and we're having a lot of fun. He's only here to see his son win the cup.' She ran her fingers through Pebbles's fur. 'Ty is not like his father. He is not all fun and games and having fun. Pavel thinks he has feelings for you.'

Faith didn't know how Ty felt. He'd never said. She knew he liked having sex with her. That much was obvious. And she knew he gave her gifts with some thought behind them. That had to count for something. But she also knew that if it came down to a choice, he'd pick his career over her. She understood that. Hockey was a part of him. It flowed through him like his own blood, giving him substance and strength and purpose. His drive and dedication were the things she loved about him.

They were also the things that would break them apart.

Game One of the Stanley Cup Finals between the Pittsburgh Penguins and the Seattle Chinooks was played on Seattle's ice. The Key Arena was filled to capacity and the cool air buzzed with the excitement of more than fifteen thousand cheering fans.

Early in the first period, the Penguins dominated the puck, but the Chinooks came back strong in the second and third frames. Faith watched from the skybox, her heart pounding in her throat as the Chinooks beat Pittsburgh 3–1.

Game Two was played in the Mellon Arena on Pittsburgh ice. Despite the Penguins' hometown advantage, Game Two was a repeat of Game One. Chinooks goalie Marty Darche stopped twenty-five of twenty-six shots on goal, while Ty scored in the remaining minutes with a one-timer shot across ice from the stick of Logan Dumont. The Chinooks once again won 3–1. The flight home from Pittsburgh was jubilant while remaining cautious.

Later as Faith lay curled up beside Ty's warm body, next to his heart, she was actually starting to feel a bit optimistic about the future. Somehow, maybe everything would work out. She wasn't exactly sure how, but once the playoffs were over, maybe they could go away together and find a solution.

She was still thinking about possible solutions the next afternoon when she returned from a meeting with Jules and the Chinooks Foundation. Perhaps their relationship could remain a secret for a few more years.

When she walked into her building, a card waited for her at the front desk. It wasn't signed but said, 'Meet me in Virgil's office inside the Key Arena at 6:00 p.m.' It was an odd request. Ty would be at the Key getting suited up to play Game Three. She knew he was as cautious as she was about being seen together, and she wondered what would prompt him to want to meet her.

At five thirty, she dressed in her team jersey and figured it had to be something really important, but when she walked into the office that night, it wasn't Ty sitting in her chair with his feet up on her desk.

'Come in and shut the door,' Landon said, a particularly smug smile flattening his colorless lips.

Faith didn't move. She looked into the cold eyes of the one person on the planet who truly frightened her. 'We don't have anything to talk about.'

Landon took his feet from the desk and pushed a file toward her. 'You're wrong about that, Layla. We're going to talk about your boyfriend and how fast you're going to sell me my father's team.'

Faith's heart slammed against her ribs as she moved to the desk and flipped open the file. Inside were photos of her and Ty. There were four of them, but the most incriminating picture had been snapped the night she'd come down from the penthouse wearing nothing but her raincoat. It had been dark outside, but the photograph clearly showed Ty kissing her while his hand was inside her coat cupping her breast. Her stomach fell and she thought she might vomit all over her desk and the front of Landon's gray suit.

'I'm thinking I don't want to pay one hundred and seventy million for the team.'

'And what happens if I don't sell?' she asked, although she figured she knew the answer.

'After I send the photos to the newspapers, I'll blow them up and hang them around town with the other billboards of you and the captain.'

She'd figured wrong. She'd thought he'd stop with the threat of sending the pictures to the *Seattle Times*. The thought of her and Ty like that on a billboard added panic to the fear in her tumbling stomach. 'What makes you think I care if people see me like that? I've suffered worse humiliation in my life.'

'I don't think you care. You're a stripper and have no morals. You're shameless, but I don't think you want to humiliate the captain and the rest of the team. Especially when it looks like they might actually win that cup.'

She believed him. She believed he'd do what he said. 'Your father always said that you were a little pissant.'

Landon's eyes narrowed. 'My father was a fool with a taste for trash.' He stood. 'My lawyers will send the papers to you tomorrow. Sign them and send them back as soon as possible or the price will go down even more. I thought about having you gift the team to me, but God forbid anyone assume we were involved somehow.'

She didn't care about the money. 'What are you going to do with the team?' She couldn't believe this was happening. Not now. Her throat closed and she licked her dry lips. 'Are you going to move it?'

He shook his head. 'That won't be necessary now that the team has had such a successful playoffs season. I'll keep it in Seattle.' He smiled again. 'I can't say the same for your boyfriend. He'll be traded as soon as I can work out the details.'

The hits just kept coming. This one right to her heart. 'Why? He's doing exactly what Virgil hired him to do.'

He tilted his head back and looked down at her through his frosty gaze. 'I hardly think my father hired Mr. Savage to fuck his wife.'

'You would trade a captain who's led this team to the final round of the championship just because you hate me?'

'Unfortunately, Mr. Savage has become involved with you, and I don't want him or you anywhere near my team.'

Faith looked at the man in front of her, at the only man on the planet she'd ever feared and she lied to save the only man she'd ever really loved. She shrugged. 'Trade him to Toronto, for all I care,' she said, mentioning one of the lowest scoring team of the season. 'I doubt they'll want him, though. He's persona non grata in Canada these days. Although that's exactly what the jerk deserves. To be forced to play on a losing team that hates him.'

'Don't tell me he got tired of you already?'

'He's decided he wants someone more respectable,' she said, giving Landon the one lie he would believe. 'Most men want to have an affair with a stripper. Few want a relationship outside of the bedroom.' She shrugged and pointed to the photos. 'Those pictures are old news, Landon. The captain and I are no longer . . . an item.'

Now it was Landon's turn to shrug. 'Which means the captain is smarter than I gave him credit for. Maybe I'll keep Mr. Savage. Depends on if he hands me the cup.'

He believed her for now. Perhaps a little too easily, but she guessed she shouldn't be surprised, considering what he thought of her.

'That doesn't change your predicament,' Landon said. 'Sign the contracts tomorrow or the photos hit the newspapers the next day.'

The thought of Landon's hands on the cup made her sicker than she already felt. She had to say something. Do some*thing* or Landon would win. 'You expect me to give up a hundred-and-seventy-million-dollar team?

Just like that?' was the best she could come up with. 'What? Over some photos that might humiliate Ty Savage and the rest of the team?'

'Yes,' he said, calling her bluff. He moved past her but stopped in the door. 'Enjoy your last night in the skybox, Layla. After tomorrow it's mine.'

Technically it wouldn't be his until the sale was final in a few months, but she was in no position to argue.

'When will you make the announcement?' she asked.

'The night I'm handed the cup.'

18

Faith sat in the owner's box as the Chinooks were announced. One by one they skated onto the ice amidst the roaring cheers of the hometown crowd. Her face felt hot and her stomach burned from pent-up emotion. Sam and Marty and Blake. Her team. Her players. The guys she'd come to know over the past two months. Tension pounded the base of her skull and everything seemed unreal as she went through the motions.

There had to be a way. There had to be something she could do to keep from losing everything. But there was nothing. Nothing at all. She had no choice.

Her first instinct when Landon had left her office was to run. Run home, pull the covers over her head, and pretend everything would be all right. But she couldn't do that. Everyone expected her to sit in the box tonight as if her world hadn't just come apart.

'Do you want a glass of wine?' Jules asked her.

She looked at him. At her assistant in his peach-and-green silk shirt, obviously still suffering from a metrosexual crisis. What would happen to Jules?

'Faith?'

'Yes.'

'Do you want wine?'

She shook her head. 'No,' she answered and her voice sounded hollow.

'Number Twenty-one.' The announcer's voice filled the Key and bounced off Faith's brain. 'The captain of the Chinooks, *Ty S-a-a-a-v-v-a-a-a-ge!*'

The crowd went wild as he hit the ice, their screams drowning out the painful sob that racked her chest. He skated around the rink with one hand in the air, and when he passed below, he looked up and smiled. Faith's heart shattered right there. Right there in the skybox. A keening little sound threatened to escape her lips and she rose to her feet. She covered her mouth to keep it inside and ran into the bathroom, practically shoving her mother and Pavel out of her way. She shut the door behind her and wrapped her arms around her stomach as the first sob broke her throat.

'What's wrong, Faith?' her mother called through the door.

'Nothing,' she managed. 'I feel sick.' Another sob racked her chest and she knew she couldn't stay there. She had to get home. 'Could you bring me my purse?' She turned to the vanity and looked at herself in the mirror. At her red cheeks and watery eyes. She ran a paper towel under cold water and held it to her hot face. Her mother entered the room and handed her bag to her.

'You don't look good,' Valerie said. 'Are you getting the flu again?'

'Yes. I have to go home.'

'I'll get Jules to take you.'

The last thing she wanted was to break down in front of her assistant. 'No. I can make it,' she said as she opened the bathroom door.

'Call me when you get home,' her mother called after Faith as she hurried from the owner's box.

She stumbled into the empty elevator and her vision blurred as she rode it down. She held it together as best she could on the short drive home, but once inside the penthouse, she broke down. Tears poured down her cheeks as she pulled her jersey over her head and she wiggled out of her jeans. Both dropped into a pile on the floor and she crawled into her bed. Jules called to make sure she got home all right and she managed to convince him that she 'sounded strange' because she was sick. Then she hung up and pulled the covers over her. She'd lost it all, and she'd never felt so desolate in her life. Landon had ripped everything from her, and she was empty. Except for the burning sorrow in her soul. Just when she was starting to really enjoy her role as owner, just when she was really excited about being involved in the Chinooks Foundation, Landon had taken it all from her. Worst of all, she'd made sure he'd taken Ty, too.

She felt like a kid again. Alone and helpless. She'd worked so hard never to feel those two things again, and here it was back.

A sob racked her chest and Layla crept into her head. She wondered how much it would cost to have someone kill Landon. He deserved to die. The world would be a better place without people like him. Of course Faith would never do it. Not only because she wasn't that sort of person, but she also had a healthy fear of prison.

Two months. It had only been two months since Virgil died, but her life had changed so drastically, it felt longer. She felt like a different person. Stronger. Confident. More sure of herself.

Two months to have gained so much, only to lose it all. Such a short time to fall completely and totally in love, only to lose him, too. And it was ironic as hell, really. For the last five years she'd let a man take care of her. Now she was giving up her team to take care of someone else.

There was just no choice. No way to save herself and Ty and keep the team. She had to give Landon what he wanted. She wiped a hand across her cheek and wondered what Ty would say if she told him about the photos and Landon's plan to ruin them. She could predict what he'd say and what he'd ultimately do. He'd want to kill Landon, just like her. And just like her, he'd do what was best for the rest of the team. In the end, she'd still have to sell the Chinooks. She'd still lose the man she loved.

She'd always known she couldn't have both. That it would end someday. That it would hit her hard and shake up her life. But it didn't have to be that way for Ty. It didn't have to affect him. And it wouldn't if she didn't tell him about the photos.

He had a good shot at his dream. At the one thing he'd worked for and waited his whole life to achieve. The last thing he needed to worry about was his picture in the *Seattle Times* and appearing on billboards. Especially now, when it was a foregone conclusion anyway. Unless she wanted to humiliate Ty and embarrass the team, she would sign those intent-to-sell papers when they arrived tomorrow and he would never know why she had agreed to sell the team.

The letter of intent was just the first step in the process, and if she remembered from the last time she'd signed the letter of intent, it would take several weeks to get approval from the NHL commissioner. After that, the sale would go forward, and once all the *i*'s were dotted and the *t*'s crossed, Landon would own her hockey team.

She threw back the covers and walked to the huge windows in her bedroom. She wore her bra and panties and stood staring at the lights of the Key Arena. Ty was in there. Shooting pucks, throwing elbows and spitting on the floor, and she longed to be there too. All her guys were there, only they weren't her guys anymore. She didn't think it was possible to have her heart break in so many ways.

Tears rolled down her cheeks and she wiped at them with the backs of her hands. She and Ty had thought they were being so careful, and they had been. Either she went to his house or he holed up in her penthouse. On the road, they never even spoke to each other. Valerie and Pavel had figured it out because they lived with them.

She thought about some unknown person following and photographing her without her knowledge. It was creepy and she felt violated. What kind of person hired someone to photograph people at three in the morning?

Someone determined to win. And he had. Landon had won and she'd lost at a game she hadn't even known she'd been playing. Only this was no game. This was her life. What Landon had done to her burned like acid in her stomach.

She pressed her forehead into the glass. Was it just this morning that she'd been happy? That she'd been with Ty, massaging his sore muscles for him? She'd always known it would end in disaster. Just not like this. Never like this. There was no way out for her, and she could see no other alternative but to give Landon what he wanted.

She loved Ty to the depths of her soul, but she didn't know how he felt about her. Other than that he liked to have sex with her, but as she'd learned long ago in life, sex wasn't love. When he found out she'd sold the team, he might be mad, but he'd get over it. When he found out she wasn't going to see him anymore, he might be a little mad about that too. But again, she was sure he'd get over it.

She turned away from the window and crawled back in bed. She stared at the ceiling and wondered how she was possibly going to get through the next week until the final playoffs game. When they heard of the sale, would they miss her?

And what about the week after that? Or next month or the month after that? Her and Valerie and Pebbles. Maybe she'd travel. Or move. Move far away from Seattle and the Chinooks and Ty. Far away from the pain of seeing them.

And Jules. What was she going to do about Jules? He'd quit his job at Boeing to come to work for her. There wasn't a whisper of a chance that Landon would keep her assistant. She could keep him on, but in what capacity? Shoe coordinator? Jules would hate that.

At ten minutes after eleven, the phone on her nightstand rang. It was Ty. After every game, she went to his house or he came to hers. Tonight she didn't answer. She turned the television to a loop news channel and saw that the Chinooks had lost Game Three in overtime and the series was now on to Pittsburgh.

At five the next morning, Ty called again. Faith figured he was just about to board the team jet. She would have to face him, of course. She would have to face him and tell him they couldn't see each other, but she needed time. Time to first face the truth and compose a good, believable lie.

Later that day, she'd convinced her mother that she had a horrible strep throat and a fever of a hundred and two. Since she looked like crap, it really hadn't been a hard sell. She laid in bed all day, and that night, she watched the Chinooks win Game Four alone in her room.

Ty called that night and early the next morning. He left messages, but she didn't return his calls. Jules visited her, and she figured she deserved an Academy Award for her performance of a sick patient. Or at the very least, a daytime Emmy. She had to tell him that Landon's family would be using the box that night at the Key, and that he and her mother would have to sit in the nosebleed section. She made up a lame lie about a promise she'd made to Virgil, but he didn't believe her. He kept asking her over and over if something had happened that he should know about. And over and over she lied.

That night at the Key, as Landon and his family watched from the owner's box, Faith watched from her living room a few blocks away. The Chinooks lost Game Five in overtime. It broke her already broken heart, but not as much as hearing her telephone ring and knowing it was Ty. She didn't think her heart could hurt anymore, but the next two days proved her wrong. Ty stopped calling, which was even more devastating than listening to his angry messages, and the Chinooks lost Game Six once again in overtime. Her team seemed to be imploding and there was nothing she could do about it.

The seventh and final game would be played in

the Key to a capacity crowd that would not include Faith.

The morning after the Chinooks' loss in Pittsburgh, Faith took a shower and brushed her teeth before noon. Her mother was with Pavel, probably at Ty's, and she was alone. She checked her phone, but Ty hadn't called. Not that she would answer. Maybe he'd moved on. Maybe he was over her. Which was good. It was what she wanted, but just not quite so fast.

At ten that morning, someone rang her intercom from the lobby of her building. 'If you don't buzz me up,' Ty said through the speaker, sounding not only tired, but pissed off, 'I'm going to call in a bomb threat and the whole building will have to be evacuated.' Her heart pounded in her chest at the sound of his voice.

'You're bluffing.'

'Grab your umbrella. It's raining outside.'

She would have to talk to him sooner or later. She'd just hoped it would be later. 'Fine.' He appeared at her door less than a minute later. He looked exhausted and angry and delectable and her heart skidded to a stop in her chest.

'You don't look like you're dying.' His brows lowered and he frowned. 'So why have you been avoiding me?'

'Come in.' She turned and he followed her into the living room. Pebbles jumped and yipped in an effort to get Ty's attention and Faith had to drag her out on the terrace and shut the glass door. She gave a thought to the dog jumping off, but her luck wasn't running in that direction these days.

Before she lost her nerve, she turned and said, 'We can't see each other anymore.'

He put his hands on his hips and gazed across the room at her. 'Why?'

Her palms were clammy and her chest ached. She folded her arms across her heart instead of running across the room and throwing herself on him. She'd thought up a perfectly good lie last night. Something about Virgil. 'I'm a widow.' That wasn't it. There'd been more.

'You were a widow the past few weeks, and that didn't stop you.' His gaze lowered to her hand. 'Where's your wedding ring?'

Damn. 'I took it off in the shower.' Wow, that was lame. She just couldn't lie cleverly with him staring a hole through her. Where was Layla when she needed her?

'You've taken a lot of showers at my house with it on. Try again.'

Behind her, Pebbles threw herself against the glass. Faith swallowed past the burning lump in her throat. 'Being with you is wrong. I can't do it anymore.' Pebbles barked and ran headfirst into the door. 'It should never have happened. You need to concentrate on winning and I need to be by myself.' Again the dog threw herself against the glass and Faith knew exactly how the little dog felt. Her nerves unraveled even more and she glanced at the dog and yelled, 'Stop that!' She returned her gaze to Ty, his beautiful blue eyes, and her heart shattered all over again. 'I can't love you anymore. Please go before Pebbles kills herself.'

His hands dropped to his sides. Instead of leaving, he looked at her for several moments before he said, 'Anymore?'

'What?'

'You said you can't love me anymore.'

Crap. 'I meant I can't be with you anymore.'

'That isn't what you meant.'

She moved across the room toward the entrance. She had to get him out of her penthouse before she fell apart in front of him. 'I don't love you and I can't be with you.'

He grasped her arm as she passed and looked down into her face. 'You keep mentioning love. Are you trying to convince me or yourself?'

She tried and failed to pull from his grasp. 'Stop.'

'I've tried.' He placed one big hand on the side of her face. 'I can't.' He lowered his forehead to hers. 'These past few days, not knowing if you were okay, have been hell.'

'I'm okay.'

'I'm not.'

His lips touched hers and she sucked in a breath. 'Ty. You have to go.'

'Not yet.' His mouth opened over hers and she felt his kiss everywhere. It poured through her, starting fires in her chest and belly. She held as still as possible, careful not to touch him or kiss him back. 'I need you,' he whispered.

She raised her hands but dropped them to her sides before she gave in to her desire to touch him one last time. A sob broke from her throat.

He raised his free hand to the other side of her cheek and he held her face as he kissed her, long and deep, and after several long, torturous moments, she placed her hands on his arms and tilted her head to the side. She could not stop herself. She could not stop the pounding in her heart or the fiery need racing through her veins, and she gave in.

He groaned deep in his throat, a sound of pleasure and possession. His tongue slid into her mouth, the kiss feeding all the hungry places in her starving heart and soul. All the places that loved him and longed to be with him. When he lifted his head, he looked into her eyes. 'Why don't you start over? Why have you been avoiding me?' His thumbs softly brushed her cheeks. 'The truth this time.'

She loved him too much to tell him. 'I can't.'

'You can tell me anything.'

She shook her head. 'It's bad.'

'Have you found someone else?'

'No!'

He closed his eyes, and when he opened them again, he looked relieved. 'Then what?'

'It's best that you don't know.'

'Why don't you let me be the judge of that?'

Again she shook her head as tears filled her eyes. 'Can't you just leave it alone? Can't you just take my word that you're better off not knowing?' Where was Layla when she needed her? The tough one. The one who could resist interrogation and come up with believable lies.

He folded his arms across his chest, the belligerent hockey player. 'I'm not leaving until you spit it out.'

Once she told him, he'd leave. He'd go away. Perhaps angry, but he'd have his answer. 'Landon has pictures of us,' she relented.

His arms fell to his sides and one brow rose up his forehead. 'Virgil's son?'

She nodded. 'I have to sell him the team or he's going to send them to the newspapers and put them on billboards, like our PR photo.'

'You're selling him the team?'

'I have to.'

A fire replaced the relief in his eyes and he said, 'Like hell.'

She recognized that fire. She'd seen it on the jumbo tran when he faced an opponent in the corners. 'I don't have a choice.'

He stepped back and took a deep breath through his nose. Pebble threw herself against the glass and he walked to the door and let her in. 'You have a choice. I'll think of something.'

'You can't solve this, Ty. He'll do it. He's not bluffing. He'll ruin you to get what he wants.'

'He can't ruin me, Faith.' He pointed to Pebbles jumping up on her back feet. 'Settle your ass *down*.'

The dog stopped barking and sat. Faith would have been impressed if she didn't have more important things on her mind. 'He planned to trade you, but I think I've convinced him that you broke up with me. So I don't believe he's going to now. Which makes your being here too risky. You have to leave. Sneak out somehow, just in case.'

She expected some sort of gratitude. Instead his gaze narrowed even more. 'And you weren't ever going to tell me any of this?'

Her eyes started to water once more. 'No.'

Deadly quiet, he asked, 'Why the hell not?'

She thought she'd made it clear. 'Because you have a lot of other things to worry about right now.'

'And you thought what? That you should sacrifice yourself and hand over your hockey team?'

She brushed a sudden bead of moisture from beneath her eyes. 'I know how important winning the cup is to you.'

'Don't you think you're important?'

She stilled and her hands fell to her sides.

'I see that you don't.' He folded his arms across his chest like he was mad at something. No, not something. At *her*. 'You don't have a very high opinion of yourself. Or is it me you don't have a very high opinion of?'

'I have a high opinion of you.' She was confused and shook her head. 'Why are you mad at *me*?'

'Why?' he asked, incredulous. 'I've been in hell these past few days. I almost punched your assistant because he'd seen you and I hadn't. I've been walking around worried and pissed off and it all could have been avoided.'

Now it was her turn to be incredulous. He'd almost punched poor Jules. 'How?'

'You should have told me about this. You should have let me take care of it. This involves me too. Do you honest-to-God believe I'd let you hand over your hockey team to cover my ass?'

She nodded and laid it all out quite reasonably for him. 'For five years I let Virgil take care of me. Now it's my turn to take care of someone.'

He laughed without humor. 'You want to take care of me?'

'Yes.'

'If I let you do that, what kind of man does that make me?'

She wasn't sure what he meant.

He cleared it up for her. 'It makes me a pussy.'

'It's done.' She'd saved his ass and he was worried about being a 'pussy'? So much for gratitude. 'I signed the letter of intent to sell.'

'If I recall, you signed one before and changed your mind.' He moved toward her. 'Do you trust me?'

'To do what?'

'Do you trust me, Faith?'

It seemed very important to him, so she answered, 'Yes.'

He shoved his hand in his pants pocket and pulled out his keys. 'Then show up for Game Seven tomorrow with your skates.'

'Landon banned me from the skybox.'

'It doesn't matter. Just show up with your skates, and when we win, come out onto the ice.'

'What are you going to do?'

'Not real sure. I'm still too pissed off to think straight, but no one threatens me or what's mine and gets away with it.' He shook his head. 'Don't ever make me crazy like you have the past few days.' He kissed her hard, then moved toward the door.

'Yours?' A smile curved her lips. A smile that lit up the dark empty places she'd been living in for the past few days. She hurried after him. 'You think I'm yours.'

'I know you're mine.' He walked out of the penthouse and headed for the elevators. 'And for God's sake, don't sign any more papers Landon sends over – eh?'

'We Are the Champions' blasted from the huge arena speakers, clashing with the sounds of fourteen thousand fans cheering and stomping their feet inside the Key. The cacophony of noise faded into the background as Ty stepped onto the ice. He glanced up at the owner's box and the rows of Duffys seated in it as if they had that right. Anger tightened Ty's stomach and lowered his brows as he looked up at the man who'd had him and Faith followed. At the man who'd hired someone to take sleazy photos and ruin their lives. Or at least try.

Landon might scare Faith, but Ty wasn't so easily frightened. He'd come up against men bigger and badder than Landon Duffy, and he hadn't lost a fight yet. He wasn't about to lose this one either. It was the most important fight of his life, and he'd thought long and hard about all his options. Short of having Landon killed, there was only one solution. Just one.

He had to win the Stanley Cup. And he had to do it without going into overtime. Pittsburgh had won the last three games in overtime.

Ty skated twice past the face-off circle and then moved inside. For the seventh time in two weeks, he faced off against Sidney Crosby. 'Sid the Kid' was twenty-two and had the facial hair of a thirteen-year-old. But the Kid's age and lack of anything resembling a beard had nothing to do with ability. He hit hard and skated fast and was already a top-five player in the NHL.

'Ready to lose, Cindy?' Ty asked.

'I'm going to kick your ass, old man.'

Ty laughed. 'I've got more hair on my nuts than you have on your whole face, Kid.' He got into position and waited for the first puck of the night to drop. Faith was out there in the arena somewhere, but he wasn't going to think about that. If he wanted everything to work out the way he'd planned, he had to focus on the game. One play at a time.

The puck dropped. Game on. Both teams had come to win. Both were determined to win the ultimate prize, and Ty knew this game wasn't going to be easy.

In the first period, Daniel scored on a Chinooks power play, but Sid the Kid tied things up in the last few seconds of the first frame, confirming what Ty feared. A hard physical game followed by grueling overtime.

In the second period, the Chinooks forwards cycled the puck along the boards, and in the first few seconds of the second period, Ty saw an opening in the ice and ripped the puck at the Penguins goal. It was deflected wide. Daniel followed the puck, shot it to Blake, who slammed it in the five-hole. As the horns blew and 'Rock and Roll Part 2' blasted from the sound system, the players crowded around Blake and pounded on his back.

Ty skated to the bench and squirted water into his mouth. The refs talked at center ice as the goal was replayed on the jumbo tran.

Faith was somewhere out there. Ty swallowed and thought about the hell she'd put him through. The truth about Landon and the photos had almost been a relief compared to what he'd been left to presume on his own. His imagination had ranged from a mysterious illness to her boredom with him to her involvement with another man. There wasn't another woman on the planet who'd ever made him feel things like Faith. Who made him feel as if his life was better with her in it. Who made him look for her in a room filled with people. Who made him feel like smiling just because she smiled.

There wasn't another woman on the planet who'd ever twisted him in knots like Faith. For two days, he hadn't called her. He told himself to forget about her. That he was better off without the distraction of a woman. Then, before he knew it, he was in her lobby threatening her with a bomb and a building evacuation.

Maybe his father was right about him. Maybe he

was more like his mother than the old man. Not the mental illness part, although the last week had made him a little crazy. Maybe his mother had felt about Pavel what he felt about Faith. A bone-deep longing that there was just no getting past.

Brookes skated to the face-off circle and Ty wiped sweat from his face. His intent gaze watched the puck drop and Crosby shoot it down ice. 'Faster, boys,' he yelled to his teammates.

The Stanley Cup was in the building, waiting to be carried out and presented to the winning team. Ty had worked hard his entire life to get to this point. He'd gotten this close a time or two, but never had he had so much riding on the outcome. More than just having his name immortalized. Tonight was about more than just doing something his old man had never been able to do.

After a minute and a half, Ty jumped over the boards and changed on the fly. Logan shot him the puck and he dumped it in. There was only a minute and a half left in the second period and Ty skated across the ice and bodychecked a Penguin into the boards. He was shoved from behind and punched in the back, and he turned and aimed for a black helmet. His punch landed and the Penguins enforcer fell to the ice. The whistle blew and the punching stopped. Except for Sam, who continued to participate in some extracurricular activity in the corner with a Pittsburgh defender. All four players were given three-minute penalties and sat out the last few minutes of the second period in the sin bin.

'Quit taking stupid penalties,' Ty said as he took a seat within the Plexiglas enclosure, 'and we just might win this thing.'

'You're in here,' Sam reminded him as he spit between his own skates.

'The ref made a bad call.'

'Yeah. With me too.'

The Chinooks sent out their penalty killers, but neither team was able to convert on the 3-on-3.

In the third frame, the Penguins evened the score and it remained tied as the clock ran down. Ty was exhausted. His legs were rubbery from long shifts and he was sucking up pond water when he breathed. God, the last thing he wanted was to go into another overtime.

On the change he took his seat on the bench and dried his face. He thought of Faith and her giving up her team to save his ass. Yesterday he'd been mad as hell about it. Today, he had to admit that he was a little in awe. Giving up a hockey team and millions of dollars was a whole hell of a lot of love.

He glanced up at the clock and the remaining two minutes before he hit the ice.

Pittsburgh dumped the puck, and the Chinooks battled in front of their own net. With only half a second left, Blake cleared the puck and Ty headed up ice. Blake passed to Vlad and Vlad shot the puck across ice to Ty. As the clock counted the seconds, Ty ripped a slap shot at Pittsburgh's goal. The puck streaked past the goalie's glove and slammed into the back of the net. The buzzer sounded and the arena went wild. The Seattle bench emptied and the players piled onto the ice and onto each other. Horns blared inside the arena, and Ty's ears rang and his heart pounded. He sucked in a breath as he fell to his knees beneath a pile of hockey players and tried not to cry like a girl.

Faith walked through the tunnel wearing her Chinooks jersey, a white flowing skirt, and the pink skates Ty had given her. She moved to the side as the Pittsburgh Penguins filed past her on their way to the guest locker room. It had taken her fifteen minutes to get through the crowd and past security. The Chinooks had already popped the first bottle of champagne and were spraying it all over each other by the time she stopped at the tunnel opening. The team had replaced their helmets with championship caps and her gaze sought and found the captain. Ty held up a jeroboam-sized bottle, took a huge mouthful, then shook it up and sprayed it on Sam and Blake. The sight of his laughter lifted her heart and stung the backs of her eyes. She had no idea what he had planned, other than she stand in the tunnel after the game. She'd spoken to him last night and that morning, but he hadn't told her, and both times the conversation deteriorated into what she was wearing and the color of her panties.

Tears spilled from her lashes as she watched the red

carpet rolled out on the ice. The three-foot Stanley Cup, polished and engraved with the names of heroes and warriors, was carried down the carpet by Hockey Hall of Fame executives Philip Pritchard and Craig Campbell, who were wearing blue blazers and white gloves. She was so proud of her team and Ty.

The executives presented the cup to Ty, and he hoisted hockey's most prized possession over his head as his teammates shot champagne into his eyes. He laughed as he lowered the thirty-five-pound cup and pressed his lips to the cool silver before he raised it once again.

The fans went crazy as Ty took off, skating around the rink with the cup above his head. For a few scary seconds, she wondered if he'd forgotten that she was waiting for him in the tunnel just like he said, but as he passed, his gaze met hers and his smile grew even bigger. He winked at her, then handed the cup off to Daniel. A microphone was shoved into Ty's face and he wiped champagne from his eyes.

'How does it feel to win tonight?' a reporter from ESPN asked.

'Wonderful,' he said and adjusted the cap on his head. 'We've all worked hard for this and we deserve it. This team had to work through some adversity. It made us all stronger, and I know that we all wish Bressler was here to enjoy this moment.'

'What gave you the edge tonight?'

'Pittsburgh is a great team. They didn't give up or give us anything. I just think we're in our own house and there was no way we were going to lose in front of this crowd.'

Sam approached Faith from behind, carrying another big bottle of champagne and with an unlit cigar in the corner of his mouth. 'Can you believe we won, Mrs. Duffy? This is fucking incredible.' He reached for the cigar and tried and failed to appear apologetic. 'Sorry about the F bomb. I got carried away.'

She laughed. 'Understandable.'

He inclined his head toward the arena and the cup being passed from one player to the next. Each player held it up and kissed the coveted prize as he was sprayed with champagne. 'Coming out?'

She looked over Sam's shoulder to Ty, who was still speaking with reporters. 'Not yet.' As Sam moved from the tunnel, she looked out at the arena and the fans still filling the seats. Then she raised her gaze to the empty skybox and swallowed past the sudden constriction in her throat. She doubted Landon had just gone home.

She was right. 'What are you doing here, Layla?' he asked from just behind her.

She glanced over her shoulder. 'What does it look like, Sprout? I'm watching my team pass around the cup.'

'It's not your team.'

She looked into his cold blue eyes and felt the tension ease from her chest. He'd done his worst to her and she'd survived. At the end of the day, she might not have the Chinooks, but she still had the only man she'd ever truly loved. 'You're tiresome.' She sighed. 'You and your whole entitled family.'

'Holy shit!' Blake said as he and Vlad stepped into the tunnel for more champagne and cigars. 'I can't believe he just did that.' He looked at Faith.

'What?'

He pointed to Ty and the knot of reporters around him. 'Saint just said he's retiring. This was his last game.'

Faith's mouth fell open and her brows rose up her forehead. When he said he'd take care of everything and get her team back, she never thought for one second that he'd give up his career. 'He better not,' she said.

'It doesn't change anything,' Landon spoke. 'If you try and back out again, I'll send the photos to every paper in town.'

Ty separated himself from the reporters and walked up the red carpet toward her.

'I won't let you retire,' she said as he approached.

'What?' He laughed and stuck a championship cap on her head. 'I can't hear you.' His smile flatlined as he looked at Landon. 'Did you tell him you're not selling after all?'

She shook her head.

'She'll sell,' Landon assured Ty. 'She signed a letter of intent.'

'Yes, and she signed one of those before. You're a businessman, Mr. Duffy; you know these deals fall apart all the time. If you want a hockey team, I hear that the Wild might be up for sale. Of course, that's just a rumor. Like Faith selling you the Chinooks.'

Landon's jaw tightened. 'I'll ruin you both.'

'You can try.' He took Faith's hand and pulled her from the tunnel and onto the red carpet. 'What an asshole,' he said through a laugh.

Faith's ankles wobbled and her heart pounded in her chest as she followed beside him. 'I can't believe you're laughing. When you said to trust you, you didn't say anything about retiring. Now you get over there and tell all those reporters that you were joking.'

He slid his hand to the small of her back and put his mouth next to her ear. Instead of doing as she demanded, he said, 'I love you, Faith.'

He smelled like sweat and champagne, and the warmth of his breath and the heat of his words crept inside her heart. Her footsteps faltered from shock and trying to balance on her skates. She looked up into his blue eyes. 'I love you, too.'

He smiled. 'I know.'

'I love you too much to have you retire for me.'

He raised his gaze from hers as Marty lumbered around in full goalie pads, holding the cup over his head. 'I've played hockey for most of my life to just get to this one moment. Now that I'm here, I've discovered it's not enough. I want more.' He looked back into her face. 'I want you in my life.'

She wanted that too. More than she'd ever wanted

anything. More than money and security and big shiny diamonds. 'There has to be another way.'

He shook his head. 'No, this feels right. I want my career to go out on a high note. Not after a few more years of chasing tonight's glory. Trying to capture it again, only to go out on a low. I don't want to be one of those guys. I don't want to be my dad. It's time.'

'Are you sure?'

'Yep.' They moved to the end of the carpet and he said, 'Which means I'll need a job.'

'Yeah?'

'Yeah, and since I have no skills other than playing hockey, I'm pretty much unemployable.'

'I saw a Help Wanted sign at a Gas-N-Go.'

He laughed. 'I thought maybe you could use another pro scout.' They stopped at mid-ice and he bent her back over his arm and looked down into her face. The crowd went wild.

'What are you doing?' she gasped.

'Making sure those photos are old news.' His mouth came down on hers and he tongue-kissed her on national television. In front of all the Chinooks and fourteen thousand cheering fans, the kiss lingered until she was dizzy and he was sure everyone got the point.

Everyone but Sam. 'My turn.'

Ty shook his head as he brought Faith back up. 'Don't even think about it.'

Alexander Dumont hoisted the cup up over his head and let out a Tarzan yell as Logan shook a fresh bottle of Moët. Within the sweet mist of golden champagne, Ty lowered his mouth next to her ear. 'There is only one thing that will make this night even better.'

'What?'

'You and me. A hot shower and really inappropriate behavior.'

little black dress

brings you fantastic new books like these
every month - find out more at
www.littleblackdressbooks.com

Why not link up with other devoted Little Black
Dress fans on our Facebook group? Simply type
Little Black Dress Books into Facebook to join up.

And if you want to be the first
to hear the latest news on all things
Little Black Dress, just send the details below to
littleblackdressmarketing@headline.co.uk
and we'll sign you up to our lovely email
newsletter (and we promise that we won't share
your information with anybody else!).*

Name: _____

Email Address: _____

Date of Birth: _____

Region/Country: _____

What's your favourite Little Black Dress book?

_____

How many Little Black Dress books have you read? _____

*You can be removed from the mailing list at any time

You can buy any of these other
Little Black Dress titles from your
bookshop or *direct from the publisher*.

FREE P&P AND UK DELIVERY
(Overseas and Ireland £3.50 per book)

TO ORDER SIMPLY CALL THIS NUMBER

01235 400 414

or visit our website: www.headline.co.uk

Prices and availability subject to change without notice.